ONCE YOU GO THIS FAR

ALSO BY KRISTEN LEPIONKA

The Last Place You Look
What You Want to See
The Stories You Tell

ONCE YOU GO THIS FAR

A ROXANE WEARY MYSTERY

Kristen Lepionka

MINOTAUR BOOKS

NEW YORK

First published in the United States by Minotaur Books, an imprint of St. Martin's Publishing Group

www.minotaurbooks.com

Library of Congress Cataloging-in-Publication Data

Names: Lepionka, Kristen, author.
Title: Once you go this far: a mystery / Kristen Lepionka.
Description: First Edition. | New York: Minotaur Books, 2020. |
    Series: Roxane weary; 4
Identifiers: LCCN 2019055285 | ISBN 9781250309372
    (hardcover) | ISBN 9781250309389 (ebook)
Subjects: GSAFD: Mystery fiction.
Classification: LCC PS3612.E62 O53 2020 | DDC 813/.6—dc23
LC record available at https://lccn.loc.gov/2019055285

Our books may be purchased in bulk for promotional, educational, or business use. Please contact your local bookseller or the Macmillan Corporate and Premium Sales Department at 1-800-221-7945, extension 5442, or by email at MacmillanSpecialMarkets@macmillan.com.

First Edition: 2020

10 9 8 7 6 5 4 3 2 1

In memory of Marie Kelly

ONCE YOU GO THIS FAR

CHAPTER 1

t happened on the first day that felt like autumn. Overnight the air turned crisp and the trees burnished into orange. It was a relief after another Midwestern summer that, emboldened by climate change, seemed determined to stick around until winter. The long, narrow parking lot behind the nature center at Highbanks was still mostly empty when I pulled in; there was a school bus at one end, a gaggle of kids in Catholic school uniforms in an unruly line beside it.

I was wearing a new jacket, a plum-colored canvas anorak that I'd been looking forward to wearing for weeks. If not for the coat, I probably would've been more pissed off that my brother was standing me up.

"Andrew Joseph Weary," I said into his voice mail. "It is nine forty-five in the morning and I am not in my bed right now, because of you. And yet, you're nowhere to be seen. Giving you five more minutes and then I'm leaving."

It wasn't like either of us to engage in traipsing about in nature. But Andrew was trying to turn over a new leaf. A week in jail will do that to a person, and his particular new leaf involved aspirations of hiking the Pacific Crest Trail. After he told me that, and after laughing my head off and asking who in the hell had left a copy of *Wild* in his apartment, I decided I should probably be supportive. Turning over a new leaf wasn't such a bad idea, not for anyone. So I'd agreed to join him in some practice hiking. Thus far, we'd actually managed to do it only once before.

Neither of us were morning people, new leaf or no.

I waited the five minutes and thought about leaving. But the crisp air convinced me otherwise. I was here already; why not take a walk anyway? I opened the car door just as a silver Chevrolet Equinox whipped into the spot next to me; I barely managed to close the door in time to avoid it getting ripped off.

The passenger window of the SUV went down. "Sorry, sorry," Rebecca Newsome said. I didn't know her as Rebecca Newsome at the time, just as a sixtyish woman with short, ashy-blond hair and a wide, thin-lipped smile. "I hate it when people do that." She got out of the car and I saw she wore dusty hiking boots and ripstop cargo pants. She opened the back door and a brown dog jumped out, small and fox-like with pointed ears that looked comically large for its head. "It's just so gosh darn beautiful out today that I couldn't wait!"

I waved her off. "No harm done," I said.

Still smiling, she tugged at an imaginary lapel. "Great coat. I like that color."

I wasn't prone to small talk with strangers either, but the weather had made me downright friendly.

I said, "I like the fact that it's cool enough out to wear it."

She grinned. The dog, antsy to get after something in the woods, strained at its woven leash. "Well, have a good one."

"You too." I gestured at my own car door. "And be careful."

Rebecca gave me a thumbs-up and set off briskly toward the woods.

That "be careful" came back to haunt me less than a half an hour later. After wandering through the shrieking middle schoolers in the nature center, I went out onto the observation platform and looked into the trees growing from the steep embankment.

Somewhere out there, a shale bluff towered over the Olentangy. But all I could see was sun-dappled gold and orange. The only sounds were foresty rustling noises and birds and the crunch of sneakers on the gravel trails and, somewhere far off, traffic.

Then I heard something that was distinctly unnatural.

A dusty scrambling, a startled gasp, followed by a series of snaps and the startled bark of a dog.

I pushed off the railing and started down the Ripple Rock Trail, calling out, "Hello? Everyone okay?"

I heard a voice but couldn't quite make it out.

I scanned the sloping path for the dog, the woman from the parking lot, or a sign of what had caused the noise.

"I don't think doggies are allowed on this trail," a voice said, lilting. I rounded a corner and finally saw someone, a woman in lime-green running gear farther down the path. She crouched before the fox-like dog, which hunkered just off the trail, tail swishing like a metronome. "What are you doing out here all by yourself?"

"It was with someone," I said.

The lady in green spun around to look at me, while the dog growled and let loose a tirade of barks that echoed through the trees around us.

"Did you see a woman? Silver hair, cargo pants?" I had to raise my voice to be heard over the dog's barking.

"No, I just came around the corner and saw this little dude. He seems terrified."

Over her shoulder, I saw a strange divot in the surface of the trail, an irregular-shaped hole where it looked like a rock had become dislodged.

"There," I said, pointing. I took a few steps closer while the dog continued to snarl.

The woman in green grabbed ahold of the leash, which had

caught on a branch. I headed for the divot. Everything on either side of the path was orange and golden and brown. Off to the right, the ground sloped gently; to the left, a much sharper drop-off to a creek at least fifty feet below.

The left side was where I saw the bottom of a hiking boot, the hem of ripstop cargo pants, midway between the trail and the ravine below.

"Oh, shit," I said. "I see her down there." I stepped off the path and nearly slipped on a pile of dewy leaves.

"The rangers' station," the other woman said. "I'll go for help."

I gingerly stepped over a moss-covered log, bracing myself against a tree trunk studded with mushrooms. "Can you hear me?" I called.

The lady from the parking lot didn't make a sound. She didn't move, either. I picked my way down the steep embankment. Now I could see signs of her fall—a patch of earth freshly exposed when another log was bumped aside, a swatch of nylon caught on a sharp root.

I nearly lost my footing twice more before I reached her. She was on her stomach, neck twisted harshly, the side of her face planted in the soft ground. I felt for a pulse at her throat—faint. She was bleeding from a gash at the right temple and her palms were scratched up, mud caked under her fingernails. As I leaned over her, I saw that her eyes were open, staring into the dirt.

I didn't know what to do—she was at an angle, meaning the blood was rushing to her head, but I remembered something from a long-ago first-aid class about not moving someone with an in-jured neck. Fortunately, I heard shoes on the gravel above me. "Where are you?" the woman in green called.

"Down here. I'm down here. She's really hurt."

"Thank you, ma'am," a new voice said, "please stay on the trail." I looked up and saw a young woman in a park ranger's uni-form coming down the steep hill. She spoke into a walkie-talkie in urgent tones. Her dark eyes swept across the scene and her expression hardened.

The beautiful quiet morning suddenly felt anything but.

They took her to St. Ann's. I followed in my car, unable to shake the sound of my own voice—*be careful*—from my head. Was I the last person who'd spoken to her before she fell? It seemed more than possible given how empty the trail had been, and it left me feeling responsible. If not for what had happened, then at least for making sure she wasn't alone now.

The woman in green had the same idea. She was waiting outside the emergency room doors, the dog's leash looped around a wrist while the creature on the other end backed itself into a bush and whined.

"I don't really know what I'm doing here," she said when she saw me. She held up the leash. "That ranger said something about calling animal control and, well, that would be terrible. You fall while hiking and your dog ends up in a shelter? But you can't take a dog into an emergency room, it turns out."

I scratched my wrist and nodded, thinking of Rebecca's open, blank eyes. I hoped the whereabouts of her dog were not beyond her concern.

"I'm Stacy," she added. She went to offer me a hand but found her right one wrapped in the leash. So she settled for a small wave.

I smiled, or tried to. My face felt weird. "Roxane."

"I can't believe a woman fell off a cliff right in front of me and all I noticed was her dog." Stacy shook her head. She had dark, ageless skin and hair pulled into a high, tight bun.

"I saw her in the parking lot earlier," I said. "That's the only reason I knew."

Before too long, a woman rushed in from the parking lot. Pregnant—very—in a striped maxi dress and a denim jacket. Her face was pale and worried as she went through the sliding doors and up to the nurses' station.

Stacy and I stood outside in relative silence, neither of us sure what we were supposed to do next. Would anyone need to know what we hadn't seen and hadn't heard? The breeze, which had felt deliciously cool earlier, now just seemed damp and chilly.

Eventually, the pregnant woman came back out outside and walked over to Stacy and me as if seeing us for the first time. Her face was bloodless, a faint spray of freckles across her nose standing out like a splash of paint. Her hair was corn silk, damp and frizzy at the temples as if she'd just stepped out of a shower. She had a tiny golden cross on a whisper-thin chain around her neck. "They said you two were— Oh, God," she muttered, noticing the cowering dog. She reached out for the leash; the dog yipped defensively and moved farther back into the bushes. The woman flinched. "What happened? Did you see what happened? Did she trip over him?"

"I heard it," I said, gently. "I heard her fall. But I didn't see anything. I'm sorry."

Stacy handed over the leash, which the pregnant woman then clutched so tightly her knuckles went white. "I'm Stacy, and this is Roxane."

"Maggie Holmer." She was looking at something behind us, or at nothing at all.

"Are you her daughter?"

A nod, curt.

"What's your mother's name?"

"Rebecca Newsome," Maggie said. "I can't believe this."

Stacy glanced at me, then tried a change of topic. "When are you due?"

Maggie didn't bite. "They took her for a, what's it called. A

CT scan. I guess I'm just supposed to wait? How is a person just supposed to wait like this?"

I glanced down at her hands; her left sported a modest wedding set. "Is there someone we can call for you?" I said.

She pulled a phone out of her handbag and promptly dropped it on the concrete. Blotches of red had appeared now on her ashen cheeks. "My husband is on his way. He'll know what to do. I can't believe this."

After that, Stacy led her back inside the ER and I took a turn with the dog's leash. I was on the lookout for Maggie's husband, James, who was en route from Findlay, where he worked two days per week for some petroleum company. I hoped the dog would like him better than it seemed to like me. While it low-key growled from its place under the bushes, I scrolled through my phone and read a series of apology texts from Andrew about standing me up. It wasn't that big of a deal, but I wasn't in the mood to reassure him.

James Holmer was bookish and flushed, dressed in a brown Carhartt jacket over a burgundy polo shirt and khakis. I knew who he was from the way he rushed past me, then noticed the dog snarling from the bushes and turned back. I said, "James?"

He stopped and stared at me from behind his frameless glasses. "Where's Maggie?"

"She's inside."

He didn't ask me who I was, just proceeded into the emergency room.

I sat for a while on a concrete bench. Eventually a Delaware County sheriff's deputy approached the door and we had a rather perfunctory conversation about what had happened. Then he went inside, and a few beats later James Holmer came back out. "You're still here."

I held up the leash.

"Thanks for watching him." He tugged on the leash and the dog came forward skittishly, whining now. "Let me put him in the car. Sorry you got stuck here—hopefully you were on your way out of the hospital, not in."

"No worries. I was actually at the park. I talked to your mother-in-law, briefly."

"Oh." He looked up at the grey-white sky over the lenses of his glasses. The dog strained against the leash, trying to retreat to the safety of the bushes, but James ignored it. "Wow. Did she say what happened?"

"No, this was before."

James nodded, his eyes drifting down to the dog. "Did you see what happened?"

"I didn't."

"I hope she didn't trip over him," James said, nodding at the dog. "He's always underfoot. I've tripped over him already once this week—she's been staying with us. Maggie's due date is tomorrow." His expression hardened, probably as he realized how the birth of his child would be, one way or another, affected by what had happened this morning. He cleared his throat. "Okay, well, thanks again, for your help."

"Of course." I found a business card in my wallet and gave it to him. "If you need to reach me for anything."

"Great. That's very kind."

He went off to one side of the parking lot, and I headed to the other.

I didn't hear anything else about it. I called the deputy twice, hoping for an update, but he didn't answer and he didn't return my messages either. I thought about trying the hospital, but I knew they wouldn't tell me anything.

Not knowing was hard for me. It always was. This was part of why I'd bailed on my plan of becoming a psychologist—I was too nosy, too hungry for the why. You can't act on people's problems as a psychologist, just talk. And talking had its place, but so did doing.

This time around, there was nothing to do. Nothing except wait out the deeply unpleasant poison ivy that developed on my hands and arms and try to move on.

never expected to see Rebecca Newsome's daughter again, but somehow I wasn't surprised when she reentered my life a month later.

She was sitting in the fourth-floor waiting area of my new office building, rocking a newborn baby in a carrier on the floor beside her. For a second I didn't understand that she was there for me, thought instead she must have an appointment with someone else in the building—what a coincidence. Then she said, "Your website says business hours are ten to five."

The whole office thing was my own new leaf, an experiment in something allegedly known as work-life balance, but the experiment wasn't going well. I apparently didn't like work-life balance. Or at least not if it involved going in to an office. So far the space was turning out to be nothing but an inconvenient location to keep my printer-scanner. I nodded, still not understanding.

Maggie went on, "I didn't know you were a detective. You gave my husband a card that day. It didn't say what you did for a living. I wanted to send you a note. A thank-you note for—for what you did. So I looked for your address online."

She had stopped rocking the baby carrier, and its occupant made a disgruntled sound. So she resumed, her face tight and exhausted. I was afraid to ask but I said, "How is your family?"

"My mother passed away," she said, and I drew in a sharp breath, involuntary. "She hung on for three days. She got to hold her granddaughter. Well, they said her brain activity—that she wasn't aware of her surroundings. But I don't know about that. I put the baby in her arms. Just because. And it was about an hour after that she slipped away."

"I'm so sorry—"

"No, I'm sorry. I didn't come here to—I don't know why I told you that. The reason I came is, well, when I saw your website, what you do. I wondered if I could hire you."

The conversation had gone to an unexpected place. "Hire me?"

Maggie nodded. "Maybe there's a reason that you were the one in the woods with her. Maybe you can figure out what happened. What really happened."

"What do you think happened?"

My office contained a desk, a printer, a chair, and a thrifted vintage love seat in a brown velvet voile that reminded me of a couch my grandmother once had. A large, empty picture frame leaned against one wall, which seemed to be emblematic of something. Maggie glanced at it but said nothing, just set the baby carrier gently on one cushion of the love seat and sat down beside it.

"This is still a work in progress," I said, "the office. And the business hours. I might've guessed that I wouldn't like having regular business hours." I took a seat in the desk chair and took a notebook out of the top drawer, wondering if I could find a pen without looking like I was actively searching for it. Good detectives should always have pens, probably. Ironically, I'd ordered a thousand pens printed with my phone number and address from a former client who owned a print shop, and someone—hard to say if it was Arthur or if it was me—had gotten the address wrong on the order form. So I was in possession of a thousand misprinted pens, but they were all in my apartment or in my Range Rover. I didn't want to keep them in the office in case a client accidentally picked one up and spread misinformation across the city. "I hope you weren't waiting for long."

Maggie shrugged. "It's good to get out of the house, honestly. I am really grateful to you, for helping my mother that day. I know you probably didn't expect to get roped into babysitting a dog outside the hospital when you woke up that morning."

"Life does have a way of surprising us," I said. "But don't even mention it. I was happy to help. Other than a little bit of poison ivy, I was no worse for wear." I casually reached into my computer bag, feeling past loose change and hair ties until I landed on something pen-shaped. "So tell me what's on your mind."

Maggie rubbed her forehead. "Well, I don't know how to say it, so I'll just say it. I don't think my mother fell into that ravine. I know she didn't."

"How do you know?" I said gently.

"My mother loved the outdoors. She'd hiked the Grand Canyon rim to rim, Bryce, the PCT. All just in the last few years. She was an experienced hiker."

I tried to write that on my notebook, but the pen scratched inklessly across the yellow paper.

"And Highbanks is not, how do I say it."

"It's not Bryce Canyon."

She smiled faintly. "No. It's not. I mean, she took the dog with her on the trail. It was hardly a real hike."

"How's the dog?"

Maggie shook her head. "He was always sort of weird around people other than my mom. Skittish, but also aggressive. But after that, he started going after people constantly. He ripped a sweater of mine, trying to bite me, and he actually drew blood from James. I wanted to keep him but with the baby, I was just afraid something worse would happen eventually. So I found him a new home."

"Do you think there's a chance she tripped over him at the park? You mentioned something like that at the hospital."

Maggie sighed. "I don't know. I know I've certainly tripped on the little dummy. Apparently dogs aren't even allowed on that trail, maybe for that very reason. But she took him with her on little walks all the time."

"Okay, so you don't buy the tripping theory. Not over the dog, and not over her own feet due to being an experienced hiker."

"No," Maggie said, her nostrils flaring a little. "Plus, she wasn't a careless person. She was a nurse. I never even knew her to cut herself accidentally while chopping onions."

I tapped the impotent pen on my notebook. "Where did she work as a nurse?"

"A private school, Horizons Academy. Part-time. But listen, it's not just that I don't believe she tripped. There are a few other things. Weird things."

"Okay."

"Her phone is missing."

"What do you mean?"

"It wasn't with her things, the things she had with her that day. And not in the car, either. So what happened to it?"

"Maybe she dropped it, when she fell?"

"Oh. Maybe."

"Sometimes the answer really is that obvious, but sometimes it isn't. What else?"

"The police—well, listen. She didn't live down here. She was down here to help me finish the nursery—she lives up in Toledo."

I tried to scratch in Toledo, waiting to hear the part about the police. "Okay."

"I told all of this to the Delaware County officer but he didn't seem to think much of it. His name was Monterrey, or Montero something like that. I'm sure I'd remember his name if he'd actually cared, you know?"

I nodded.

"Anyway, apparently, the day it happened, the police were at her house up there. That afternoon. Mom's neighbor told me. Her name is Arlene French." She reached into her own bag and handed me a pen without pausing. "I have no idea what they were doing at the house, and they won't tell me."

Functioning pen in hand, I quickly jotted down a few notes. "They won't tell you?"

She shook her head. "That brings me to the last thing. Her ex-husband, Keir Metcalf. They've been separated for years but just finalized the divorce in January."

"So she changed her last name back after the divorce?"

Maggie shook her head. "Newsome is my maiden name, my father's last name. My mother kept it, even after she married Keir. Yet another thing they fought about. Their relationship got a little ugly. So that's why I think he might know something. Of course, he's like this with the police department up there." She held up two crossed fingers. "He's a former cop. And an asshole."

"A current asshole, I take it."

Maggie gave me half of a smile. "Yes."

"Is your father still in the picture?"

She shook her head. "My father abandoned us when I was a baby. I've had like three conversations with him in my life. He's long out of the picture."

"And you think, what, your former stepdad might have been involved in what happened to your mom?"

"Stepdad," she muttered. "Yeah, I do."

"Anything concrete behind that? Threats, an ongoing dispute?"

"All I know is that there was a lot of bad blood between him and my mom, and I can't stop thinking about it. I think about it all day, every day. Wondering. My husband says he's afraid the baby is going to pick up on it, my anxiety. And anger. He walked in on me talking on the phone to someone in the Delaware County coroner's office the other day while I was—" She stopped, blushing faintly. "I was breastfeeding her. I wasn't thinking. But

I need to not be doing that anymore. The anger I carry can't be good for my child."

I nodded. I knew exactly what she was after. "You want to give custody of that anger to somebody else. Outsource the worrying about it."

"I have this whole giant Dropbox folder of stuff that I can share with you. Like the autopsy report. And the hospital stuff. I keep looking through it, over and over." Her baby began to squirm in the carrier beside her. "I just need to stop. For her." She lifted the baby—swaddled in pink and brown polka dots—into her arms and peeled back the outermost layer of blanket, revealing a pruny, round face.

"Aw," I said, sensing that it was expected. "What's her name?"

"Beatrix," Maggie said. "Bea for short."

"Hi, baby Bea."

"Do you want to hold her?"

I put the borrowed pen down. "If you need a break, I am happy to hold your baby. My ovaries do not ache to do so, however."

Maggie laughed. "I think that's the most honest thing anyone has ever said to me."

"I try."

She stood up and plopped the baby into my arms. "I'm like that about other people's kids. I always was. And then when she was born, when I first saw her—it was like a switch flipped in my brain, it turned on this animal instinct. You always hear about maternal instincts, a mother's love and all. *Love* isn't even the right word. It's so much fiercer than that. It's like I immediately knew that I would kill for her. Isn't that effed up?"

I jostled baby Bea, hoping she wouldn't start screaming. "No, I think that's honest too."

"I'll never get the chance to ask my mother if that was how she felt, too."

"I'm so sorry."

We looked at each other for a long time.

"Do you think you can help?"

"I can't promise I'll find anything," I said, "but I can promise to take care of looking."

Maggie nodded. "That will be a huge relief."

I knew I had saved the business card the sheriff's deputy gave me that afternoon at the hospital. I knew because I hadn't done laundry for a minute, so it had to be in a pair of jeans in my apartment somewhere. The problem was, I had a lot of somewheres in my apartment. I spent a while digging through a basket in my dining room, checking pockets without success. Then I spotted the plum-colored coat at the bottom of the basket. I hadn't worn it since that day—tainted—but now I figured it was safe to wear it again, even if the business card wasn't in its pockets either.

I heard voices in the backyard, followed by the telltale rattle of a spray paint can. I pulled the coat on and dashed outside, but it was just Shelby, my upstairs neighbor and surrogate niece, and her friend Miriam, at work on a patchwork of pink and white poster boards in the rough grass.

"Craft hour?" I said.

Shelby grinned at me and peeled up a heavily duct-taped stencil to show me her handiwork: WOMEN'S BODIES ARE MORE REGULATED THAN GUNS. "There's a gathering at the statehouse tomorrow, so we're making signs."

The current round of attacks on women's health clinics were indeed disturbing. I nodded to Miriam. "What does yours say?"

"It's not as good." Shelby's friend held up her sign, a more modest PROTECT REPRODUCTIVE RIGHTS in black paint. "I wanted to make uterus cookies but I guess those aren't going to be very impactful."

"I told her she should make some anyway. In case Constance is there."

"Constance Can is not going to eat cookies that some random girl made. Even if they're delicious and perfectly shaped. Right, Roxane?"

"Well," I said, "I don't think she's going to have a Royal Taster or anything like that, so you're probably right."

Constance Archer-Nash was a homegrown lightning rod, a thirtysomething tech entrepreneur who'd gotten fed up with the way politics in Ohio were going and decided to challenge Rob Portman for the Senate seat he'd held for nearly a decade. Overnight she became a household name, with videos of her speeches going viral and thousands of people in line to hear her speak at events. Her campaign materials all said "Constance CAN"—her initials—in bold pink letters.

"I think both signs are instant classics," I said. "But what about the rest?"

Shelby looked down at the unpainted cards at her feet. "Extras in case there are people who don't have signs."

Miriam gestured at the small village of spray paint cans standing at attention in the yard. "You know our Shel. Pathologically generous."

"That's a good thing to be. Well, have fun, don't inhale."

"Love you, mean it," Shelby said.

I went back inside and sat down at my desk. It was emptier than it used to be, given that I'd moved my printer and a lot of random paperwork into the office. Now the front room of my apartment felt like a space recently vacated by someone. Me, I supposed. I'd thought that creating some separation between home and work would allow me to focus better while working and relax more at home. Specifically, that I could stop reliving the blurry memory of Elise Hazlett drowning in front of me earlier in the year, her icy blue skin and white teeth and pink puffer coat sinking into darkness.

It was more than just that memory, though. Everything about winter felt wrong and bad. Only bad things happened when it was cold out, as it was becoming now. Elise Hazlett. Catherine's decision to move to the East Coast with or without me—or, rather, definitely without me, since she hadn't even broached the subject before deciding. And my father's death, of course, the thing that split my life into two halves and divided time now into the months leading up to the anniversary and the months looking back at it.

Like a change of scenery could come close to touching any of that.

It seemed stupid, but I'd signed a yearlong lease. So it would continue to be stupid at least until April.

Maybe until then, I would convert my front room into a home gym.

The thought made me laugh out loud.

gave you the password for this." Kez rolled her eyes at me when she came by the office after her exam. "Did you even try?"

I looked over her shoulder at the website she had built for me. "You know I can't keep track of passwords. I mean, obviously." Despite my very irregular use of the office, I had still managed to make an impressive pile of papers.

Kez rolled her eyes harder. "I didn't write it on paper, Jesus, I emailed it to you."

"Email is even worse."

"Are you ninety years old?" Kez said, even though I knew her to be a year older than me.

"Any day now."

She grinned at me and clicked a few keys. "There. Done. Office hours are a thing of the past. Is that all you called me over here for?"

"Actually," I said, pulling myself into a sitting position on the ugly love seat, "no. We have a case."

Kez leaned back in my desk chair and put her Doc Martens up on the paperwork mountain. "Tell me."

Kezia Denniere wasn't interested in investigative work long-term—her real interest was in bail-bonds enforcement—but she had a record, something that made it hard for her to line up a criminal-justice practicum as required for her degree from

Columbus State. A felony-weight drug-possession bust will do that to a person, even if the only thing she'd been guilty of was terrible taste in boyfriends given that he left her high and dry to serve a one-year prison sentence. But that had been a long time ago, and I could tell Kez was scrappy and smart when I met her on a case at the beginning of the year. So I was willing to sign off on her hours in exchange for some tech help and the occasional backup.

I explained about Maggie and her mother and the very full Dropbox folder.

"You want me to read an autopsy report?"

I was paying her twenty bucks an hour but felt weird about asking her to actually do things. "Or you can pull some background on Keir Metcalf."

"Yeah, I'm gonna do that one instead."

She turned back to my laptop. I watched the screen as my own website was replaced by that of AA Security and Investigations in Perrysburg, Ohio. "Ew. Somebody else needs a web designer, I see."

"Is there no such thing as loyalty anymore?"

Kez clicked on the About tab and pulled up a photo of Rebecca's ex-husband. He was a standard-issue ex-law-enforcement type: salt-and-pepper buzz cut, sharp jawline, the sort of bulk that could be fat or menacingly muscular depending on his mood. He wore a neutral expression and a polo shirt embroidered with his own name.

"Trust me," Kez said, "I have no desire whatsoever to work for someone like this. And I am sure the feeling is mutual."

"Find out what you can about him," I said, "and I'll take the autopsy report."

"Do I get paid extra for this?"

"No."

She shrugged. When I met her back in January, she was working at the desk of a shitty hotel in Whitehall and selling stuff left behind in the rooms on eBay. "Worth a shot. I gotta go, but I can come in tomorrow morning. Cute coat, love the useless zippers."

"They're not useless," I said as she left, demonstrating by unzipping the breast pocket. And there it was—the business card I'd been looking for.

Deputy Carter Montoya. I left him yet another voice mail, imagining my three messages as the only ones he'd ever received. Maybe it wasn't anything personal; maybe he didn't know his passwords either.

Modern life was hard.

Autopsy reports aren't especially gross—just boring. The first line contained a succinct summary of what I would find if I pored over the entire forty-page document: *From the anatomic findings and pertinent history I ascribe the death to: intracranial hemorrhage due to traumatic brain injury.* The mode of death was listed as Accidental.

I skimmed through a physical description of Rebecca's body—laceration at right temple, abrasions on palms and knees, bruised hip, fractured wrist, fractured clavicle, allergic contact dermatitis on hands, ankle, and neck, old scars on abdomen (cesarean) and lumbar (laminectomy and spinal fusion). I was obviously no forensic pathologist, but all of that seemed consistent with a fall over a steep embankment.

Especially the allergic contact dermatitis—the fancy name for the poison ivy that had plagued me for three solid weeks after the incident.

I stood up and closed my eyes, trying to picture myself on the trail. Would Rebecca have been holding the dog's leash in her right hand, or her left? I opened my eyes and flipped through the autopsy report; the coroner had noted more developed musculature in her right arm. So she was right-handed, but I wasn't sure what that meant in terms of holding a leash. I looked out my window onto Gay Street and spotted a man with a leashed pit mix in the crosswalk at Third Street. He had the leash in his left hand. Statistically speaking, he was probably a righty. So I held the imaginary leash in my left hand and closed my eyes again, picturing the golden-orange forest and the sloped hiking trail. If Rebecca had been going down the path, the area to which she fell was to her left.

But the majority of the injury had occurred on the right side of her body.

I turned around, eyes still closed, and imagined walking up the hill instead. This put the ravine on her right, which made more sense. But why would she have been going up the hill already, given that she'd just set out on the path a few minutes before?

I sat back down at my desk and flipped through the autopsy report again. If Rebecca had stumbled on the path—with enough force to cause her to fall and become unable to stop herself—wouldn't there be an ankle or knee injury? She had the skinned knee and bruised hip, but no swelling or ligament damage to indicate a twisted ankle or blown ACL. I reread the description of her broken wrist: fractured distal radius with volar displacement.

I had no idea what that meant.

A quick Google search told me this was also known as a *Smith's fracture*, an injury that specifically occurs in a fall on a flexed wrist. I held up a hand and bent my palm toward my body, then away. Which was flexion and which was extension? I was clearly out of my element here, and not just in terms of the pathology report. Trying to solve a mystery that I myself had more or less witnessed when it happened was going to be difficult, if not impossible. If I hadn't noticed anything suspicious all those weeks earlier, I didn't know how I was going to find anything at this point.

Most of the leaves were off the trees by now. The golden glow of that morning had been replaced by ashy twilight, and the crisp chill in the air was just damp and cold. "I think it was here," I said, pausing in the middle of the gravel trail. "I saw some lines in the dirt, here. And a divot, like from a rock or a shoe. Then I looked down and saw her."

Tom followed my hand as I swept it across the path in front of me. "What kind of marks?"

"I don't know. What kind of marks does a person make when they trip?"

"I think it depends on the person—no need to investigate that one empirically though."

I felt myself smile. "No pratfalls in the name of science? It's like you know me or something."

"I am vaguely familiar."

I stepped aside to let a jogger pass, and Tom brushed a hand against the small of my back. There was nothing sexy about standing here talking forensics, but I was a little turned on. I said, "Do you see the tree right there, the bendy white one? How far down do you think that is?"

"The bendy white one—the birch tree?"

"Obviously I don't know what it's called, Cub Scout. How far?"

"Twenty feet, I think."

I took a few steps closer to the edge of the trail and Tom's arm went rigid. "What?"

"Nothing."

"Are you afraid of heights?" I said.

"What? No. Not *afraid*, per se." His hand found my wrist and gently tugged me away from the overlook. "I just would prefer not to be right on the edge of a cliff."

"I can't believe I didn't know this about you."

"My last remaining secret."

I backed off the edge and spun around and he kissed me, long and slow and deep. I always had an impulse to pull away and tell him that this was going nowhere, that I was going nowhere, that if he wanted to go somewhere with someone he should get the hell away from me and do that before the world ended. But such warnings hadn't fazed him yet and really, I was enjoying myself. Another jogger huffed past us and we both cracked up. "So how, exactly, does someone fall there," I said, pointing to where I'd seen the marks in the path, "but end up over here, facedown, with injuries only to the right side of her body? Did she *roll* across the path?"

"What are the famous Weary instincts telling you?"

"That if she was walking down the hill and fell here, she would have ended up on the other side of the path. The non-ravine side." The other side of the trail was lined with soft-looking bushy things, with no incline whatsoever. A fall there would have wounded Rebecca's pride but little else. "Or, she was walking up the hill. Which would be strange because she had literally just started the trail."

"Maybe she was going back for something she left in her vehicle. Or because she wasn't feeling well," Tom said. "Maybe she passed out. A stroke."

"That would have been in the autopsy."

"True."

I thought back to my client's worries, to the smug face of Keir Metcalf. So proud of himself for naming his business AA Security because it would show up first in the Yellow Pages that way. Did the Yellow Pages even exist anymore? If not, the joke was seriously on him. "Maybe she turned around because she encountered someone or something she didn't want to mess with."

"Some*thing*?"

"A bobcat? A snake? The ghost of her own failed ambition?"

"Show me the wrist thing again."

I held up my arm and flexed my palm toward my body, having watched a YouTube video in order to determine that this position equaled flexion.

Tom took my elbow and guided it out and down. "What if she fell backwards?"

He turned me around so that my back was to the ravine Rebecca had fallen into. "If she was standing like this, and she fell backwards, that could break a wrist. It's a sort of submissive posture, don't you think? As opposed to defensive." He let go of my arm and held up his own hands, palms out, in a *don't shoot* gesture. "I could see an animal, maybe. Though I don't think there are bobcats out here. And you didn't see one, either."

That was the problem with any theory that involved Rebecca encountering some*one* or some*thing* on the trail—neither Stacy nor I had seen it.

"But doesn't it seem like there are more questions than answers here? Isn't that what *undetermined* is meant for?"

"It seems," Tom said, "that your client wants there to be a big bad. It's so much easier to blame a villain than it is to blame bad luck and gravity."

He wasn't wrong. "That could be said about a lot of my clients. Most. Maybe all. I think that makes me want to help them more, not less."

The sun had dipped farther below the trees, and it was getting hard to see the edges of the trail. "I guess we can go. I'm not going to figure it out standing here."

We hiked in silence for a while. Tom was thinking about my father. I could tell because I was, too.

Later, in my bed, I thumbed my phone through a list of animals common to Ohio on the Department of Natural Resources website. "There are too bobcats around here," I said. "And coyotes, black bears . . . it could have been anything."

"Don't bobcats lie in wait for their prey?"

I glanced over my shoulder at him. We were halfway spooning, me on my side, Tom on his back, a hand resting on my hip. "You're the one who said there weren't any bobcats in Ohio. But now you're suddenly an expert?"

"I didn't say there weren't any bobcats in Ohio. I said I didn't think there were any in Highbanks."

"Maybe a least weasel, then."

He rolled over so that his mouth was right at my ear. "Let me see this list."

I held up my phone.

"Least weasel," he read. "As opposed to the short-tailed weasel and the long-tailed weasel."

"The woods contain multitudes."

"Least shrew."

"That's me."

He laughed, the kind of laugh that seemed to take him by surprise. I loved the timbre of that one. "Do you think you'll have to go to Toledo?"

I sighed. "I don't think I'm going to get an answer for Maggie with a list of small woodland mammals. So probably. Maybe tomorrow or the next day."

"We've fallen into a nice little rhythm here."

I scrolled back up through the list. "Indeed. But you can feel free to see your other girlfriends while I'm gone. I'm sure they miss you terribly."

"Roxane."

"That's my name."

"You say stuff like that and I don't know what to think."

"Think whatever you want. Do whatever you want."

Tom took my phone and put it on the nightstand, screen-down, and the room plunged into darkness except for the glowing stars on my ceiling. "I'm just the worst, for being so transparently available, is that it?"

I tipped my mouth up to his for a kiss. "I wouldn't go that far."

CHAPTER 4

Kez brought crullers and information, two of the better things a person can offer at a morning meeting. "I think he's a real asshole, Mr. AA Security," she said. "His company has a LinkedIn profile that posts nothing but Bible stuff and Constance Archer-Nash hate memes." She spun the laptop around to show me the screen—earlier that morning, Keir Metcalf had felt the urge to share with the world a picture of the candidate superimposed with text that said: "Life's a bitch—don't elect one."

"I think he may misunderstand what LinkedIn is for," I said. "And also the Bible."

"Well, he also got canned from the Toledo Police for repeatedly handing out Jesus pamphlets at traffic stops."

I laughed around a mouthful of doughnut. "What?"

Kez clicked around on the computer and then cleared her throat. "This is from 2010, the Toledo *Blade*. 'A Toledo police officer has been fired after multiple drivers complained that he issued more than tickets after pulling them over—he also shared a little religion on the roadside, in one case asking a woman if she had accepted Jesus Christ as her savior.

"'The department's spokesperson said on Friday that the officer, Keiran Metcalf, a twelve-year veteran, was let go on Thursday for repeatedly proselytizing and for handing out religious materials to speeders.

"'The authorities said his termination was based on a complaint in January that said he had questioned a driver's religious affiliations after pulling over the vehicle—the second time in the past year that the department was aware he had done so. After a similar episode in 2009, officials said, Officer Metcalf was formally told not to question drivers about their religious beliefs or try to convert them.'" She looked up from the screen. "Can you imagine?"

"Did he issue tickets after all that?"

"It doesn't say."

"I'd be pissed if I got an inappropriate question about religion *and* a ticket."

"Fortunately, the dude has moved on to subtler forms of persuasion." She opened a new link, this one an article entitled "Harry Potter: Harmless Christian Novel or Doorway to the Occult?"

"So I think it's at least safe to say he's a crank. But in my experience, religious types generally frown upon throwing ex-wives off ravines."

"Also divorce, for that matter."

"Touché."

"What else did you find?"

"Well, prior to joining the Toledo PD in 1998, he was a deputy with Delaware County."

"Really," I said. That meant the jurisdiction that oversaw Highbanks was his former employer. I remembered what Maggie had said about Metcalf being connected. "What was his story there?"

"He was put on leave for misconduct, along with three other guys, after the mishandling of a domestic-violence issue. Seemed pretty clear-cut, but I can go on if you want."

A twenty-year-old resignation seemed unlikely to matter here, so I just asked Kez to save the paper trail in Maggie's Dropbox in case we wanted to refer to it later.

"Now do I get paid extra?"

"No. But good work."

She took her boots down off my desk and picked up her bag, a canvas messenger festooned with enamel pins that said things like MISANDRIST and DON'T FUCKING TALK TO ME. I admired the direct approach. "I have to go. TBH, this office makes me sad. Maybe you could hang that up or something?"

I looked at the frame propped against the wall. "I need something to put in it first."

She squinted at it. "Fuck me, I thought this was some sad, artsy picture of a beach that you took on vacation. Here," she said, scribbling something on an orange Post-it. She placed the square of paper over the bar code on the frame and walked out.

I had to laugh when I saw what she'd written: *Cheer up, beach.*

I met Deputy Montoya at Coffeeology, where I bought a muffin and a mint tea for myself and a white chocolate mocha for him. "Black coffee hurts my stomach," he said, as if his beverage choice required an explanation.

"No judgment," I said, although the image of the burly, armed cop stirring an additional packet of sugar into his whipped-creamy drink was a bit amusing.

We were sitting at the barstools in the window facing Sandusky Street, which was caught in midday bustle. The Delaware County courthouse—a new, generally empty and silent fortress—loomed one block over.

"Look," Montoya said. "I do feel bad for Maggie Holmer. What an awful position to be in, about to have a baby and her mother has this accident. But whatever she told you about it not being an accident? She didn't say a word until well after the fact."

"I think it was a slow-burn kind of conclusion."

"Conclusion." Montoya wiped foam off his upper lip. "My sister-in-law," he said, "when she was on maternity leave with her second kid. She started losing her shit, thinking the traffic signs were a code telling her that her baby had been switched at birth.

She was diagnosed with, what do you call it. Postpartum. Postpartum psychosis. She had to spend three weeks on a psych ward. Hormones, you know?"

"So Maggie's making all of this up because hormones?"

"You're one of those feminist types, I take it."

We glared at each other.

"I'm just saying. It is not unheard of for these . . . things to happen. To a woman right after she has a baby. If she truly thought that something suspicious had happened, why did she wait so long to say anything?"

"Perhaps because she was shocked, and distracted, and once she actually had a chance to think about it, she realized it didn't actually make any sense."

Montoya made a face like his stomach hurt anyway. I figured that was my fault and I wasn't sorry. "Accidents are called accidents for a reason. You can't say there's no chance someone *accidentally* fell. The word means it was unintentional, out of anyone's control. And besides, the coroner's findings were consistent with an accidental fall."

I found myself flexing my wrist, still wondering exactly how Rebecca's Smith's fracture had happened. But instead of asking the deputy about it, I said, "So what's your explanation of the Toledo Police showing up at the victim's house the very day of the accident?"

Now Montoya just seemed annoyed. "Rebecca's neighbor, have you talked to her yet?"

I shook my head.

"Well, she's about a thousand years old and she has no idea what she's talking about. Toledo PD don't have a record of going there."

"An official record."

"Who's paranoid now?"

"You do realize that you're quick to dismiss anything a woman says as unreliable."

"No—"

"And for someone in the business of finding out the truth, that's pretty messed up."

A blotchy red bloomed across his cheeks. "I have three daughters. I do not dismiss anything that a female says."

"But when was the last time you actually gave a damn about a woman's opinion?"

"Would you talk to your dad that way?"

He hadn't mentioned that he knew Frank until now. Sometimes I wondered if half the folks who claimed to remember him really did, or if he was just a part of the collective unconscious now. Maybe a vague knowledge of Frank Weary came with every badge in the state. I said, "Probably, or worse. What's that got to do with anything?"

"I would've thought a cop's kid would have more respect, is all."

"Think again."

"I need to get back to the courthouse."

"One more thing. Keir Metcalf."

"What about him?"

"You know him?"

"Not personally."

"Would you just take his word for it, whatever he said? Because he used to wear that same star?" I nodded at his chest.

"I told you, I don't know him. But he had an alibi, with twenty-some witnesses. He was at a church breakfast that morning anyway." Montoya stood up.

I said, "Listen to your daughters now. If you don't, they'll never trust you."

That took some of the wind out of his sails. He politely shook my hand before he walked out.

needed to talk to Rebecca's neighbor. Montoya obviously hadn't liked me much, but I doubted he would lie about there being a police visit to the house on the day she fell. There were other explanations: maybe the neighbor had been wrong about the day, maybe the visit had been from some other law enforcement agency, or maybe from an off-duty cop.

Maggie and her husband lived in Powell, a few blocks to the north of a small downtown area that called to mind the setting of an Andie MacDowell rom-com. The Holmers' house was big and old and white, featuring a wraparound porch and an expansive yard. Maggie answered the door with a sleeping baby Bea in her arms. "Come in," she whispered, and shut the door gently behind me.

I kept my voice low too. "I was hoping to take a look at your mom's things that she left here. And hopefully get a house key. I'm going to head up to Toledo."

A sad sort of relief—or relieved sadness, if there was a difference—slid over Maggie's face. "So you don't think I'm crazy."

"I don't think you're crazy, and I do think there are still some questions. Like I said the other day, I can't promise you results, but I can promise you my time."

"That's all I ask. Well, and preferably for you to be out of here before my husband gets home—I just don't want to get into all of it with him again."

"Understood."

Maggie gave me her mother's keys—recovered from her jacket pocket—and showed me up the steps to the guest room. "I've been driving her car—it's so much easier than mine, with the baby. Feel free to look at that too if you want, as long as you don't judge me for all the Starbucks cups."

It said something about the world, that people were afraid of being judged about something as insignificant as their caffeine habits.

The guest room where Rebecca had been staying was about ten by ten, with creaky wooden floors and old, plaid wallpaper, the kind that had gone out of fashion so long ago that it was back on trend again. One wall featured a framed picture from the young couple's wedding and another sported James's diploma from the University of Michigan, chemical engineering. The double bed was pushed against the sloping attic ceiling on one side, with an abutting nightstand on the other.

"I haven't touched anything in here," Maggie said. "I actually haven't really come in here more than a couple times since, since it happened." She looked down at her sleeping daughter. "I'll be downstairs."

"Thanks, Maggie."

I closed the door and leaned against it. The attic was slightly stuffy from the warm sun streaming in through the skylight in the slanted ceiling, particles of dust seemingly caught in a midair snow globe. The white chenille bedspread was smoothed out on the bed and expertly folded under and over the pillows. The nightstand offered a lamp and a digital clock, which was flashing 3:02 in red numerals. I opened the nightstand drawer—a Bible and an extra set of sheets. I opened the closet—women's clothes, summer, presumably Maggie's prepregnancy wardrobe. A rolling suitcase was on its side on the floor of the closet, unzipped.

I sat down on the floor and pulled the suitcase out so I could see its contents. Jeans and sweaters, hiking socks, a blue plastic pill tray with only Sunday's and Monday's medications missing. I opened Tuesday and peered in—an oval cream-colored tablet, a pale pink round one no wider than the hole in a drinking straw, two halves of an oblong white one. I was making a mental note to ask Maggie what her mother was taking, but then I found a trio of pill bottles in a mesh suitcase compartment: sertraline, propranolol, and an unpronounceable statin, respectively.

I wrote these down in my notebook and moved on to the dresser: a dog-eared copy of *Big Magic* and a fraying phone charger, a bottle of Merle Norman foundation and a packet of makeup-remover wipes for dry, mature skin. A small television sat on one end of the dresser, so I flipped it on—NBC. The early news was airing right now, and the screen showed a jumble of white and pink poster boards on the statehouse lawn. I looked for Shelby and Miriam, but it was impossible to make out any particular faces. The disembodied voice of a reporter was saying, "Due to security concerns at the outdoor event, Ms. Archer-Nash canceled a scheduled appearance here this afternoon with promises to return to central Ohio before Election Day."

I turned it off and stood hunched under the skylight, taking in the room from the opposite angle.

I noticed the strap of a canvas tote bag poking out from under the bed and bent to pick it up. A knitting project—baby booties—a tin of mints, a linty ChapStick, a five-dollar bill and two ones folded around a cashout voucher from Caesars Hotel and Casino in Windsor, Canada.

Maggie didn't know anything about it. "She wasn't a gambler. Not at all."

"Well, not much of one, anyway," I said, tapping the total printed on the paper slip—seven dollars and fifty-one cents. "What about Keir, is he a gambler?"

"I don't know. His hobbies tend towards guns and whatnot."

"And proselytizing at traffic stops, I take it." I explained about the Toledo *Blade* article.

Maggie bit her lip. "Boundaries were definitely one of the problems Mom had with him."

"What were some of the other problems?"

"He's a very, I don't know, he's flirtatious. With everybody. I think it's his personality, and I know it bothered her, and they'd fight about it."

That seemed a little thin to be the basis for a murder accusation. "Why'd it take so long for them to get divorced? Trying to patch it up?"

"Maybe a little. But when I found out I was pregnant, she wanted to make sure that everything she had would be for Bea someday. Rather than anything Keir could lay claim to."

And that sounded like a reason that Metcalf would not have killed Rebecca, if the divorce was already a done deal. "Did she have a lot of assets? I can't imagine being a school nurse is terribly lucrative."

"She loved working at the school. Loved it. But she also had some property, rental property."

"Any problems with tenants?"

"Not that I ever heard about."

"Do you have the addresses for the places she owned?"

Maggie sighed. "Somewhere. This is one of those things that I need to deal with but can't quite seem to manage."

"You can outsource dealing with her estate to somebody else," I said, "just not to me. I would like those addresses if you can find them."

She rubbed her forehead. "I must seem like a lunatic to you. My priorities are really out of whack."

I touched her arm across the kitchen counter. "Not at all. I know what it's like to lose someone. Your thoughts might not always make sense, but that doesn't mean they're wrong."

The corner of her mouth tipped up. "Thank you for saying that."

I peeked in Rebecca's silver Equinox on my way out—I knew which vehicle was hers because it had nearly taken off my own car door that day. Coffee cups in every cupholder. I got in and started the vehicle to check the in-dash computer to mine for information in place of having Rebecca's missing phone, but the screen simply told me that Rebecca's iPhone was not connected.

I closed the door and patted around the inside, imagining the natural place to leave clues. The glove box was always a decent contender, but it—boringly—only contained the owner's manual and the registration and a multi-tool to use to cut one's seat belt in an emergency. Other than Starbucks cups, the console held a Michael Bublé CD case, empty, and a pack of gum. A silver chain dangled from the rearview mirror, one of those car charms that said *Guardian Angel, Protect my passengers and all who pass by. Keep us safe under your watchful eye.* I liked that Rebecca was hopeful, but practical—the guardian angel was wishful thinking, and the multi-tool was just in case. I checked the pockets on the back of each seat and found nothing, but the small pop-up trash can in the backseat revealed a discarded piece of gum tucked into a folded valet ticket for a place called the St. Clair Club in downtown Detroit.

I was feeling around in the bottoms of Rebecca's reusable-grocery-bag collection in the back when James Holmer got home. He did a double take when he saw me. "Oh, it's you," he said, "what are you doing here?"

"Oh, I just stopped by to see how Maggie is doing."

He nodded. He wore the same tan jacket that he had on at the hospital. "That's sweet. It's been tough on her, it really has. But our daughter is perfect. So that helps. But, um, what's going on with the car?"

I would have had no problem lying to him, but nothing

immediately came to mind to explain being elbow-deep in his mother-in-law's Trader Joe's bag. I said, awkwardly, "I thought I saw something moving back here."

"Something moving?"

"Yeah, but I guess not. Must have been a reflection, I guess."

"Must have been," he said.

My brother Andrew didn't work at the Westin anymore; he'd gotten fired for missing more than a week of work after he was arrested back in January. But maybe it was for the best—being a hotel bartender maybe didn't go so well with the whole new-leaf situation. A situation that seemed to include less drinking.

There was something depressing about being the last drinker in the family, though. Our oldest brother, Matt, had been sober for years—some unpleasantness in college—and my mother barely drank even when my father was alive; now that he was gone, long gone, the legendary booze cart in the living room long depleted, she hadn't bothered restocking. Even the contents of Frank's office upstairs had been slowly but surely drained. Andrew used to be counted on to bring a bottle over during our family dinner, but that seemed to be changing now.

Tonight he brought over a murky-smelling mason jar of CBD tincture with the intention of making us each some sort of honey-tea digestif after dinner, but my mother wasn't having it.

"I told you, it's not marijuana, Mom," Andrew was saying. "It's not. Roxane, help me out here."

"It's not," I said, "but I still don't want any."

"It's cannabis," my mother said gravely. "That's what they said on the news."

"Yes, it's cannabis—"

"You know how I feel about all that."

"Listen, hemp is also cannabis. All that macramé shit you used to have?"

"Language."

I smirked and resumed scrubbing the dregs of turkey chili out of the slow cooker.

"CBD is perfectly legal, Gen." My mother's boyfriend—man friend?—Rafael Vega was a cop like my father had been, but the similarities stopped there. I actually liked him a lot, and not only because he was drying the dishes for me.

From the living room, where the television was tuned to a Cavs game, my other, least favorite brother said, "Personally, I would never. I take sobriety seriously."

Andrew met my eyes with a roll of his. Matt was in rare form tonight, showing up in the new, gargantuan F-250 he'd bought since starting his own construction business and subjecting us all to a detailed litany of its features despite the fact that no one cared.

"That's all well and good," Andrew said, "but this has nothing to do with sobriety, because it's not a drug."

My mother gave the mason jar a sniff and shook her head. "Nope. I can't do it. I'm sixty-four years old. Why try drugs now?"

Andrew said, "It's not marijuana," at the same moment Rafael said, "You've *never* tried?"

Scandalized, my mother said, "Of course not! Have you?"

Rafe didn't miss a beat. "I was young once, if you can believe it."

When the Scrabble board came out, it was time for me to go. Matt became even more annoying—if possible—when zero-stakes competition was in play.

Andrew followed me out onto the porch and lit a cigarette, unwilling to resist that vice, at least. He said, "I feel like you're still mad at me. About Highbanks."

"Why, because I didn't want your gross tea?"

"No, because I've barely talked to you in like a month, and you're standing there with your arms crossed." I was doing that. I put my hands in my pockets. "*And* because you wouldn't try my gross tea."

I shook my head. "No, I'm not mad at you. Now Matt, on the other hand," I said, nodding at the truck. It was so large that it took up the entire space between my mother's driveway and the neighbors'. "How many miles per gallon do you think it gets? One?"

"Oh, at least." Andrew exhaled toward the night sky. "But come on. Something is up."

I sighed. "Not really. It's just—you're going on a journey, with all this stuff. You both are. Your new ambitions. Matt's new truck. And I'm not. I'm just here."

"A journey." My brother exhaled toward the night sky. "I'm not going full-on hippie or anything. I'm just trying to do something else with myself. With my life. I mean, Christ, you could have died in January, because of my bullshit. Honestly, you should be fucking furious with me. Like I am."

We watched each other, the only sound the faint crackle of his lit cigarette.

"It's not like that," I said finally. I hadn't even told him about what had happened at Highbanks the day he stood me up, so maybe it was like that on some level. "And I know you're trying to do something else. It's just, well, I want to go home and enjoy a drink, and I would like to do it without the taste of pond water in my mouth. That's all."

He rolled his eyes. "You can drink in front of me, come on. Is that what this is about?"

"I'm not about to be the only person drinking here."

"Okay, that's fair. But seriously, I'm not Matt, I'm hardly Mr. Sober Living or anything. As long as having a drink is something you enjoy . . ."

He trailed off and I knew why. I wished I didn't.

He'd had a come-to-Jesus moment in jail, and strangely enough, I had too. I remembered the beige cell in the Belmont police station a few years ago, feeling like I might actually die because I hadn't had a drink in twenty-four hours. That wasn't about drinking, though. It was about being unhappy. And I was less unhappy now, or at least less direly so. Now at least I had Elise Hazlett's face to keep me company in addition to my whiskey. "I do," I said, "and I'm going to go do that, right now. Please never ask me to smell that jar again."

Andrew grabbed me by the shoulders and planted a kiss on the top of my head. "Mind if I stop by your office to print some labels this week?"

"You still have a key, right?"

He nodded.

"Print your heart out then. Labels for the gross jar?"

"I'll be on *Shark Tank* someday with this jar."

I held up two sets of crossed fingers as I walked up the block.

CHAPTER 6

The drive to Toledo was two and a half hours on a good day. Thursday wasn't an especially good day. I sat in standstill traffic on 23 for seemingly no reason until Bucyrus, and then sat in stop-and-go traffic from there on because it started to rain and no one could deal. But I made it by lunch and knocked on Arlene French's door just in time for egg salad sandwiches.

"Poor Margaret," she said, slathering bright yellow eggs on white bread. "I just feel so awful for her. Obviously it's never the right time, but this really isn't the right time."

It took me a beat to realize that she was talking about my client. "You know Maggie well?"

Arlene was a stately woman in her twilight years, with feathery grey-white hair and a shuffling walk inside a billowing fleece housecoat. But her eyes were bright and her voice was strong. "Oh yes," she said, "she grew up next door. Rebecca and Margaret lived there for years. Of course when Rebecca got remarried, she had renters in." Arlene plated my sandwich and pushed it across the counter to me. "I wasn't sorry to see them go, those renters."

"I'm sure," I said. Her regard for renters seemed low. I didn't mention that I, too, was one. "So Rebecca moved back in after her divorce?"

"That she did. Sweet woman, Rebecca. They both are. Were. It was such a shock to hear about what had happened. Oh, you'd see Rebecca walking hither and yon, always preparing for some big trek. She was mad about walking." Arlene looked sad at the mere thought of walking and/or renting.

I took a bite of my sandwich—pickles, but they were sweet—and chewed. "So tell me about the day you saw the police over there."

Arlene nodded. "Well, Rebecca had asked me to get her newspapers and just keep an eye on things while she was down your way. So I did. Her mail goes in through the slot but it just lays there where anyone could see it, so I'd gather that up too and turn some lights off and on and whatnot—she had the one light on a timer, but I don't think that's enough these days. But anyway, I saw the cars pull up out that window, right there." Arlene pointed to the square of light above her kitchen sink.

"Cars, plural?"

She nodded.

"And these were cop cars?"

"Yes."

"Patrol cars, like black-and-white ones?"

"That's right. Two of them."

"What happened then?"

"Two officers got out of one car, a man and a woman, and another man got out of the second. He went around to the back. The other two went to the front door and knocked. They were on the porch for a while, but no one came to the door, so they left. I called Rebecca right away because she'd had a few problems with the ex-husband. But of course by then she was already, well . . ."

I nodded. "When you say problems, do you mean police problems?"

"She would never call the police on him, so I had to. Twice, since she moved back here. He'd be standing in the yard, screaming for her to come out."

I wrote this down. On paper, Keir Metcalf didn't have any recent entanglements with the law, so it seemed possible that Maggie was right and the cops were doing him a favor. "When was the last time?"

"Sometime in the spring. It had been a while. But when I saw them out there, I just assumed that it was related to him again. She's never had problems with anyone else."

"What about the renters?"

Arlene smiled. "They were simply annoying, never taking their trash cans back inside. They never had the police or anything."

"So you called Rebecca right away."

"Yes."

"And when was this?"

"It was September the eighth, about eleven in the morning. I was just sitting down to watch that nice-looking Drew Carey on *The Price Is Right.* I like him a lot."

"And she didn't answer," I prompted.

"Correct. So then I called Maggie—Rebecca had given me her phone number on a piece of paper before she left. I just figured Rebecca needed to know, if things were starting up with that ex-husband of hers again. But Maggie didn't answer either. Then I thought that maybe the baby had come already and I decided not to bother them with it anymore. It was only a few days later when Maggie called me back that I heard about what had happened."

"You're positive about the date and time?"

Arlene nodded again. "I certainly am." She stiffly got to her feet. "I even wrote it down." She shuffled over to her refrigerator and slid a magnet off a sheet of typing paper. "I wrote, 'Toledo police, two cars, October third, eleven oh five a.m. Gone by eleven twelve.'"

She handed the sheet of paper to me. Her handwriting was blue-inked and wobbly. It also detailed the lights she had turned on and off: front table, back porch, dining room.

I said, "Did you show this to Deputy Montoya from Delaware County?"

"Show him? No, but I told him about it when he called."

I felt myself frown. He had given me the impression that he actually came up here to do his—admittedly very cursory—investigation. Perhaps that was my own wishful thinking.

I snapped a picture of Arlene's log and thanked her for the sandwich, then left her with a business card in case she remembered anything else.

I had packed thoroughly for this trip—a handful of the misprinted pens, not caring so much if misinformation was spread around up here, my passport in case I wanted to make a trip to Windsor, the casino slip and parking pass from among Rebecca's possessions, and a house key from Maggie.

I made use of the latter and let myself in through Rebecca's back door.

The small house was neat and orderly, though a fug of expired melon was coming from the fridge. I walked through the kitchen and into a dining room that seemed to have too much furniture—a large china cabinet, a table with space for eight, a mid-century banquette, and a desk with a framed picture of a middle-school-aged Maggie with her arm around a dog, not the one that had growled at me at the hospital, but a similar variety. I took in a living room with a modestly sized flat-screen TV and several bins of yarn, as though Rebecca intended to make baby booties for the entire city. She had a *Real Simple* magazine and a bottle of clear nail polish on the end table. Bedroom: clothes in a practical, functional vein, books that ran the gamut from The Cat Who mysteries to Melody Beattie to Nicholas Sparks. Bathroom: pink and devoid of clues. Basement: a dank place with a terrifying open shower like my grandmother's house used to have. Upstairs, a half bathroom and two small guest rooms. One had a double bed and a sewing machine. The other had a single bed and a treadmill and a low row of built-in bookshelves below a window that looked out onto Arlene's roof. The top shelf was full of yearbooks from the school where Rebecca taught, Horizons Academy. They were arranged in descending numerical order by year; she had one for each year since 1996.

On my way out, I paused at a portable phone that sat on a table in the short hallway. It was unplugged from the wall. I plugged it back in and turned on the handset, hoping for the broken dial tone that indicates a new voice mail, but just heard the regular one so I turned it off.

Then I reconsidered and hit redial.

The line rang three times before a woman answered, already angry. "This has to stop."

"Who is this—"

"Do. Not. Call. This. Number. Again."

She hung up.

jotted down the phone number in my notebook to look into further.

I wanted to talk to Keir Metcalf in person, but I wanted to have all of my facts straight first. So my next stop was the records department at the Toledo Police headquarters, a long row of bank-teller-esque windows and oddly fancy tile flooring just inside the entrance. I didn't want to wait for the results of the query, and I left my email address with the clerk and headed a bit south to Perrysburg, where AA Security ran an office from a small strip-mall storefront between a mattress store and a bookshop called Gathering Volumes. The glass front of AA's office was tinted black, impossible to see into.

The door chimed as I went inside; the interior was all grey industrial carpet and beige cubicle walls. It looked like the office of a second-rate financial-services group that had turned me down for a small business loan once. A receptionist sat at an L-shaped desk to the left of the door, reading a magazine.

"Hi there, are you hiring?"

"For what, sweetheart?" Her expression said that AA Security only had space for one vagina and it was hers.

"Investigators," I said.

"You want to be a detective, sweetheart, you need to be licensed."

"I am licensed." I showed her my laminated ID from the state.

"Oh." She put down her magazine, which appeared to be something to do with homesteading. She was a Clairol blonde in a camo dress, her eyes rimmed in electric-blue liner behind cat-eye glasses. Everything about her confused me. "I don't know."

"Do you have an application or something I could fill out?" I knew there was no chance this place had a job application. "I'd really appreciate the chance—I'm new to town, and it's, you know, hard. Or could I speak with the owner, maybe?"

I could hear someone on the phone toward the back of the office. He seemed to be talking about boat refinishing.

The receptionist sighed and got to her feet. The camo dress was complemented by towering camo heels. Without them she'd be shorter than me, but with them she had me by three inches. Hands on her hips, she strode down the hallway with a model's posture and disappeared through a doorway.

I glanced around the small waiting area. Two orange burlap chairs that looked borrowed from a seventies bureaucracy, a low glass table with an ashtray and no magazines. It had been years since you were allowed to smoke inside a business, so who knew what the ashtray was for. It was clean as a whistle. I lifted up the corner of the receptionist's magazine—*Hobby Farms.* Her desk was separated from a small conference table by a row of shoulder-height filing cabinets, the top of which was adorned by a potted plant and a glossy black statuette with a gold plaque at the bottom. I couldn't tell what the statuette depicted—a crashing wave? a dustpan?—or what it said, and I withdrew from it as the receptionist reappeared and did her runway walk back in my direction.

"Have a seat," she said. "He's on the phone."

While I waited, I checked my email and found a message from a Toledo records clerk. *We have two run sheets for calls from Mrs. Arlene French, no corresponding reports.* That meant that a formal report hadn't been taken, and charges hadn't been considered. The first run sheet was dated in March and said "Nature: Domestic disturbance." *RP heard an individual shouting "bad words" up at a neighbor's window. Responder found homeowner engaged in civilized conversation at the time of arrival. Nothing to follow up on at this time.*

I smiled. "Bad words" did sound like a description that Arlene might use.

The second report contained even less info: *RP stated that her neighbor's ex-husband was ringing neighbor's doorbell "ceaselessly." Neighbor not home.*

These incident sheets didn't exactly crack the case wide open. But they did tell me that Deputy Montoya's investigation had definitely been less than thorough.

I put my phone away just as Keir Metcalf approached from down the hall. In person he was six-four and he wore a tweed blazer over a black button-down and jeans. Cowboy boots. The shirt was untucked, and it was undone one button too far from the collar; a wiry patch of grey chest hair tufted out above a pair of mirrored aviators that he had hooked into the front of the shirt. He smirked vaguely, pleased with himself. "Keir Metcalf, how are ya?"

I shook his hand and followed him back down the hallway. "You know, I'm not hiring right now, but I've never thought about getting a female investigator so I thought I might as well hear your story."

"Not sure you're allowed to say that. *Never thought about getting a female.*"

His eyes narrowed at me like he was trying to decide if I was being funny or not. Then he decided that I was and he laughed. "You know what I mean."

"Sure," I said. "And you know that there are places only a woman can go. And certain people are much more likely to open up to me than they are to you."

Metcalf was terribly amused by me. "Mostly what we do is

security. Personal protection, corporate services, special events. VIP detail. We did Luke Bryant not too long ago."

"Wow. That's amazing."

"You carry a gun?"

"It's in my car, but yeah."

"See there," Metcalf said. "That's why I don't have any females. What on earth good is a gun gonna do you in the car?"

"Well, I wasn't planning on shooting anyone in here."

He laughed again. "You're sorta cute. You married?"

Oh, I hated this man. I hoped Maggie was right about him just so I would have the pleasure of watching him get arrested. As if anything had ever been that simple. "Divorced," I said.

"Me too. Some things, they just don't work out, right?"

"Now there's someone I wouldn't mind shooting."

Metcalf's expression remained neutral. Conspicuously neutral? I wasn't sure. "I bet you've never fired that gun of yours outside of your CCW class."

I smiled at him. "I have to be honest about something."

"What's that?"

"I'm not looking for a job. I work for your former stepdaughter, Maggie Holmer."

The amused smile stuck around but his eyes went hard. "What's this, now?"

"It's about Rebecca."

Strangely, his expression seemed to relax on that. "May she rest."

"Yes, about that. Maggie seems to think that there was a lot of *un*rest between the two of you."

Metcalf twitched his mouth like he was checking his teeth for poppy seeds. "We had our troubles. But all of that was over."

"When was the last time you saw her?"

"The day of the last hearing. Divorce court, downtown."

"When was the last time you talked to her?"

"Same time, same place. Why is Maggie hiring a PI? I thought what happened to Rebecca was an accident."

"There are still some questions."

"Who has these questions? Just Maggie?"

"And now me."

He scowled. "So she's saying, what, that somebody murdered Rebecca?"

"Like I said, there are some questions."

"Maggie's a—she can be difficult. I always wondered if something was wrong with her. She was in high school when Rebecca and I got married and she was always moping around like she was five minutes away from slitting her wrists."

His compassion was inspiring. "She was depressed?"

"Nah, she just needed to get over herself."

"Any idea why she'd think you might have something to do with Rebecca's death?"

"Rebecca was a fine woman, and I'm sorry she's gone. I'm sorry our marriage fell apart. She probably tripped over that goddamn dog, to be honest."

Everyone kept saying that. Which made me much less likely to believe it.

"But listen," Metcalf added, "if you want a piece of unsolicited advice, don't trust somebody like Maggie. She's the type of girl who says, *I don't like drama.*" He made his voice go shrill on the last four words. "But actually she loves it. So if you work for people like that, you aren't going to have a future in this business."

Despite his memes and his Bible pamphlets, the Christian spirit did not appear to be especially strong within Keir Metcalf. After I talked to him, I sat in the car in front of the bookstore and tried to figure out the owner of the phone number Rebecca had last dialed from her house. My searching wasn't immediately successful, which told me it was a cell phone but little else. I was still sitting there thinking about it when the door of AA Security opened and Metcalf came out, sunglasses on, a phone of his own to his ear.

I rolled down my window to listen.

"—unbelievable. After everything I've done for you? Oh, really?"

Then he got into his car, a deep blue Escalade, and I couldn't hear the rest.

He peeled out of the parking lot and I decided to follow.

Metcalf stopped for gas, then drove north through rush-hour traffic—surprisingly heavy for a city of this size—and into a municipality called Ottawa Hills, according to Google Maps. We went down a long road lined with new-build subdivisions and Metcalf eventually stopped on a gravel driveway, where a red pickup truck was already parked. I drove past and took the next turn, another driveway about a hundred feet away. "I'm home," I murmured and got out my binoculars.

Metcalf and another white guy, tall and thin with white hair, were standing in the first driveway, talking. The older guy pointed at something in the distance, drawing a line with an index finger in midair. Metcalf nodded.

I scanned the area through the binoculars, but there wasn't much to see; the driveway where the trio stood seemed to cut across a mostly empty lot with the skeleton of a large construction project just getting started far back from the road. I could make out a concrete elevator shaft and a huge mound of dirt.

I watched the men for close to an hour. I couldn't hear anything and as the daylight began to wane, I wondered what I was doing there. I grew increasingly concerned that the owner of the driveway where I was lurking would notice me, especially when my phone rang—the call from a Columbus number I didn't recognize—through the car's Bluetooth.

I quickly put my window up and whispered, "This is Roxane."

"Why are we whispering?"

"Who is this?"

"It's Cat."

I felt my teeth grind together. I could never get used to calling her that—she was always Catherine to me. But I didn't know why on earth she was calling me. "What do you want?"

"Ouch."

"What's this number?"

"Wystan's cell."

I watched the men through the window. More pointing, nodding, and Keir Metcalf wrote some stuff on a clipboard.

"The house sold, finally," Catherine said. "We're clearing everything out this week. I have some things that belong to you. So that's why I'm calling."

I would've liked to tell her to throw it all away, but I knew what I'd left there—my Kindle, a nearly full bottle of Midleton that I'd nicked from my father's office, my beloved black leather jacket, and several bras. I had actually thought about dropping by the house in Bexley more than once and went so far as to drive past it back in March or April, but the FOR SALE sign freaked me out and I didn't stop and I didn't go back.

"Roxane?"

"Sorry, what?"

"Can I come by tonight to drop it off?"

That was a terrible idea. "I'm in Toledo."

"Until when?"

"I don't know."

"I'd love to see you. Not sure when I'll be back in Ohio."

I rubbed the center of my forehead. "See me for what?"

"I just have no fucking idea, Roxane."

"It's not a good idea."

"When did that ever stop you from wanting me before?"

"Catherine, I'm not doing this."

"What about your stuff?"

"Can you put it on my porch?"

She huffed. "Put it on your porch?"

"Like drop it off?"

"Whatever."

She hung up on me, offended that I hadn't said yes, come over, I'll race home from northwestern Ohio so you can fuck with me in person. I shook my head and rolled the window back down.

It was nearly dark by the time the men got into their respective vehicles and drove back the way Metcalf had come.

I followed, hoping to get a license plate number for the red truck. But both vehicles went to the same place, a brick building with a giant mural proclaiming MANCY'S STEAKS CELEBRATING 100 YEARS.

The steakhouse was an old-fashioned joint, all white table linens and orangish lighting and low, arched brick doorways. Keir Metcalf was at a round table with the man from the gravel driveway and another guy, this one a bit younger, mid-forties, stocky build, tan suit. I lingered near the bar and ordered a club soda and eavesdropped for a while. But though the restaurant seemed like the ideal place for a good old boys' network meeting about nefarious deeds, they seemed to be talking about fences.

I thought I was doing a good job of being a wallflower. Then, about thirty-five minutes into the discussion, I felt a tap on my shoulder. "I thought that was you," Metcalf said. "What, are you following me?"

I decided to play it straight. "Sure. Either that or I heard this place makes a mean club soda."

He was back to finding me amusing. "Why don't you come and sit down? You'll be able to hear the conversation so much better."

I wasn't sure if he thought that would intimidate me into walking away or if he thought that would convince me he had nothing to hide—or if he just wanted to see if I'd do it. But it took more than being casually arrogant in a steakhouse to intimidate me. "Great, I'd love to," I announced.

Metcalf looked a little surprised, but he held out a hand toward the table.

"Crazy coincidence," he said, his eyes locked on mine. I remembered what Maggie had said about his personality. "But I just interviewed this young lady for a job today. Say hello, honey."

"Hello, honey," I said because I knew they would like it, and they did. "I'm Roxane. Just moved here from Columbus."

"Scooter," the guy in the red pickup said. Up close, I saw his hair was spiky with gel like he was a teenager.

"Joel Creedle," the tan suit said. He resembled a low-rent Russell Crowe—the rounded face, indistinct stubble, thin lips, dark hair almost curling over his forehead.

Scooter said, "What part of the city are you in?"

"Oh, by the mall," I said vaguely.

Joel said, "The Franklin Park Mall?"

I nodded, feeling Metcalf's eyes boring holes into me. I hoped this was his personality and not his idea of foreplay.

"Maybe we're neighbors," Joel added.

"I have a feeling you live somewhere nicer than me." I gestured around the steakhouse. "I can't afford to eat here."

"Or drink, apparently." Metcalf pointed at my club soda. "You want something else? On me."

I went for demure. "I better not."

Scooter was still giving me a thorough once-over—I wasn't

sure what was taking so long. "There's no way Lindy's letting you hire another gal to work in there."

"Roxane's a detective, not a secretary." Metcalf winked at me. "Or so she says."

Now the whole group was amused by me. "A woman private dick? Metcalf, you ever hear of such a thing?"

Metcalf nodded. "I've met some at conferences and whatnot. Bull dykes, every last one of 'em."

A chorus of disgusted "hmmm"s went around the table. The consensus on bull dykes was not favorable.

"But you got to be able to work with people of all stripes in this business," Keir Metcalf added, magnanimously, like this made him the resident liberal of his peer group.

Going for a change of subject, I said, "So you aren't all PIs, then?"

"Nope," Scooter said, and tapped his chest. "State trooper." He pointed at Joel. "Preacher man."

"Excuse me?"

Joel Creedle smiled indulgently. "I like to think of myself as a shepherd."

Metcalf said, "Joel's a pastor. Are you a believer, Roxane?"

"That's none of your business."

"Ooh, she's a feisty one."

"You should have heard Lindy talking to her today. Talk about feisty . . ."

I sat there and listened to them shoot the shit for a while, growing increasingly tired of them. If Metcalf's goal had been to bore me to death, it just might work. When the entrées came, I stood up and thanked them for the company, since obviously nothing of substance would be discussed in my presence.

It was almost seven when Metcalf finally came out of the restaurant, and I followed him at a safe distance, but he just went home to a stone house in Sylvania on a wedge-shaped property. I lingered on the main road and used my binoculars to see what he was up to, which turned out to be watching Fox News with his pants unbuckled.

"Great," I muttered, and pulled a U-turn and sped away.

CHAPTER 8

The motel I had checked in to that afternoon had felt vaguely cheery with natural light, but now that the sun was going down it seemed a little bleak. I sat at the small wooden desk and flipped open my notebook to the number that belonged to the hissing woman Rebecca had apparently been calling. I briefly wondered about Lindy, Keir Metcalf's secretary, who seemed more than capable of hissing. But when I dialed the number from my cell phone this time, it rang and went to voice mail, no recorded name.

"Hi," I said into the ether, "my name is Roxane West and I'm calling from *The Columbus Dispatch,* working on a piece about Ohio women, and I was given your name as someone who may be interested in sharing her story." Everybody had a story, and most folks were pretty eager to share it. I was hoping that the mysterious hissing woman would be one of them.

I looked through the rest of my meager collection of clues—the cashout slip from Caesars in Windsor and the parking voucher from Detroit. It was late enough to call it a day, but too early to call it a night, so I decided to follow up on these two items instead of spending the remaining hours of the evening in the bleak motel room with my thoughts.

I'd been to Windsor once before, back in college, in the days before you needed a passport and could get across the border with whatever you had in your wallet. You could also drink and gamble there at nineteen, which appealed to my rebel streak, and casinos seemed exotic and forbidden, since we didn't have any in the area anyway. Now they were all over Ohio, so the temptation for random border-crossing by today's youth was no doubt vastly reduced.

I parked on the sixth floor of the parking garage and looked out. The huge red Caesars sign shone pinkly on the brackish river below. In my recollection of the place, the Canadian side of things featured the casino, an all-night Chinese restaurant, and not much else. But now I saw it was far more expansive than I remembered, with high-rise hotels, a waterside garden—grey in the fading daylight—and a massive attached arena. It was raining softly and not many people were out. Across the water, the gap-toothed Detroit skyline looked like something from another time period with its gritty old buildings, so unlike the modern glass landscape of Windsor itself.

Although I'd had the hour-long drive from Toledo—plus twenty minutes spent in line for Customs—to think of a plan for once I got here, I hadn't come up with anything better than simply wandering around. So I wandered across the gold and red gambling floor of the casino slowly, hoping something would occur to me in the noisy space. The massive banks of slot machines were a third full, maybe less, but the lights and carnival-ride sounds of it all gave the illusion of vibrance, simultaneously sensory overload and sensory deprivation—all casinos were like this, and I could have imagined I was anywhere.

I would not have said no to a comped whiskey from a cocktail waitress. But like the casinos at home, and unlike Vegas, the booze wasn't free. I settled for a Coke, changed a twenty-dollar bill for twenty-six Canadian, and mindlessly pulled the lever on a slot machine called Diamond Dust for a few minutes, or seconds, really, since that was all it took to run through it. The next time a waitress passed by, I flagged her down and showed her a photo of Rebecca on my phone.

"I was just wondering, have you seen my friend around here?"

She gave the image a cursory glance. "I've barely seen anybody here tonight. It's dead."

"I don't mean tonight. I mean, is she someone you've seen here regularly?"

Now she looked annoyed. "How am I supposed to remember that?"

"Maybe you're not. It was just a question. Her name is Rebecca Newsome."

She studied the photo again. "She looks like a real nice lady but I've never seen her."

Something had rippled through her face, though, a faint flick of her eyes to something above us.

After she walked away, I looked up; she had glanced at the beady round eye of a security camera.

The security operations office was on the ground floor of the casino, near a giant buffet that smelled of prime rib and Italian dressing, and was cleverly disguised as a lost-and-found. No one was at the little counter, but the mirrored wall behind it no doubt contained a room full of surveillance equipment—i.e., answers to at least some of my questions.

But even if I managed to convince someone to allow me to take a look at security footage, there was no telling how long it would take to find Rebecca on the screen, or if it would even yield any useful information if I did. I wandered away from the desk and used my phone to pull up LinkedIn, where I searched for *security director Caesars Windsor.*

Who happened to be a man named Barry Newsome.

I called the main casino number and asked for the man, but he wasn't in this evening. That was fine with me; I was just happy to have an angle to pursue. Maggie had indicated that her father was long out of the picture, but it seemed like that might not be true.

Hoping to make it two for two, I drove back through the tunnel and stopped at the St. Clair Club, the place where Rebecca had parked at some recent point.

I pulled to a stop at the curb. A guy in a blue-green windbreaker emblazoned VALET came up to my window. "Good evening, ma'am," he said.

I looked up at the building I was parked beside. I could make out red brick and a dark-colored stairway awning.

I put the window down. "Hi. What is this place?"

"Are you dining with us or staying?"

"Is this a restaurant?"

The guy looked mildly offended. "This is the St. Clair Club, ma'am."

"Which is?"

Headlights flashed in my rearview mirror and the valet guy glanced behind me. "Are you valeting your vehicle this evening?"

"Sure," I said. I gave him my name and watched as he scribbled it down on one end of a tear-off valet ticket. He detached the other end and gave me a spiel about allowing fifteen minutes to have my car brought around. "I have a question."

"Yes?"

"Do you keep a record of which vehicles are parked here and when?"

"A record?"

"Like if I had a valet ticket from a few weeks ago and I wanted to know when exactly it had been used."

"So, wait, you have been here before?"

"No, I'm just curious. If you have a system for keeping track of that info."

The valet guy nodded at a key cabinet mounted underneath a podium that sat just below the awning. "That's our system."

I thanked him and went up the steps. A doorman in a black suit over a black dress shirt opened up for me. "Good evening, madam."

Madam, now. My, my. Once inside the door, I was standing in a two-story lobby done up in dark, polished wood and plush blue velvet. To the right were a hotelesque counter and a bank of gilded elevators that looked like they might contain white-gloved operators. To the left, a hostess stand and a coat check, behind which was a curtained doorway that led to a restaurant from the sound of it, although I couldn't see it. The counter to the right was unattended, so I opted for the restaurant.

The hostess intercepted me, smiling politely. "Good evening, madam." The smile, bulletproofed by the kind of long-wear lipstick that you have to use olive oil and sandpaper to remove, stayed in place. "May I suggest that you may be more comfortable if you went back up to your room and changed?"

"Pardon?"

"We don't allow denim in our dining room." She pointed to a small framed card on her podium: THE RESTAURANT AT THE ST. CLAIR CLUB APPRECIATES YOUR ADHERENCE TO OUR BUSINESS-CASUAL DRESS CODE.

"What exactly is business casual?"

"Our female dinner guests typically feel the most comfortable in a dress or a skirt."

I said, "Do they, now."

I had a pair of black pants back in the motel room, but not in the car. I sighed and thanked her and went over to the hotel counter instead. Still empty. I peered over the ledge and found the countertop to be conspicuously clean; a computer screen featured a bouncing-ball screensaver, which flipped to a login gateway when I may have nudged the mouse a tiny bit. A bin on the floor, labeled OUTGOING MAIL, contained windowpane envelopes—probably credit-card bills for a bunch of executives who didn't want their wives seeing what they bought and wondering who it was for—and a dozen or so white padded envelopes with neatly typed addresses. The only papers on the desk appeared to be application forms for joining this establishment.

I took one and tried to call the elevator, but it required a room key to do so.

Opposite the desk was a row of small cubicles, presumably for making private phone calls—but they were all empty.

Whatever Rebecca had been doing here was going to remain a secret for now.

My motel was on Route 20, across from a Chipotle and a liquor store. The room had barely cost twice the price of a burrito, guac, and three plastic airline bottles of Jim Beam, but the accommodations seemed clean and smelled like laundry soap, which was a far better smell than some motels. I poured one of the whiskeys into my half-full Coke and reflected on my evening as I ate a late dinner.

One for two wasn't bad, as far as useful trips go, but I was annoyed that a wardrobe issue had prevented me from getting into the restaurant at the St. Clair Club. I made a point of putting my black corduroys into my computer bag to put into the car in case I found myself going there again. Then I spent a while looking at Barry Newsome's background: divorced from Rebecca in 1995, remarried to a current wife, Sofia Calvet, a Canadian citizen, also in 1995. It appeared they'd lived in Montreal for a time, then moved to Windsor a decade ago. Barry Newsome had served in the Gulf War, then worked as a security guard at the Toledo Public Library and a string of hotels, worked his way up the ranks in the loss-prevention division of Holt Renfrew, then turned up at the casino.

It seemed that Rebecca had a type—law enforcement.

I was reading up on the St. Clair Club when Tom called. "Did you know that private social clubs still exist?" I said by way of hello.

He was used to me by now and didn't miss a beat. "Are you saying that you wish to join one?"

"Are there any in Columbus?"

"I'm sure. Not that either of us have the right pedigree."

"What are you implying about my pedigree?"

I heard him smile. "So what brings private social clubs to mind?"

"I was just in this place, the St. Clair in Detroit."

"You're in Detroit?"

"I was. Also, Windsor. But now I'm back in Toledo."

He sighed. "You're in Toledo." It wasn't a question.

"Should I have told you that I was going?"

"I don't know about *should,* but you might have mentioned it. I was going to stop by your office with Ho Toy."

"Shit. Tom, I'm sorry." It hadn't occurred to me to tell anybody before I came up here, but I could see his point. Like he'd said the night before, we had fallen into a nice rhythm, one that included frequent dinners together at odd hours in my office. "Garlic chicken with extra green peppers?"

"I know what you like."

"I know you do. I'm sorry—really."

"How's the human-trafficking capital of Ohio?"

I winced in the semidark. "Toledo?"

"Yes. It's the proximity to the border. You probably saw how easy it is to get over the border and back just today."

"It used to be even easier."

"Yeah, it did. I remember once, when I was in college, I got across with a student ID and a Sears card."

I laughed out loud. "Like a store credit card?"

"Yes."

"Why did you even have a Sears credit card in college?"

"A girl told me I needed to stop dressing like Kurt Cobain's gardener if I wanted to get any traction with her."

I was sipping my drink when he said it and I almost snorted. "You've always been a lady-killer."

I heard the smile in his voice from a hundred miles away. "When are you coming home?"

"Soon."

"Will I talk to you before then, or are you just going to show up here at some point?"

"Hard to say." I cracked open another of the airplane whiskey bottles. The tiny mouth made it impossible to drink it fast, giving me the sense of admirable restraint. "No, I'll call you tomorrow."

CHAPTER 9

Rebecca's boss was named Sharon Coombs, and she was the Horizons Academy's vice principal. We went to her office, which resembled mine in its unfinishedness. "This is my first year in the school administration," she explained. "I taught English here for almost twenty years."

"Congratulations."

Sharon shrugged. She wore her greying hair in neat box braids and no makeup. Despite the greying hair, her warm brown skin was unlined. "It's bittersweet, to be honest. It's been a difficult school year already. What happened to Rebecca is just terrible. For many of us, personally, of course, plus she was really beloved by the students. So it has been hard, trying to act strong for them when really I just feel like bawling every time I see the flowers kids are putting down there by her office. Maggie really thinks that someone . . . did this?"

"She just wants to be sure," I said. I was sitting on a small, low-to-the-ground love seat, probably the scene of many tough conversations. I could see no fewer than five tissue boxes in Sharon's office. "She was about to have her baby when it happened. Now Maggie is worried she missed something. There are definitely some questions."

"Well, I don't know what I can do to help, but I'd sure like to try."

"The police never spoke to you?"

Sharon shook her head. Her earrings made a faint rustling sound. "Should they have?"

"I don't know. It's true that it did appear to be an accident from the get-go, but it only takes a minute to make a phone call. Any chance someone else from the school would have spoken with them?"

"No, I would have heard about it. We've been having weekly meetings with the whole staff. Someone would have mentioned it. But I don't think there's anything we could have said that would be useful, though. Rebecca had been off for the previous week or so." Sharon smiled. "She felt so bad, asking for two weeks off right when the academic year had just started. But she never takes time off." The smile faltered; I could tell she was mentally correcting the verb tense.

"So she didn't have any problems here at school?"

"No, not at all. I know it's a cliché to say she was universally beloved, but I mean, she was. Kids would talk to her about things they'd never bring up to an English teacher, say, or the administration. She just had this openness."

"Any particular kids?"

Her expression turned ever so slightly stern. "I can't talk particulars about our students, of course."

"Right, of course. But no problems?"

"None."

"Can you tell me anything about Rebecca's divorce?"

Sharon looked uneasy.

"Maggie told me her version, but maybe you have a slightly different point of view as Rebecca's friend."

"Well . . ." She trailed off, debating. "Rebecca was on her own for such a long time. When she told me she was going to marry Keir, I remember being surprised. He seemed like a perfectly nice man but I was just surprised that she'd want to uproot her life for him at that point."

"Uproot how?"

"Oh, like how they had to live in his house, some place up by the lake. I just remember Rebecca being disappointed that they weren't going to get a new place together, that she had to move to his place. And I know he wasn't happy that she kept her house and rented it out, rather than selling. I don't know. I saw less of her after they got married, too."

"Was he controlling?"

"I don't know if it was controlling so much, just, the pairing seemed unlikely. Rebecca was no bra-burning feminist or anything but Keir was traditional, I guess that's the word."

"And Rebecca wasn't?"

"I'm not sure how to explain it. Her faith was very important to her—to both of them. She belonged to the Keystone Christian Fellowship and I believe that was how they met. But over time I think Rebecca started turning a bit more moderate in her beliefs. For example, she didn't take his last name—I remember her talking about that. For her it wasn't a statement or anything, because Newsome, that was her first husband's name. But after so many years, it became her name. You know? She didn't want to do that again, the identity change."

I nodded. "The first ex-husband, he still in the picture?"

Sharon shook her head. "Not that she ever mentioned."

"Was Keir ever violent? Emotionally abusive?"

Her expression went a little shocked. "No, nothing like that. He's a very friendly guy, almost too friendly. You know how some men can be. They don't know how to turn it off. That was the impression I always had of him." She cocked her head as something else occurred to her. "But like I said, she started socializing a lot less, after they got married. I thought part of it was that his house was so far out, it made for a long commute to come to work, a long drive just to have dinner on a weekend or whatever. I guess that could be its own kind of abuse. Isolation?"

"For sure. Do you know why they split up?"

"Well, I'm not completely sure. I don't even know that she would have told me, as in confided in me. But she actually was worried about her job—we're a Christian school, and some people on staff are less than open-minded."

"About divorce?"

"You'd be surprised."

"But isn't the stat something like fifty percent of all marriages end in divorce?"

Sharon shrugged. "Sad, but true. And necessary in so many unhappy cases."

"So you're plenty open-minded."

"In my opinion, Horizons is a *modern* Christian school. Nothing rigid can stand."

"What doesn't bend, breaks," I said, quoting Ani DiFranco.

She didn't appear to get the reference, but she nodded.

I said, "So she mentioned that she was getting divorced and hoped that she could still keep her job. Then what?"

"I think I just said I was sorry to hear that and asked if she was doing okay. She said it was all for the best and that you can't expect people to change after you marry them. But looking back, I'm not sure if she was talking about Keir, or about herself."

Lindy, Keir Metcalf's secretary, was done up in a lime-green tunic over pleather leggings. "You're back," she said, less than thrilled to see me. She was filing her nails with an emery board that matched her top.

"Is he in?"

"No."

"Yes, he is, his car is here."

She stared at me. We had reached an impasse. But then I heard Metcalf's voice from down the hall. "You can come on back."

Lindy resumed work on her nails without another word.

In Metcalf's office, I sat in the same chair I had occupied yesterday. "I can't figure you out," I said. "Are you being cooperative or just trying to confuse me?"

"I'm a cooperative guy." He leaned back in his chair, both thumbs hooked through empty belt loops. "What do you want?"

"I wanted to know if you ever met Rebecca's first husband."

"Nope."

"Know anything about him?"

"Nope." He rocked a little in the chair, relaxed as anything. "He ditched her to shack up with some French-Canadian model before they'd even been married two years."

"So you do know something about him."

"That's the sum total of what I know."

"So you didn't know that he works at a casino in Windsor?"

"Nope." He shrugged.

"Or that he's also in the security business?"

"Really?" Metcalf sat up. "Heh. How about that."

I didn't like him, but I had to admit that I believed him. I said, "You and Rebecca ever go to Windsor?"

"No, why would we?"

"Detroit?"

"Occasionally, when Cleveland played the Tigers. Oh, and we saw Paul Simon once, at the Fox Theatre. Great show."

"Ever hear of the St. Clair Club?"

"Nope."

"Why's Maggie hate you so much?"

The change of tone caught him off guard, like I hoped it would. "Pardon me?"

"Yesterday when I told you why I was here, you practically bristled when I mentioned her name. And you kind of relaxed when the subject changed to your dead ex-wife. I'm just curious as to why that is. Since you're such a cooperative guy."

He shook his head. "I can't help you. I have no idea what happened to Rebecca and that's the truth."

"Why does Maggie think you did?"

His face began to pinken up beneath the tan. "She and I had a disagreement a long time ago. That's it."

"What kind of disagreement?"

"It doesn't matter."

"Maybe it does to me."

"I told you yesterday, she's unstable."

I said, "The more you tell me it doesn't matter, the more I'll want to figure it out. So if it truly doesn't matter, you'll just tell me and save us all a lot of time."

"You're a pushy little bitch."

"Yes."

Metcalf got up and closed the door. He was wearing a different pair of cowboy boots, these ones bone-colored with steel tips. He said, "I've played guitar my whole life. I used to lead a youth ministry at our church. A devotional rock band, I suppose you could call it. Maggie wanted to be a singer when she was in high school. That was how I first got to know Rebecca, because Maggie was in the group."

I waited.

"Maggie likes drama. Attention. I kept finding myself alone with her—her doing. She had this whole thing in her head, that we were going to be together someday. I had to be firm with her. Very firm. I didn't intend to embarrass her, but I think I did. She never liked me after that."

"So she hires me to prove that you killed her mother because ten years ago she had a crush on you?"

"I told you, there's something wrong with her."

"And you didn't do anything to lead her on."

"No, of course not."

It wasn't hard to imagine Keir Metcalf leading someone on. I'd seen flashes of that myself—last night at dinner, the piercing eye contact that had felt almost like foreplay. But of all the reasons that Maggie had for believing that her mother's death was not accidental, I found her belief in her former stepdad's involvement to be the least convincing.

There were still plenty of other questions that required an answer.

CHAPTER 10

When I got back to my motel room, I inserted the key into its slot but nothing happened. I tried it again, flipping the key over—no dice. Figuring I had demagnetized the card in my pocket somehow, I went down to the lobby and got a replacement from the deeply apathetic clerk and went back up to the second floor.

Once I got the door open, I froze.

The shower was running.

I definitely had not left the shower running that morning.

I closed the door gently and returned to the car for my gun. Then I went back into the room and set my computer bag down on the desk and looked around carefully. Clothes tossed every which way. Muffin wrappers on the nightstand. Scraps of paper from the tiny motel notepad balled up on the desk and floor. All of that tracked, even though I'd only had the room for one night. I listened for sounds of splish-splashing or singing in the shower, but the only sound was the steady spray of water.

Maybe a plumbing problem that had caused the shower to turn on spontaneously?

It seemed feasible, but then there was the issue of the key card.

I crept over to the bathroom, still listening hard.

The bathroom door was closed, the lights off.

Gun drawn, I opened the bathroom door slowly.

I was greeted by a cloud of steam, but it was easy to see that the shower was empty, its dingy curtain pushed aside like I'd left it.

I reached in and turned the water off. Then I hit the lights, and that was when I saw the writing superimposed over my foggy reflection.

STOP.

"Hi again," I said to the clerk, "somebody was in my room today."

"Housekeeping goes through between nine and three," the clerk told me, answering a question I hadn't asked.

"They wrote 'STOP' on my mirror."

"Housekeeping did?"

"I didn't want any housekeeping. I had the sign up. And my key didn't work."

"How do you know someone was in there if your key didn't work?" He was devastatingly stoned.

"I was just down here, you made me a new key? Like five minutes ago?"

He nodded. "Right, right. So what's the problem now?"

"Somebody entered my room, turned on the shower, and wrote a message in the steam on the mirror."

"Housekeeping goes through between nine and three?" he repeated, more of a query this time.

"I had the sign up. And the bed wasn't even made."

"Did you want the bed to be made?"

I set my computer bag down on the floor at my feet. Clearly this was going to take a minute. I tried a different tack: "Has anyone other than me come by to say they lost their key?"

I was thinking that if I needed to get into a hotel room that wasn't mine, I might try just that, especially in a place like this. Especially if they're busy—or stoned—hotel employees sometimes code keys as blank master keys, which are designed to open the next room they're inserted into, then programmed to that room.

But the clerk just stared at me.

"Nobody came through here trying to get into room two-fourteen?"

"Are you, like, someone important?"

"No, just someone who is distressed by someone breaking into my room."

"I just don't know what to tell you, ma'am."

I sighed. "Would I be able to switch rooms? The, um, heater is too loud, if you need an official complaint."

This seemed to cheer him. "Yes, I can do that."

My new room was on the third floor and looked over a row of rusting Dumpsters instead of the parking lot. I threw my stuff on the bed and sat down and sulked a minute. Stop what? It wasn't the most helpful of messages, but if the object had been simply to unnerve me, it was a raging success.

I had one tiny whiskey bottle left from last night, but it was only the middle of the afternoon, and I didn't want to go there. Not yet.

During the room-swapping saga, I'd missed a phone call. I used the little electric kettle in the room to heat up water for tea and listened to my voice mail while it rasped to life.

"Hello, my name is Marliss and I received your media inquiry. I'm touching base on behalf of Constance Archer-Nash . . ."

My thoughts snagged on *media inquiry*—it took me a minute to recall that I'd left a message last night for the woman Rebecca had called, invoking some lifestyle article that my journalist alter ego was desperate to write—and I almost missed the name Constance Archer-Nash completely.

I listened to the message again. It said the same thing the second time through.

I had thought there was a fair chance this gambit would get results, but I hadn't been expecting it to be outsourced to the hissing woman's media inquiry person, and I really hadn't been expecting the homegrown lightning rod to be involved.

I called the media coordinator back and got her voice mail.

"You've reached Marliss Scott, media coordinator for Nora Health. I'm on the phone or away from my desk . . ."

I'd heard of Nora Health in passing; it was Constance Archer-Nash's company, but I wasn't sure entirely what it was, so I looked it up now.

What if health care was easy, affordable, and actually made you feel better? We bring real doctors and real care to you, exactly where you are.

The website was all HDR photos and millennial pink.

I read on:

Nora Health is an innovative network of women's health professionals dedicated to providing in-office and remote health care at reduced rates, because no one should go without.

On the About page, Constance Archer-Nash smiled out at me, a woman in her late thirties with short, dark hair and a row of piercings around the outside of her left ear.

But why was Rebecca Newsome calling her?

I made a mental list of reasons the Christian school nurse could be harassing Constance Archer-Nash over the phone: anti–birth control, anti–liberal politics, anti-doctor? The bitter end of a torrid affair, a lease dispute, a plain old wrong number?

I left a message for Marliss. The phone rang a beat later and I answered quickly, hoping it was her.

But a shaky voice said, "Oh, hello, dear, this is Missus Arlene French."

Rebecca's neighbor. "Hi there. What's up?"

"I'm sorry to bother you after business hours," she said.

I smiled. It was five thirty. "No problem. What's up?"

"Well, it's just that the police are at Rebecca's house again."

"Right now?"

"Yes, dear."

Before I left the room, I rigged up a low-tech security system by crumpling up a bunch of pages from the tiny notepad. I went into the hallway and closed the door almost all the way, leaving a gap only as wide as my arm, and then I tossed the paper balls onto the floor just inside the door, like dice. Then, without moving the door, I snapped a photo of the random configuration of papers and made a mental note to do the same when I returned. If someone came into the room while I was gone, they'd move the papers just by opening the door. If no one did, my "before" and "after" pictures would be identical.

It wasn't exactly scientific, but it would work.

There was a motto to put on my website.

CHAPTER 11

The cops were gone by the time I got over there, but Arlene French explained their appearance thusly:

"Just one car this time, but two officers knocked on the door for probably five minutes. I was in the bath when I called you, you see." She patted her damp hair. "Otherwise I would have gone out there and made them stick around for you. But by the time I got my shoes on and made it outside, they had already left. I'm very sorry."

"Don't even worry about it," I said. "You did great."

She beamed at me.

I went into Rebecca's house; nothing appeared out of place. But what would cause the police to show up again, over a month after she died? I wandered through the living room and immediately noticed that the phone cord was unplugged from the wall again.

I crouched down on the carpet and examined the jack. It had been unplugged yesterday, but I'd plugged it back in when I hit redial. I hadn't unplugged it again, at least not intentionally.

I reached back to the baseboard and returned the jack to its proper place, noting that the faceplate had been painted over so many times that it seemed virtually impossible for the thing to become unplugged accidentally.

I hit redial once more. I could already hear Constance Archer-Nash's angry hiss in my ear, but the line rang three times and a voice said, "Marco's Pizza, help you?"

At this moment, someone knocked on the back door behind me. I practically threw the phone across the room. Hoping it was Arlene, I parted the curtains and looked out to see a pimply kid in a humiliating Marco's hat.

"What the actual fuck," I muttered. I opened the door a crack. "What do you want?"

I immediately felt bad, because the kid looked terrified. "I, um, I have your all-the-meats sub and a Mountain Dew?" His voice quavered like an opera singer's.

I let out a breath. "Why did you come to the back door?"

Stricken, the kid said, "I'm really sorry if that was wrong. It's just what they wrote down, is that not what you wanted?"

"Wrote down where?"

He thrust a grease-spotted receipt at me. It listed Rebecca's address and phone number, the order the delivery kid had just rattled off, and a handwritten note: *GO TO BACK DOOR ONLY.* This last part was underlined twice.

I tried to sound a little less intense. "Do you know who placed this order? Or when?"

Wordlessly, the kid pointed to a string of numbers on the top of the receipt. "It looks like five oh three. We're slammed tonight, I'm so sorry, um . . ."

I gave him a twenty and told him to keep the change and I closed the door behind him. Then thought better of it and left it open a crack. I quietly opened kitchen drawers until I found Rebecca's cutlery, and I picked out the biggest knife she had.

There was someone else in this house.

The basement steps were dark and rickety. I tried to go down them, but some animal instinct in me overrode my brain. It occurred to me that I hadn't set foot in a strange basement since Jack Derrow's house, and I wondered if I ever would again. Now I grabbed a chair from the dining room and wedged it under the doorknob, just like Derrow had.

Exploring that particular corner of my psyche would need to wait.

The house was small, and there wouldn't be a ton of places to hide. I flipped lights on in the dining room, bathroom, and first-floor bedroom, went back to the kitchen, and started going through the rooms clockwise, starting with the dining room. It contained the table, a china cabinet, and a dry sink. Nobody was hiding in, under, or beside any of these.

From there, I passed the steps that led to the second floor and stood in the living room. Sofa, armchair, television, empty. I kept going—bathroom, empty. I flung open the door of a hall closet and found it stocked with folded linens. Bedroom—empty. I even lifted the edge of the dust ruffle and peered underneath the bed itself.

One floor down, two to go.

Knife in hand, I went up the ivory-carpeted steps. I was either being very silly or very reckless, or maybe a combination. The second floor of Rebecca's little house held two bedrooms and another bathroom. I checked the bedroom to my left first—empty. The bathroom was decorated in a beach-house motif, sand dollars and driftwood. I yanked aside the blue-and-tan-striped shower curtain—empty.

I started into the second bedroom but changed my mind when I saw that the corner of the dust ruffle was snagged on itself, revealing a small section of bedframe and whatever was below it.

Given how impeccable Rebecca's housekeeping seemed to be, I doubted she had left it like that.

I crouched down in the bathroom and pressed the back of my phone against my thigh while I turned on its flashlight function. Then I snapped my arm out and shined the light through the open doorway into the bedroom. From my position on the floor, I had a good view of whatever was under the bed, which turned out to be a stunned, blinking, young person's face.

He recoiled from the light, jerking up with such force that the mattress shifted. The figure scrambled to his feet and into the wall, blinking, one hand to the back of his head.

"Don't fucking move," I said, the knife outstretched.

I realized he was a teenager, probably no more than fifteen or sixteen. Sandy hair, longish, an oversize black hoodie and ripped jeans, dirty Vans, a few bristly mustache hairs that stood out from his greasy, pale face. His eyes were wide and glued to the knife.

"What are you doing in this house?"

He looked from the knife to me to the doorway. I took a step closer. "Don't even think about it. What are you doing here? Who are you?"

"Who are *you*? Where's Rebecca?"

"You first. What's your name?"

"A—" he said. "A. My name is A."

"This isn't *Pretty Little Liars*. What's your name?"

He seemed to deflate. "Aiden."

"I'm a friend of Rebecca's family."

"When is she coming home?"

The bravado in his voice was fading. I started to feel a little bit bad. "She's not."

"What?" Aiden's face went from scared to bewildered, a subtle but meaningful shift.

"I'm sorry to be the one to tell you this, but Rebecca died."

"What are you talking about?"

"There was an accident—"

"No, no, no, she's just in Columbus with her daughter, she's pregnant, she said she was coming back—" He stopped abruptly, expression hardening into a sneer. "How do I know you're not one of them?"

"One of who?"

"If you were really a friend of her family, you'd know."

"Okay, listen. I'm a private investigator. Rebecca's daughter

Maggie hired me, to try to figure out what really happened. Do you know something about what happened?"

"I don't even know what you're talking about, lady." He was still trying to sound tough, but his eyes grew foggy with tears. "Oh man," he whispered almost under his breath. "Shit, shit, shit."

"What are you doing in her house?"

Aiden just stared at me, his expression defiant even as his upper lip trembled.

"Are you in some kind of trouble?"

"No. I just don't like being cornered in here by some strange woman." He swiped at his eyes.

"I'm not cornering you. I just want to know what's going on."

"I can't tell you. I don't even know you."

"I'm going to show you my license. So you know I'm telling you the truth."

I got out my wallet and flipped it open with one hand—my other hand was still holding the knife.

"Whatever, like you can't just make one of those yourself."

I tossed one of my business cards onto the bed. "Google me."

He picked up the card but didn't look at it. "Are you just going to hold me here at knifepoint forever?"

"Until you tell me what's going on. You're here, the police were here—what do you know about that?"

"I don't know anything about anything."

"It sounds like you do, if there's something you don't want to tell me."

"I can't believe him."

"*Who*, Aiden?"

The kid clutched at his temples. The bewilderment had turned to panic. "Rebecca's supposed to help me."

"Help you with what? Aiden, if you talk to me, maybe I can help you."

He shook his head.

"Why'd you unplug the phone?"

"So they can't trace it."

"So who can't?"

Nothing.

"Look, Aiden, I've got all night."

"Can I eat my sub first?" Now his voice was plaintive. He did look like he hadn't been eating much lately. "I'm so hungry, dude. My blood sugar is like super low."

I sighed. "You can eat your sub while you talk, how about that?"

We went down the steps in the dark. Instead of going through the dining room, which would have been shorter, the kid led me the opposite way. I didn't have time to think about why before he flung open the hall closet door in my face. I banged right into it, and in the second or two that it took me to extricate myself from the door, Aiden managed to get out through the back door, sandwich in hand.

went back into the house and up to the shelf full of yearbooks. The most recent was called *Hello, Horizons!* It had a cheery sunglasses-wearing sun on the cover. But what were the sunglasses protecting it from, itself? Assuming that a random teen in Rebecca's house had to be someone she knew through school, I paged through the pages of identical school-day pictures, looking for Aiden's skinny face. Everyone looked about the same in their uniforms of white Oxford shirts embroidered with the school logo, though the occasional bit of flair showed through—a necklace, a colorful undershirt, an inspired hairdo, an earnest grin or a bad-boy smirk.

I finally found him near the top of last year's sophomore class. Aiden Brant.

Unlike his peers, Aiden Brant just looked lost. His skinny frame swam in a polo shirt at least two sizes too big, and the expression on his face was more easily defined by what it wasn't than by what it was: not a smile, not a smirk, not a moody stare or a class-clown antic.

I paged through the Clubs section but found no sign of him there. No sports, no extracurriculars. He did not seem to be engaged in the culture of the Horizons Academy, modern Christian school that it was.

"Aiden Brant, yes, of course, he was a student until a few weeks ago." Sharon Coombs sipped from the glass of white wine that she'd been working on when I rang the doorbell of her down-town condo. "A junior this year but his parents pulled him out of school, oh, at the end of September to send him to a boarding school in Michigan, I believe."

"Do you know why?"

"He needed structure that we don't have. He's a bright kid, maybe too bright. The kind of smarts that manifests as being difficult, I guess you could say." She gazed out her window to the Maumee River below. "Now that you mention it, Rebecca had been a little concerned when that happened. His withdrawal from school."

"How so?"

"She asked for his home address. Which I gave her. I didn't hear anything else about it."

"Do you think she could have gotten mixed up in something, maybe through trying to help him?"

"We have established protocols for issues with students," Sharon said. "Suspicions of abuse, trouble at home, et cetera. Rebecca always followed them."

That was the thing about mysteries—no one ever deviated from the routine until the moment they did.

"So the trouble with Aiden Brant wouldn't have been something she was involved in."

"I can't say for sure that he never went to see her, but he wasn't one of the repeat offenders, you know, the kids who end up in the nurse's office every day. His trouble was more along the lines of sassing his teachers and refusing to do his assignments. I fully supported the parents' decision to find a new school environment for him. What makes you ask about Aiden Brant?"

"Something Maggie said." The lie rolled off my tongue so easily, I was a little disarmed by myself. I was racking up the fibs so far on this case, something I'd possibly worry about if they weren't so damned effective.

"I'm surprised Rebecca would have mentioned him to her."

"Well, I think they were very close."

That eyebrow flicker again. "I'm glad."

"Do you disagree?"

Sharon smiled. "They had their own rough patches. Maggie was too smart for her own good too. But it sounded like getting ready to have a baby of her own made her rethink some of the attitudes she had towards Rebecca."

Beginning to wonder if my own client was telling me the whole story, I gave Maggie a call but had to leave her a message. If people didn't start picking up the phone when I contacted them, I was going to develop some kind of complex.

It was around seven when I left Sharon's house. Still vaguely suspicious of my motel, I posted up at a Starbucks nearby and tried to see what I could see about Aiden Brant. I looked for social media profiles, finding a private Instagram and a public but abandoned Twitter account where he retweeted skateboarding videos until the summer before last, when he just stopped posting. I also found an obit from the Toledo *Blade* from the same time, for Geoffrey Brant, age forty-one, who died following a short illness, survived by his wife, Nadine, and his children Aiden and Katie.

I followed the thread of these names for a while. Katie Brant was an apple-cheeked fourth grader who attended a gifted and talented school and had come in third in the Ohio statewide spelling bee earlier this year—she went out on the word *amelioration*. I found Nadine's current address, a big white house in Ottawa Hills, just below the nature reserve. It was an architectural wonder, this house, as if the builder had set himself the challenge of adding every possible style in suburban home design to the façade of this one structure. A circular driveway, a turret, a portico, a two-story entry, a sky-lit garage, and a black wrought-iron fence with a painted-brick base. The yard was cleared of fallen leaves but the once-colorful chrysanthemums around the front porch had been neglected to death. I rang the doorbell, which sounded with a chimey rendition of the first bars of "Ode to Joy." It was that sort of place.

The doorbell's serenade was interrupted by a barking dog, which made itself visible in the panes of glass that flanked the door—a white and floofy creature with a shiny black nose. It looked big.

I took a step back, which afforded me a glimpse of the ruffling curtains in a window to the side of the door.

The dog retreated, accompanied by the sound of nails scampering on tile.

The door opened and I found myself looking at the down-market Russell Crowe from last night's dinner.

He looked positively shocked to see me. Hopefully I hid my own shock a little better as I said, "Well, how about that, we are neighbors."

"Hi, uh, Roxane, was it?"

I nodded. "This is just such a coincidence, Joel, I can't even believe it. But I was driving down the street here, just out here," I said, pointing over my shoulder and stalling for time, "and I ran over this." I pulled the yearbook out of my bag and brushed at the cheerful sun on its cover as if to wipe away the tire tracks. "I just thought, someone's going to miss this."

Joel laughed, a little uneasy. "Well, that is quite the coincidence."

"Do you know who this might belong to?"

"My sons go to Horizons."

"Well, how about that."

He was holding a stack of mail, which I casually glanced at; an

AmEx bill was addressed to Joel Creedle, care of Keystone Christian Fellowship. He said, "So you were just driving by?"

"I got turned around after I left the nature preserve. Such a great spot for hiking."

He nodded. "It's great."

"This seems like a wonderful area for kids."

"It is."

"You said you have sons?"

"Twin boys. Preston and Porter."

I vaguely remembered seeing those names in the yearbook, possibly one year behind Aiden.

"Great names. Just the two kids?"

Joel nodded vaguely and fanned the pages of the yearbook and I was suddenly seized with worry that someone had signed it like *Have a great summer, Nurse Newsome!* But if anyone had, he didn't let on. "Well, thanks for this, I really don't know how to explain how it got out there, but I'm sure the boys will be glad to have it back. I don't mean to be abrupt, but I was in the middle of something."

"Of course," I said, "you have a great night."

I walked back to the car wondering why Joel Creedle didn't count Aiden and his sister Katie among his kids, step or no, and why a pastor's stepson was hiding out in a dead woman's house, certain she was going to help him.

started the morning with a rather tense phone call from my client. "Aiden Brant," Maggie said over the Bluetooth connection in my car. The day was overcast and chilly and felt like a biting rain was inevitable before the sun went down. "No, I've never heard the name."

"She never mentioned a student from her school that she was particularly close to?"

"I mean, maybe she mentioned a student here or there, but she never said that he had been to her house. Why would she ever have a student at her house?" In the background, baby Bea started to cry. Our conversation had started on the high note of Maggie locating the addresses for Rebecca's other rental properties, but things were going downhill quickly.

"I don't know. So your mother tended not to confide in you?"

"What does that mean?"

I wasn't sure what it meant. "I spoke to a coworker at the school," I said. "Sharon Coombs. She was under the impression that you two had been through a rough patch."

Maggie didn't answer right away, and when she did, her tone was measured. "Was I a perfect daughter? No. Did we have a perfect relationship? No. But we loved each other and we both knew it. Isn't that good enough?"

Only Maggie herself could answer that one. I said, "Do you know anything about a man named Joel Creedle?"

She cleared her throat. "Well, of course."

"Really?"

"The Fellowship is a big part of my life."

"The Keystone Christian Fellowship?"

"Yes."

"How so?"

"Well, James and I moved down here to be a part of planting a Columbus church."

"Planting?"

"That's what it's called. Starting a new church."

"So you know Joel Creedle personally?"

"No, no. Someday I hope to hear him preach in person but for now, just the worship stream."

"Worship stream?"

"Why are you asking these questions about the Fellowship?"

"Curiosity. What's a worship stream?"

"They can beam the service on the internet. So we can watch, no matter where we are."

It was an odd description of the technology for a twentysomething. I said, "Was your mother a member of the Fellowship too?"

"She was for a long time, but she disconnected."

"Disconnected."

"It's what we call people who leave the group."

"Why'd she leave?"

Maggie sighed. "It was around the time she split up from Keir. She was going through some things."

I thought about that. Five or six years was a long time for a church-related vendetta. "Did she know Joel Creedle personally?"

"Oh no, she had left already by the time he took over. But I know that he has children—maybe she knew him through the Horizons Academy?"

"Maybe," I said. "Okay, what about the St. Clair Club?"

"No."

"Detroit?"

"Well," Maggie said, her tone getting a little sharp, "I'm sure at some point she mentioned Detroit for some reason or another."

"You know I'm trying to help you."

She sighed. "Yes. I'm sorry. It's just . . . well . . . it seems . . . improper. That some kid from her school was in her house. I didn't think that you were going to find out something bad about her, but I guess that's the way this works."

"You never know what might be out there. But I don't know what's going on with this kid yet. There very well could be an innocent explanation."

Maggie didn't say anything.

I felt for her. What she'd really hired me to do was to ease her mind, allay her fears, prove that nothing was wrong after all. Reassurance, plain and simple. That was still possible, but that wasn't the same thing as likely.

"I did find out something interesting, about Windsor," I continued.

"Oh?"

"Your dad is the director of security at the casino there."

"What?" If her voice was tense before, now it was practically fraying apart. "Did you talk to him?"

"Not yet."

"So maybe it's some coincidence."

"Maybe, but I tend to think not—"

"I don't want to hear anything else about him."

"I understand that it's a sensitive subject for you."

"If my mother got back in touch with him, that's really her business. But I don't want anything to do with him."

"Okay. You don't have to."

"Keir Metcalf is the person you're supposed to be looking at anyway. Not Pastor Joel and not Barry and not this Aiden whoever."

"Maggie, I know."

"Well? Have you spoken to Keir?"

"I have." I cleared my throat. "He mentioned that you two had a disagreement—his word, disagreement—when you were in high school."

She went quiet.

"I'm not saying that you're wrong about him, but I did want to check in with you to see if that could be why you're so certain that he's involved."

"A disagreement."

"Like I said, his word."

"I'm certain he's involved because he's a creep. Look, I have to go. Bea needs me."

She hung up just as it started to rain.

Despite Arlene French's general disdain for renters, I didn't think they had anything to do with Rebecca's demise. But I wanted to check the places out anyway. There were two, both in Old West End, both brick Victorians on a tree-lined block of Scottswood Avenue. A kid in a University of Toledo sweatshirt answered the door at the first, rubbing his eyes blearily.

"Your landlady," I started.

"Rebecca?"

"Yeah. What do you think of her?"

"She's sooo nice."

"Yeah?"

"I mean, who can say they have a nice landlord? We're lucky. Especially because she hasn't cashed our October rent check yet and there was a bit of a cash-flow shortage in September, know what I mean?"

"When was the last time you talked to her?"

The kid thought about that. "Forevs ago. May, I think, when the air conditioner crapped out."

So at least I could cross one thing off my list.

I went to the second property, which looked a little bit neglected—the grass was long but also matted and brown. The windows didn't have curtains, and the view from the front porch showed an empty space with glossy wooden floors.

There was a notice stuck to the front door, a bright orange rectangle from Toledo Edison that advised YOUR ELECTRIC SERVICE IS SCHEDULED TO BE DISCONNECTED ON OCTOBER 10, which had come and gone.

I went around to the back of the house, past a tangled mess of bushes and three empty trash cans. The long driveway terminated in a carport, under which a white Chevy Lumina was parked. I glanced in: a mess of clothes and shoes and fast-food wrappers and soda bottles, most notably from a Marco's sub and a twenty-ounce Mountain Dew.

I watched the house for two hours before anything good happened.

At least I made good use of my time—I found home addresses for Constance Archer-Nash and Barry Newsome, since I had yet to connect with either of them, and I did some digging re: the Keystone Fellowship.

It was a modern-looking church with a logo in a handwritten script at the top of its website to show how hip it was. The site also featured a lot of photos of smiling white twentysomethings in matching neon shirts, doing various good works in the community such as descending en masse upon a food bank and posing for pictures with dented cans of stewed tomatoes.

The website was an elaborate network of overlapping groups: home churches, lifegroups, worship streams. In the News section

I found a picture of the dirt mound where Keir Metcalf had met with Scooter, the guy in the red pickup, on my first night in Toledo. *Breaking ground on our new multimillion-dollar Fellowship campus!*

"Damn," I said to myself.

I found Joel Creedle's face on the Elders page. The photo showed him with the twins, Preston and Porter, and a tall but dainty-looking woman in a white dress.

Aiden and his sister were not present.

The text accompanying the picture read: *I am a husband and father of two kids, serving as lead pastor of Keystone Christian Fellowship, which is a house church planting ministry. My wife is Nadine, and my kids are Preston and Porter. We're all involved in this wonderful Christian community, growing together as God uses us to bless others. Nadine serves in our Women's Ministry and is a horticulture expert at Bloom. Preston and Porter (the twins, as we call them) seek to lead their own home churches someday.*

I've been a member of the Fellowship since I was in college. I had recently come to faith in Christ and left the party lifestyle to follow Him. I have served in this group from the days it was a small Bible study and watched it grow into a church of almost 2,000 people, made up of nearly 300 house churches across Ohio, Michigan, and Indiana. Unlike a lot of home church networks, we have an eldership and weekly worship meetings too.

I clicked on the Beliefs tab and felt my eyes narrow. Despite the modern look of things, this church was evangelical in nature:

We believe that the Bible is the Word of God, without error, and is the final authority on faith and life.

We believe that marriage is a purposeful union between one man and one woman that exists for God's glory as a picture of the covenant between Christ and His bride, the Church. God has commanded that no sexual activity be engaged in outside of a marriage between a man and a woman.

I was naturally suspicious of organized religion. But did any of this have anything to do with Rebecca Newsome's death?

Finally, the white Lumina backed out of the driveway.

Aiden was at the wheel, still wearing the black hoodie. I followed at a safe distance and we headed out of the neighborhood and to the west. As we drove, I realized that I had been this way before, just last night; he eventually pulled to a stop half a block away from Joel Creedle's house.

He got out and stood on the street, hands balled into fists.

I watched as he took a few steps toward the house, turned around, muttered something, got back in the car, got out again, lather, rinse, repeat. He seemed to be trying to talk himself into something, or out of it.

I wanted to see what would happen between the two of them. Hopefully it would be a conversation that I could overhear and not, for example, a murder. But in the end Joel Creedle came out of the big house and got into a blue Audi and drove away.

Aiden gave his stepdad a head start, then followed.

I did the same.

The three of us got on the outerbelt and then picked up 75 going north. Aiden wasn't a bad tail; he was maybe one car length closer than I would have been, but the Audi seemed oblivious. That told me that perhaps Joel Creedle hadn't seen the car before—maybe it was a recent acquisition—or that he was very much expecting his stepson to be safely away at boarding school in Michigan.

As we continued to head north, I started to wonder if that's where we were going. But as the sun began to set through my driver's-side window, we went into the Detroit metropolitan area, past the warehouses of Delray and the eternal construction of the interstate on the Michigan line.

But after going through the space-age tunnel that ran below

the convention center, the train led by Joel Creedle hooked left on Washington Avenue and away from the river. It was getting harder to follow now—the early start to rush-hour traffic in downtown Detroit clogged the streets. I hung back and got caught at a red light at Fort Street while Joel Creedle and Aiden turned left. "Dammit," I muttered. I turned off the radio—why did that always seem to help a person concentrate in traffic?—and squinted in the sun and up the block as Aiden's distinctive taillights, oblong and slitted like the eyes of a snake, turned right at the next intersection and disappeared.

When my light turned green, I made the turn as well and slowly approached the intersection where Aiden had turned. I no longer saw his taillights. But I was on the same block as the St. Clair Club.

The Audi was nowhere to be found—maybe Creedle had opted for the valet service—but as I passed Lafayette, I saw Aiden's taillights, illegally parked in a bus lane.

I drove up another block, pulled a tight U-turn as quickly as I could, and headed back toward the St. Clair Club. I found a parking spot on the opposite side of the street from Aiden so that both he and the club were to my left.

Checking the binoculars again, I saw Aiden digging around in his backseat for something. Then he got out of the car and, shrugging into a white button-down shirt, ran toward the St. Clair Club, stopped just short of it, and seemingly disappeared in the time it took for a bus to drive past the building.

As I got closer, I saw a narrow alley cutting to the back of the red brick building. A service entrance? Two men were standing next to a doorway, smoking, and they watched me warily.

"Hi," I said, "did you just see a kid in a white shirt come through here?"

One of the smokers stared at me with cold eyes. He had long-ish fingernails, either a guitar player or a pervert. He didn't say anything.

Did Aiden work here? It seemed unlikely, but I tried, "Is there an employee here named Aiden? Sixteen, blond hair?"

"We got cheese that's sixteen years old, maybe," the other guy said. He had a thick beard and eyebrows like caterpillars. "But no employees."

"So no one came through this way."

I could tell that neither of them could care less. "The main entrance is back that way," the pervert said.

"Right, thanks."

Aiden was a sixteen-year-old kid, so maybe the service entrance was his only way into an establishment such as this. But I was an adult lady, which meant I could go through the front.

hurried back to the vehicle and found the pair of black corduroys I had thought to put in my computer bag yesterday.

I looked around; cars idled at the traffic signal in front of me, but no one appeared to be paying any attention. Detroit had no doubt seen stranger things than a woman changing her pants in the wayback of a Range Rover, so I took off my boots and got to it.

The suited doorman greeted me with *madam* once again. The lipsticked hostess from last night—or another just like her—nodded at me. "Good afternoon, madam, do you have a reservation?"

"No."

"I'm sorry, we don't have any available tables."

I smiled right back at this infuriating person. There was always some reason that I could not gain access to the St. Clair Club. "Could I have a seat at the bar, then?"

"Of course."

Finally, I was allowed to enter the inner sanctum. The restaurant was roughly the size of an airplane hangar and just about as noisy as one too. Every linen-clothed table and stately dining chair was full. My hostess friend carried a menu that resembled a leather-bound photo album, but I didn't need to look at it to know that this was the type of place that served six cuts of steak and one salmon entrée and the rest of the menu was a wine list. There appeared to be plenty of wine being consumed at the tables that we passed on the way to the bar, which ran along the right wall of the restaurant and sported a gold-veined mirror behind the tin-soldier formation of liquor bottles.

The hostess placed the menu down at a seat on the end, smiled again—or still?—and said, "Enjoy your meal."

I looked at the room's reflection in the mirror. The servers all wore white button-down shirts and black pants. Some of them looked like they had worked here for decades. The lighting was low, and the tables offered flickering candles in translucent blue orbs, so everything was soft-focus and vaguely dreamy. The patrons were mostly men, mostly in their middle fifties and wearing sports coats. Some of them had second wives with them. Some were possibly on to their thirds. But I didn't see Joel Creedle among them, and I didn't see Aiden, either.

I flagged down a bartender, who turned out to be the caterpillar-eyebrows guy from the alley, and ordered a whiskey and Coke—I needed to keep my wits about me.

"We meet again," the bartender said. "I see you found the front after all."

"I did, thanks. What even is this place?"

This question confounded him. "It's . . . the St. Clair Club."

"Yes, I know, but what exactly is that?"

He was clearly offended that I didn't know what the St. Clair Club was. "Detroit's first, and oldest, social club," he advised. "Founded in 1896, and we've hosted the likes of Henry Ford, Lee Iacocca, Empress Zita of Austria, Edward G. Robinson, and, once, Madonna."

"Wow."

"It was built in the Romanesque Revival style, and beautifully restored just last year."

I sipped my drink and went back to studying the mirror.

"So you're new here, then."

"You could say that."

"What do you do?"

"I'm a dental hygienist. Do you know all the members?"

"I don't know about all."

"Most?"

"Sure."

"Do you know a man named Creedle?"

He squinted. "Creedle? No."

I showed him a photo of Rebecca. "You ever see her in here?"

"You ask a lot of questions for a dental hygienist." But he looked at the image and shook his head. "Sorry."

I finally spotted Aiden on the other side of the room. He was lurking near a ficus, conspicuously idle. He appeared to be scanning the room too, and without success.

Aiden went through the swinging doors that led to the kitchen. I left a twenty on the bar and went back out into the lobby, down the steps, and around the corner into the alley. The guy with the long nails was still back there, smoking another cigarette and scrolling through his phone.

He looked at me like I had two heads. "What are you doing?"

I said, "Ten bucks if I can go in this way."

He shrugged and held out a hand, and he stepped away from the door when I slapped my ten-dollar bill into it.

Compared to the size of the dining room, the kitchen was tiny. The air was hot and heavy with grease and the smell of meat in various states of doneness. A small hallway ran behind the kitchen wall, with two offices and two unisex restrooms on the other side. There was a small porthole-like window in the center of the wall that looked into the cooking area, presumably so that a boss person could keep an eye on the staff while in the office. The glass was greasy, but I could still see through it. Amid the bustling activity, shouted orders, and flaming grills, I saw no sign of Aiden.

At the end of the hallway, I could go to the right—into the literal fire—or to the left, which offered an elevator and an order-entry terminal that had a bouncing blue diamond as its screensaver and a long strand of receipt paper dangling from the machine like an untied shoelace. I lifted it up and tried to read it, but the printer was nearly out of toner and had rendered a day's worth of orders as faint grey lines.

I turned my attention to the elevator. The row of indicator lights above the sliding doors showed that the car was currently on the seventh floor. I checked the tiny kitchen again but still didn't see Aiden. So if he wasn't in the kitchen, and he didn't leave through the service entrance, maybe he went up to one of the guest rooms?

The elevator had buttons for floors three, four, five, and six. Two apparently didn't exist, and seven's button was a long white oval that said PENTHOUSE. I pushed it, then hit the one that made the doors close before anybody saw me.

This particular elevator was out of sync with the feel of the St. Clair Club—rickety, slow, and drably industrial. When it opened on the seventh floor, I found myself in a utility room with house-keeping carts and a dumbwaiter stuffed with rolls of toilet paper. I stepped out of the elevator and listened, but the small room was quiet except for the rattling of a vent in the ceiling.

Next I opened the door a crack and listened again—nothing.

I opened the door further and stuck my head out. The hall-way was carpeted in thick blue with taupe-colored walls and dark wood wainscoting. Framed photos and newspaper articles hung in ornate frames. There were two doors, marked PH1 and PH2, and the guest elevator at the end of the empty hallway.

I stepped out of the utility room and crept over to PH1. I could hear low voices murmuring inside, unintelligible. PH2 was quiet.

The area in front of the elevators was also empty.

I glanced at the framed newspaper articles on the walls. HIS-TORIC DOWNTOWN CLUB GETS A NEW LEASE ON LIFE, a headline said. *Thanks to investments from regional titans like Ford, Marathon Oil, and General Dynamics, the long-defunct St. Clair Club is getting a top-to-bottom renovation. . . .*

A fascinating trip down memory lane that didn't tell me anything about what Joel Creedle and Aiden were doing in this place.

I tried to go back into the utility room, but the door had locked behind me.

"Fuck." I yanked on the lever, frustrated, then mad at myself for forgetting to be stealthily silent.

I crossed the hallway to the door to PH1 and listened.

The murmuring voices had stopped.

The strip of light in the crack between the bottom of the door and the plush carpet suddenly went dim as someone stepped in front of it. I dropped to a crouch and crab-walked away from the door and hopefully out of the peephole's fish-eye view.

A voice said something—the doors here must have been soundproofed, because I still couldn't tell what it was. The shadow lifted from the light at the foot of the door.

I stayed where I was, clocking the locations of the security cameras in the hallway. If the staff of the club was watching them, I'd look pretty suspicious. Maybe it would be more natural to loiter in the hallway standing up? I was still debating this point three minutes later, my quads burning, when the door to PH1 opened and Joel Creedle strode out.

It was my good luck that he didn't glance toward the end of the hallway where I was lurking awkwardly. Instead, he just headed toward the elevators at the opposite end, pushed the button, and got in.

Whoever had been in there with him stayed in the room.

I unfolded myself and slunk over to the windows. The drapes were blue, and I was wearing black and purple. But maybe there was a way to blend in. Then I felt the floor vibrate faintly as the service elevator came back up to the seventh floor and the utility room's door opened.

A man stepped out, black suit, black shirt, earpiece. He looked right at me.

"I think the Wi-Fi is down," I said, ineffectually waving my phone at the window. "And I can't get a signal."

"Ma'am, can you come with me, please?"

No more polite *madam* for me. My luck had run out.

"I'm—"

He shook his head, cutting me off. His neck was thicker than his jaw, so the effect was owl-like. "This floor is reserved for members and their guests, and we both know you're neither. Let's go."

"Where are we going?"

"You're leaving."

There wasn't really much I could say to that. But I wanted to see who would come out of the penthouse suite, so I tried to stall. "Okay, you're right. Busted. But it's harmless, I swear."

I thought he would ask me what was harmless, but he just stared at me.

"I'm playing a game with some friends, a scavenger hunt—"

From the other end of the hall, the elevator dinged.

I turned to look just in time to see a man disappearing into it. How had he gotten out of the room without me seeing him?

It dawned on me: "These rooms are connected, aren't they?"

The security guard didn't acknowledge that. "You're trespassing. What happens next is up to you."

I put my phone away. The St. Clair Club wouldn't be approving my application to join anytime soon.

The lobby was still empty. Across from the check-in desk was the row of private phone booths, outfitted with a VoIP handset and a LAN hookup. I glanced in each one as the security guard led me toward the door, but they were all empty. I saw no signs of Joel, or Aiden, or the mystery man, and when I got back to Lafayette Street, I saw that Aiden's car was gone.

Following people is supposed to give a detective answers, not tons more questions.

Clearly I was doing something wrong.

Since I was this far north anyway, I decided to go back across the border to the casino and then on to Barry Newsome's house if he wasn't working. I'd already tangled with one security staffer this afternoon; why not make a whole day of it? He proved to be somewhat more cooperative than I expected, but still not very.

"Yes, I received your phone messages," he said once we were sitting in his office. "All of them."

"The way it works is, you answer and I stop calling."

Barry Newsome gave me a patient, practiced smile. He was well-dressed for ex–law enforcement, a tailored tan suit over a sky-blue shirt and a navy tie. He had brown hair, threaded with silver and receding slightly, and a broad, friendly face. "No need, I guess, because here you are."

"I want to talk about Rebecca."

He clasped his hands in front of him. He wore a gold wedding band on one hand and a large class ring with a garnet stone on the other. "I don't know what I can tell you about her."

"Do you know that she passed away recently?"

"Yes."

"How'd you hear? I know Maggie didn't tell you."

"No." His expression remained neutral, but his jaw might've tightened a little. "A friend of mine in Toledo heard it on the news and told me."

"What's this friend's name?"

"Not important."

"Maybe to me it is."

He shook his head.

I said, "Maggie was very surprised to hear that her mother and you were in touch again."

"We weren't, not really."

"Was it just a coincidence that she happened to come here?"

"Lots of people come here."

"Did you see her when she did?"

"We spoke, briefly."

"How did that shake out—you just happened to run into her?"

"No, she told me she was in the Windsor area and we met for coffee."

"Why was she in the Windsor area?"

Another shake of the head. "She didn't say." He wasn't a terrible liar, but he wasn't a particularly good one either.

"And you didn't ask?"

"We were just catching up. It wasn't a big deal. We had coffee and spent about fifteen or twenty minutes talking. Then I had to get back to work and that was that."

"Did you talk to her after that?"

"No."

"No phone calls or texts or emails?"

"No."

"Messages by carrier pigeon?"

He smiled indulgently. "Like I said, I don't have anything useful to tell you. It was several weeks ago and very brief. It was nice to see her after so long, but that was all it was. A quick catch-up between people who used to know each other a lifetime ago."

"So she forgave you, for abandoning her and Maggie."

"I don't know about forgave, but she'd moved on. It was a quarter of a century ago and Rebecca wasn't one to dwell on the past, really."

"She just contacted you out of the blue and wanted to have coffee for exactly no reason."

Newsome nodded. "Pretty much."

"You're lying."

"I assure you, I'm not."

"Oh, in that case, I'm totally convinced."

"I was very sorry to hear that Rebecca passed away, but I don't have anything to add."

"Aren't you even curious about what happened?"

"It was a hiking accident, wasn't it?"

"And things are never more than they appear, are they?"

"Sometimes, but not usually. And not this time."

Aiden wasn't at Rebecca's house or at the Victorian on Scottswood Avenue, nobody was home at the Brant-Creedle place, and Keir Metcalf's office was locked up tight. I got a Cuban sandwich to go from the restaurant a few doors down and returned to the motel to consider what I'd learned today.

It had felt like a lot in the moment, but when I looked at everything together, it still didn't make any sense.

Keir Metcalf didn't trip my bullshit detector when he said he didn't know what had happened to his ex. Barry Newsome did but I couldn't explain why. My client seemed to hate both of them but was of the opinion that only the former was involved here. I didn't know what to think about Joel Creedle's visit to the St. Clair Club, a place Rebecca herself had gone at some point, nor about his stepson's presence in both her house and an empty rental property she owned. And the biggest question of all may have been Constance Archer-Nash, who had been getting harassing calls from Rebecca for some time.

I thought about Aiden Brant and his strange belief that unplugging a landline was enough to keep the police from tracing a phone call and wished everything were that simple.

"Why was he worried about that in the first place?" I muttered to the motel room.

I spent a half hour on the phone with CenturyLink in order to get Rebecca's phone records for the past month. I had a whole story ready but the customer-service rep just asked me for the last four of Rebecca's Social, which I had on her death certificate in the paperwork Maggie had given me, so it just became a matter of convincing them to send a copy of her recent calls to my e-fax number.

When I dialed the first, I realized it was the same sub shop that Aiden had ordered from the other night.

When I dialed the second number, it didn't ring, just went into the recorded greeting: "Hello, you've reached Rebecca Newsome . . ."

I slapped my phone down on the desk, a stab of pain behind my eyes.

I pushed away from the desk and went over to the window and looked down at the Dumpsters. I couldn't help Rebecca. But I still had the chance to help her daughter, and I wasn't going to do that by calling numbers at random.

I called down to the desk clerk to ask if I could print a document; he said no. I turned to the tiny notepad again and started writing down numbers and key dates, making notes beside them.

September 30—when Rebecca had left Toledo for Maggie's house.

October 3—the date of her fall.

I crossed out the numbers I could identify—R for Rebecca, S for subs—and then I went back through and tried out the 800 numbers.

A Visa gift card balance-check hotline, a calling card access number.

I paused there to turn to my computer. I didn't know calling cards still existed, but apparently they did—or at least their phone line did. *Welcome to Call Link Worldwide,* the recording told me. *Please enter your PIN.*

According to their website—which bore the look of a site created back in the day when calling cards were common—Call Link Worldwide prided itself on providing unparalleled quality and reliability within the prepaid telecommunications industry. *With communication facilities located all around the world, the company is able to provide exceptional long-distance service at a fraction of the cost.*

I drew a question mark beside that number on my notepad.

That left only local Toledo phone numbers.

I found the date when I'd gone into Rebecca's house and hit redial on her phone, adding a star next to the number of Constance Archer-Nash's cell phone. There were about thirty calls in between the day when Rebecca left to visit Maggie and the day that I first went to her house, and at least half of them had been to the candidate's phone.

Aiden was making those calls.

I grabbed a blank sheet of paper and quickly scribbled out a calendar for September and October and plotted the calls on it accordingly, something needling at me about these dates.

On October 2, Aiden called Constance.
On October 3, the day Rebecca fell into the ravine, Arlene saw the police at Rebecca's house.
On October 11, Aiden called Constance three times.
On the twelfth, Arlene saw the police at Rebecca's house.
On the twentieth, *I* apparently called Constance.
And as with the other calls, the very next day, the police were at Rebecca's house.

There hadn't been police reports or run sheets for these visits—not because they took place off the books, but because they weren't in response to dispatches. They were probably follow-ups.

I needed to check for police reports filed by Constance Archer-Nash, and now I had the dates to go on.

I was expecting a quiet night emailing my new pal at the Toledo Police records department, my last remaining whiskey bottle keeping me company.

Then my phone rang.

"Hi, um, Miss—Mrs. Weary, I'm calling from the Commerce Building security."

I'd never gotten a call from the security staff at my office building before. In fact, the desk was usually unattended, and I'd always assumed it was for show. "Hi, what's up?"

"There's a—suspicious package—your office—calling the police."

I was on my feet without having any recollection of having done so. "What?"

"There's smoke and—oh, no—wh—oh, no."

"Hello?" I said, my heart in my throat.

The next thing I heard was a whoosh of ignition and a blast so loud it hurt my eardrums even through the phone.

"Hello?"

The line went dead.

CHAPTER 15

My thoughts went in a spastic cycle through everyone I knew and whether they'd have any reason to be at my office today. Kez—the most likely. Andrew—maybe, he'd mentioned stopping by to print something. Shelby too. Computer bag slung over my shoulder, I practically tripped down the cement steps of the motel and was in the car and three miles down 75 before I took a second to breathe.

Phones existed. I didn't have to drive for two and a half hours assuming the worst.

I pulled into the parking lot of a rest area.

Kez didn't answer.

Shelby didn't answer.

Andrew didn't answer.

Tom didn't answer.

My chest hurt.

I dialed the number that had called me, but a recorded message told me the subscriber was not available. No voice mail—a prepaid phone?

I started on a second round of calls and Kez picked up this time.

"Are you okay?" I was standing next to the Range Rover, one foot on the running board, a hand gripping the top of the doorframe.

"What—yeah, fine."

I let out a huge breath.

"How'd you even know something happened?"

She sounded like herself, impatient and slightly annoyed. Not shaken up. I said, "What happened?"

"I don't know. I just heard a big pop-bang and the lights flickered and the fire alarms went off."

Now I was confused. "Were you in the lobby?"

"What?"

"Where were you?"

"Are you tripping?"

I rubbed the center of my forehead. "Were you in the office when it happened, Kez?"

"Yeah."

"And you didn't see it?"

"What are you talking about?"

I got into the car but left the door open. The adrenaline spike made me feel like throwing up. "I just got a really weird phone call. Someone telling me that there'd been an explosion in the office."

"A phone call? From who?"

"From someone on the security desk."

"Bob or Joe?"

"What? I don't know. Some guy."

"How do you not know?"

"He didn't say his name. He just said he was from security and there was a strange package outside my office."

"There wasn't."

"But there was an explosion."

"I don't know what it was. I thought a blown fuse or something."

What I heard over the phone hadn't been a blown fuse. "What's going on now?"

"I don't know—I left a couple minutes ago. I didn't see a point to standing around on the sidewalk when I could go not work somewhere else. But," she said, an uncharacteristic note of concern in her voice, "I'll just turn around and go back and see what's the what."

I sat in the car in tense silence for what felt like an hour but was probably a minute or two.

Then Kez said, "Oh, man. Rox, there's a coroner's van here."

I spent the entire drive from Toledo obsessing over every last detail about it. The voice—did it sound familiar? Did he actually say my name, or could it have been a wrong number? As a result, I could no longer remember the phone call at all, only my attempts to recall it.

The coroner's van was gone by the time I got to the Commerce Building, but there were still a number of cops hanging around. The counterterrorism unit owned the scene but Tom was waiting for me at the intersection of Third and Gay as I parallel-parked badly, too shaky to have good command of the wheel.

"I don't know what I'm doing right now."

Tom came over to the curb and touched my arm through the open window. "This is fine. Don't even worry about it. Hey—look at me."

I looked.

It was raining softly, and his overcoat was spattered with droplets of water. His day was probably going on twelve hours at this point. But his warm brown eyes locked on mine and some of the nauseous tension I'd been driving with for the past hundred-plus miles faded away.

I put the car in park. The street would just have to deal with my bumper hanging out into traffic. "Thanks for meeting me here."

"You don't have to thank me."

As I got out of the car, he waved at someone standing under the narrow awning of the building, a woman with short grey hair and glasses in a CPD windbreaker. Tom touched the place between my shoulder blades and led me over to her. "Mari, this is Roxane Weary. I'm sure you remember Frank—this is his daughter. Roxane, Mariella Zervos, Counterterrorism."

I shook the woman's hand, feeling strangely detached from my own body.

Zervos said, "I always liked your dad, honey."

I nodded. That wasn't helping the disorientation.

We went into the building and sat in the big conference room, just Zervos and me. She said, "So tell me about the phone call."

I showed Zervos the number on my phone.

The call had lasted all of seventeen seconds.

"And you don't know this number?"

I shook my head. "I called it back but it just had a recording, no voice mail."

"The wireless subscriber you have dialed not in service, yadda yadda?"

"Yeah."

"May I?" She pointed at my phone, and I nodded. As she wrote down the number, she hit the call button and we heard the same tinny recorded message. "Could be some prepaid SIM kit."

"Who was the—who?" I said.

"Do you know a lot of the other tenants—er, is *tenants* the right word?"

"Sure."

"Is that a yes to knowing the others who rent in here?"

"No, it was a yes to your word choice. No, I don't really know the other businesses. Maybe just to say hello in the elevator."

"How long have you had office space in here?"

"Almost six months." I felt judged, though it might have been by myself. "I'm still getting the hang of it, having an office. I don't come in every day."

"Every week?"

"Not every week."

Zervos wrote something down.

I said, "You're not going to tell me who died. Are you?"

"If you don't know anyone anyway, does it matter?" But then her features relaxed. "I'm sure the name has already been on the news. Benjamin Gaskell, substance use addiction counselor on the first floor."

I didn't know him, had never even seen his name, but some of the ragged-edged panic I'd felt in the car earlier rushed to the surface. I kept picturing Elise, again. I could still feel that cold water rushing around my collarbones if I thought hard enough about it, or even if I didn't.

I shivered.

Zervos asked me what I'd been working on in Toledo, and I summarized the Rebecca Newsome case. Zervos didn't appear impressed. "So you didn't really make enough progress to make any enemies, it sounds like."

I nodded.

"What about here. Enemies here?"

"Enemies? Does anyone ever say yes to that question?"

"Okay, not enemies. People who dislike you in a vague but meaningful way?"

"I'm sure. But I haven't had any dustups with anybody recently."

"Heitker mentioned Vincent Pomp."

"Well, there's him." I put my hands in the pockets of my coat. "But that was back in January. We haven't crossed paths since then."

The detective jotted something down in her notebook, then

flipped it closed, signaling the end of the conversation. "We'll probably need to chat again at some point, okay?"

Tom's place was off of Kenny in the liminal space between the nice houses of Upper Arlington and the endless plazas of Bethel Road. The complex was called The Homes at Cliffton Heights as if it were a row of mansions overlooking a grand vista rather than a dozen or so semidetached condos, but inside, I liked it. He had replaced some unfortunate brown carpet at some point with laminate flooring and redone the kitchen to include a tile backsplash and a bar-height peninsula with a smooth granite countertop, on which I now rested my forehead in an attempt to soothe the pounding behind my eyes.

"What can I make for you?" Tom said from the other side of the counter.

"Just a drink, please."

"You should eat something."

"I don't know if I can."

"Whiskey never actually solves anybody's problems."

"And eating something does?"

"Honestly, yes."

But he poured me an inch of Crown Royal over a few ice cubes from the refrigerator door and set the glass in front of me. Without lifting my head, I patted the cool marble of the countertop until I found the drink and then slid it toward me.

Tom opened the fridge and retrieved a cardboard carton of eggs and a block of cheddar. "Breakfast for dinner," he said, looking at his watch, "for breakfast? Does that sound okay?"

It was after one o'clock at this point. I lifted my head and nodded and watched as he heated a skillet on the stovetop.

"Zervos was part of a joint task force a while back with the homicide unit," Tom went on. "Six, seven years ago. When we had that sniper on 270. She and Frank used to drive each other crazy—Frank and his hunches, versus Mari and her dedication to legwork." He drizzled oil into the skillet and tilted it back and forth to coat the surface. "Not that Frank didn't do legwork. He did. But he didn't need to prove that something was a dead end. Is this helping?"

"No. I don't know."

"Do you want to talk?"

"I just can't shake this feeling that everything is connected. Everything that has happened. I don't mean actually connected. I just mean, a pattern. A bad pattern with me at the center. Rather than a string of unrelated events. Does that sound crazy?"

Tom set the skillet back on the burner and turned around to face me. "You've been through a lot."

I shook my head. "No, that's not what I mean. I'm talking about people getting hurt and me not being able to stop it." But as I said it, I realized that made even less sense.

"People are always going to get hurt, and you're never going to be able to stop it."

"Well, fuck."

He turned back to the stove and cracked two eggs neatly into the skillet. "You're saying you feel like it's your fault."

"Isn't it?"

"Roxane, you've chosen a profession that puts you into situations where bad things are going to happen sometimes. So have I. So did your dad. None of us can stop things from happening—all we can do is try our hardest to put the pieces together. And you do that. You have to know that."

I finally picked up my drink and swallowed the entire thing. "But a man died tonight. Because of me. Because he was unlucky enough to have an office in the same building as me. I've got no business having an office. I should live and work in an underground bunker, a hundred miles from the nearest town. What if this particular nastygram had been sent to my apartment? What if something happened to Shelby—" I stopped there and put my head back down on the counter.

Tom turned away from the stove and leaned over the counter next to me. "You can't play the what-if game." His voice was a whisper. "You don't want to." He smoothed my hair against the back of my neck. "Now, I have an important question. Mayo or sriracha?"

It was in moments like this that I felt it in my bones, how good we were together.

CHAPTER 16

My own apartment felt long-abandoned in the morning. I bolted the dead bolt behind me and opened the door that led to my bricked-in porch, hoping that Catherine had left the bottle of Midleton for me.

She hadn't.

I poured a shot of Crown Royal in my kitchen and drank it down and got in bed fully clothed. I needed to think, and it was a scientific fact that I did most of my best thinking while in my bed.

Morning sunlight shone around the edges of the mini blinds in sharp contrast to the dark purple walls of my bedroom. It wasn't a wall color I would have chosen for myself, but a previous tenant had gone for bold hues in each room. When I moved in, the landlord was supposed to have repainted for me, but he didn't, and eventually I got used to the colorful rooms. Now, after spending a few nights away, the purple walls were a bit jarring.

It was 7:41. I decided I would give myself until eight, and then get up and figure out what the hell was going on.

When I opened my eyes, the light in the room had changed. A lot. It was eleven o'clock already, and instead of doing my best thinking, I had only achieved a fitful, dream-riddled midmorning sleep.

I rolled over, my anorak twisting around me.

A dream fragment developed in my mind—I was back in my

motel room, the first one, since the bathroom was on the left. I needed to write something down but I couldn't find a pen.

"Oh shit," I said in the waking world.

I flung the covers off and made a beeline for my computer bag and its pocketful of misprinted pens. Instead of listing the suite correctly as 4-L, the pens said "Suite A-1"—which didn't exist in the building. But it occurred to me that Mariella Zervos hadn't told me which office Benjamin Gaskell inhabited, only that it was on the first floor. I opened my laptop right there in the hallway and found Benjamin Gaskell's website, which listed his office as "Ste 1-A."

"A misprinted pen?"

Zervos didn't seem impressed with my theory.

"But what's *your* theory? That someone intended to call Benjamin Gaskell and got me instead?"

Zervos slid a sheet of paper across my desk—the phone list that had hung behind the desk in the lobby of my office building. All six floors' worth of offices were crammed onto a single table, arranged by suite number. I squinted at the small print. Gaskell's name was first on the list, while mine was in the second column and three rows below his. "What," I said, "you think someone accidentally confused our phone numbers based on proximity?"

"I think that's a bit easier to swallow than the pen thing."

"Did anyone from the security staff attempt to call either me or Gaskell?"

"No."

"Then?"

"I just don't buy this." She tapped the pen on the edge of my desk. "I mean, your office is listed correctly in your website. How does it come to pass that somebody only has this pen?"

I leaned back in my desk chair and thought about that. "It's not like I give these pens out. They're in exactly three places—my car, my apartment, and my computer bag."

Zervos gave me a look like *so what.*

"I had my computer bag with me in Toledo. In my motel room. I know I mentioned this last night, but the other day, someone had been in my room."

"Right, and they wrote you a secret threatening message in the shower steam. I remember."

I sighed. "Well, whoever it was could have seen the pens and got the address from there?"

"Why, though? Your explanation requires more motive."

I didn't know the answer to that. I said, "Is the guy on the security cameras?"

"That was my next question for you." She slid a printout from the back of her notebook and over to me. "Do you know this guy?"

I picked up the image, a grainy black-and-white camera still. It showed a man—dressed in shoes, pants, and a jacket, ball cap pulled low over his eyes—in the lobby of the building. Only a narrow segment of his face was visible. He could have been anybody.

"What was the explosive?"

She scrolled to a picture on her phone, this one of what appeared to be a twist of burned-up masking tape with plastic melted to it.

"What's that?"

"The explosive. What's left."

I stared it at.

Zervos said, "My guess, it was some homemade Tannerite and a firecracker."

"It looks like a piece of tape," I said, and the detective nodded. "What's Tannerite?"

"It's used to make exploding rifle targets."

"What, like clay pigeons? Skeet? Except illegal?"

"No, perfectly legal. Tannerite is a mix of aluminum powder and ammonium nitrate. It's sold as two separate packs that you then mix together yourself—it's called a binary explosive. Completely stable before it's mixed, and pretty much stable even after. But shoot it with a rifle and you get a nice big boom."

I looked at the picture again. It still didn't make any sense to me.

Zervos said, "People will mix up some Tannerite and fold it up into a little packet with tape and use that as a target. It only takes forty or fifty grams. Of course, the more you use, the bigger the boom."

"And the firecracker?"

"Tannerite needs some kind of ignition to set it off. A rifle shot is probably harder to pull off in an office building. But stick a firecracker in there and the whole setup is the size of your palm."

"That's it? That's enough to—to *kill* someone?"

"If it was just on the floor when it went off, I wouldn't think so. It would make a big noise and a lot of smoke, but it wouldn't blow down a door or anything. In this case, the scene kind of tells me that Mr. Gaskell may have picked it up."

"What do you mean?"

Zervos put the phone and the security-camera picture away. "It looks like the mystery man may have shoved it under the door, or Mr. Gaskell opened the door and picked it up. It exploded from the inside of the office, and Mr. Gaskell was holding it."

I felt my teeth grinding together and said nothing.

"My point is, the device looks like something you might use to scare somebody. Not kill somebody. Good news for you, not so good for Mr. Gaskell."

"So what does any of this mean?"

"A prank gone wrong, maybe. Someone trying to scare you.

Or, if you believe in innocuous coincidences, maybe nothing to do with you at all."

I was pissed at myself for not writing down the details of that call before I called Kez. "I'm surprised to hear that you do believe in innocuous coincidences."

"I believe in evidence. That's all."

I could see what Tom had meant, about Zervos and my father driving each other nuts with their different approaches. I, personally, wanted to scream at her right now.

"There's a chance that the phone number will help us figure out who called you. It can take a few days to get the data from the wireless provider, but we're working on it."

We rode down in the elevator together. Although she didn't strike me as the warm and fuzzy type, she patted my arm when we reached the lobby and said, "We'll find this guy."

"You don't know that."

"Optimism. That never was Frank's strong suit either. Or Andy's, from what I can tell."

"Do you mean my brother? God help you if he hears you call him Andy."

Zervos frowned, something unnamable entering her face. "You have a brother named Andy too?"

"What on earth are you talking about?"

"Your sister."

I laughed. "I don't have a sister."

"Okay, my mistake."

"What are you talking about?"

Zervos sighed. "There's a girl, new to the force this year. Looks exactly like your dad. Like you. I assumed she was his daughter. But I was wrong. So it doesn't matter. I gotta run."

"And her name is Andy?"

But she practically ran back out through the revolving door, a hamster in a wheel.

CHAPTER 17

'd wondered before if my dad ever got some woman pregnant. We knew about a few affairs—the whole family did—and I'd assumed that if there was more to it, we'd have heard about that too.

I immediately went back up to my office and hauled out my computer. A rookie cop named Andy should be easy enough to find, and she was; a class had graduated back in July, and I found a photo on the *Dispatch* website. Out of fifty-some cadets, there were six women, and one of them was petite, dark-haired, with a strong nose and eyes that looked icy blue.

I stared at this person. She looked exactly like my aunt, my father's older sister, Cynthia, in pictures I'd seen of her when she was young. Cynthia was long dead—a car accident—but she had three kids of her own, all of whom would be old enough to have their own adult children. That branch of the family tree had lived in Erie and we rarely saw them.

I spent a while looking for a list of the academy grads' names, didn't find it.

I called my brother. "I talked to a cop this morning who said the weirdest thing, about Frank."

"Oh?"

"She said there's some rookie cop, a girl named Andy, who he thought was Frank's daughter."

"Andy?"

"I thought she was talking about you, I even said, god help her if you ever hear her call you that. But then she told me this girl looks exactly like Frank, and I found a picture, and she really, really does. I'm sending it to you now."

Silence radiated through the connection while he waited for the text message to come in. "Holy crap, you know who this looks like?"

"Cynthia."

"Exactly. Think she has a granddaughter who lives in town?"

"We would have heard about that. If we had a cousin here. A grandcousin? Second cousin?"

"First cousin once removed, technically. What are we supposed to do now?"

"About this? Um, I don't think we're supposed to do anything."

"What if she is Frank's kid?"

"That would be none of our business. You know?"

Intellectually, I did know that. But the qualities that made me a decent detective were, also, the same ones that made me an impossible person, and I knew it. I said, "We should ask Mom."

"Mom and Cynthia hated each other."

"No, that was Mom and Victoria."

"I think it was both. Dad's sisters were, well, like the female version of him, which is to say, drunk and mean and petty."

"Sexism aside," I said.

"You really don't know her name? Just Andy?"

"That's all she would tell me."

"Not much to go on."

"No."

"So that means not much to do."

I sighed. "Yeah."

"I love you."

"Yeah."

I hung up and frowned at the picture leaning against the wall. Kez's *Cheer up, beach!* Post-it was still stuck to the glass.

I wasn't kidding—I didn't know what to do, about anything. I knew deep down my brother was right—Zervos's comment didn't make this person any of my business, even if she was related to us. And regarding the rest of it, she'd told me to sit tight and wait a few days to see what their investigation turned up, but I didn't feel like sitting tight, and I didn't want to wait a few days either. But beyond doing a Google search for the phone number that had called me, there was little else I could do.

I tried Constance Archer-Nash's media person; no answer. So I tried the cell phone that Aiden had been calling and to my surprise, she picked up this time.

"Bruce?" she barked.

"Sorry—no."

"Fuck." A deep breath. "Sorry."

"Well, aren't we just two ladies apologizing for nothing," I said, and she laughed.

"*Sorry*, who's this?"

"I'm a private detective and I think I have some info about the calls you've been getting on this number."

Silence. Then, "Really. What kind of information? Actually, no, I'm not doing this. Give me your number and I'll call you back after my security person says it's okay."

While I waited for that to happen, I emailed the records department to ask for reports filed by Constance Archer-Nash or the staff of Nora Health in the last month. Then I got into the shower and stood under the stream of hot water for a long, long time. It was almost relaxing, until my thoughts drifted back to the unknown person who'd been in my motel room.

Stop *what*?

Were showers going to be triggers for me now? Mirrors? Motels?

The light changed in my bathroom as someone passed by the window on the stairs at the back of the building.

The water turned to ice on my skin.

I turned the shower off and listened; footsteps near my back door. I bolted from the shower and pulled on jeans and a sweatshirt from my laundry room, grabbed my gun, and squinted through the peephole to see who the fuck was out there.

Catherine Walsh, a box balanced on a slim hip.

I sighed and the peephole fogged up.

Catherine looked right at me, her expression going tense. "Hello?" she said.

I opened the door. "What on earth are you doing back here?"

We stared at each other. You always hope that the first time you see an ex after a breakup you'll look amazing and they'll look like shit, but that hope was only realized for Catherine today. She was radiant in a burnt-orange wool blazer and a houndstooth blouse and jeans, and I was dripping wet from the shower, dressed in dirty laundry, and holding a gun.

"I have some questions myself," she said, nodding down at it.

I set the revolver on the kitchen counter behind me. "It's a long story."

"I have time for a story."

"If this is your way of expressing concern, everything's fine."

"Oh I know. You're always perfectly fine, is that it?"

"Something like that."

"You've been happier to see me, that's for sure."

"Well, when I said porch, I figured you'd opt for the front."

"Yeah, well, I tried that, but I'm not tall enough to reach the ledge even in these." She waggled a dove-grey ankle boot and hefted the box. "I didn't think you'd want me to just chuck this crap over the wall so I decided to come around the back. I figured *you* would be in Toledo, since that was your excuse for not seeing me."

I took the box and could tell right away it was too light to contain anything other than clothes.

"What?"

"Nothing."

"Something."

"No."

I set the box on the floor. "If it was just a bunch of clothes, why not chuck it over the wall?"

Her pale green eyes flashed a warning and I could tell she knew what I was thinking about. "It's in the queer bill of rights that when your lover ditches you in the dead of winter, you get to drink her whiskey and not feel bad about it."

"It wasn't even mine."

"Oh?"

"It was my dad's. And to be clear, *I* didn't ditch *you. I* didn't decide to move to Rhode Island without consulting my girlfriend."

"*You* decided to throw my house key in my face."

I bit my lip so hard I tasted blood. "I did not throw it, Catherine, and if you think that's what happened, you've obviously rewritten a lot of history."

"Metaphorically, you threw it. Anyway, I didn't come here to relitigate the entire thing. I came here to give you your stuff back."

"Great. Thank you."

"Well, okay."

"Take care of yourself."

"Okay."

Catherine moved off the porch and onto the stair that creaked like a haunted house when anyone stepped on it. I saw her stiffen but she didn't say anything.

"Catherine."

She turned around.

"Do you really want the last thing you ever say to me to be *okay*?"

"Do I want it to be the last thing I ever say to you? No."

"Then?"

She turned and walked down the narrow path that ran the length of the fenced-in yard and ended at the gate along the alley. Then she looked back over her shoulder at me. "I'll see you when I see you."

She lifted the latch on the gate and stepped into the alley and walked away.

I went back into the apartment and dumped the box out on the top of my washing machine. A hoodie I'd forgotten about, a bra that wasn't mine, and three pairs of wool socks.

"What a crock of shit," I said to no one.

I had an email from my new best friend at the Toledo PD records desk with two run sheets that outlined visits the cops had made to Constance's office at Nora Health.

RP indicates that her cell phone has been receiving disturbing phone calls from [number redacted]. Caller is a teen or young adult male who always says he needs to meet with her. When informed that this won't be possible unless he gives his name, he hangs up. Office already has caller ID and UC private security staff. Call to nonemergency line today because caller indicated that he "has information [she] wants or else people will die." Detective F/U on phone number recommended.

And then just the other day, the day after I'd hit redial on Rebecca's phone: *RP has been dealing with harassing phone calls for several weeks but it seemed to have tapered off until another call yesterday. F/U on address.*

The second police visit that Arlene had seen must have been the follow-up, or maybe Constance or her staff had contacted a detective directly when more calls came in.

I was still contemplating this when Constance finally called me back. "I'm going to Chicago in the morning for a business meeting," she said, "but if you can come by the Nora Health office this afternoon, we can talk. My security guy says you're not a crank."

"Well, I don't know about that."

She laughed. "Are you in Toledo?"

I was already shoving my computer into my bag. "Close, I'm close."

CHAPTER 18

Nora Health's headquarters occupied a two-story brick building outside of the city. The exterior looked like it could've been any type of business, from a call center to a medical clinic, but it had been redone inside in that warehouse-chic style that was popping up everywhere, exposed ductwork and polished cement floors. Behind the front desk was a massive flat-screen television on which Constance Archer-Nash's face was floating while I waited for her to be available—*She changed the way you receive health care,* read the text. *Now, empower her to change the way the health care industry works. Constance CAN!* The slideshow went on to inform me that Nora Health started as a tiny organization called the Northwest Ohio Reproductive Alliance run out of Constance's parents' basement.

When Constance finally granted me an audience, she wasn't what I expected. The woman in the photos on the website had been put-together and manicured and easy-breezy; in real life, Constance was lying in the dark on a leatherette sofa with an ice pack across her eyes, flush-faced and stressed, nail polish flaking off in jagged chunks.

"Things are intense right now," she said, which was clear from the attitudes of everyone inside the office. Phones were ringing, screens were flashing, and I saw at least two people weeping openly at their desks on the other side of Constance's fishbowl of an office. "I wish I could go back in time and tell myself that mounting a Senate campaign is a full-time job and not the smartest idea when you already *have* a full-time job."

"Is it really a surprise?"

"I guess that's the worst part—no. But you know, my parents raised me to believe I can do anything, including run for the US Senate while also running a multimillion-dollar start-up."

"It'll be worth it, when you win."

"Yes. You're right. If I win. But on top of all that, our CRM platform had another attempted data breach overnight. I have a migraine and I just cannot at the moment." Despite her beleaguerment, she was impeccably dressed in a wool dress, navy, with gold buttons at the collar. "But I'm really very interested to hear what you know about these phone calls."

"Your CRM what?"

"Customer relationship management platform," she said. "Basically, what's under the hood of what we do. User data, profiles, medical information. We use a company based in Chicago that does this for Nora Health *and* my campaign, plus a lot of other campaigns and progressive causes—that's where I have to go tomorrow to deal with this mess, something I so don't have time for right now. But if it's bad here, I'm sure trash cans are on fire over there."

"Medical information was exposed?"

"*Attempted* data breach." Constance touched a hand to her forehead. "As far as they can tell, everything is okay. But this type of thing is terrifying, you know? Data warfare. It's unreal. It happens somewhere every day—you hear it in the news all the time, such-and-such data breach, check to see if your info is posted on the dark web. The 2016 election broke the way things are done in this world, it seems like. But it also opened the door for scrappy nobodies like me, so."

I gestured around the warehouse-cool office. "A nobody doesn't start all this."

Constance smiled. "Okay. True."

"So tell me about these phone calls. I want to hear your theories before I tell you mine."

"We can't prove it but I'm sure it's the fetus-van people."

"Excuse me?"

"You've probably see them. They set up on freeway overpasses and public events with these giant, graphic photos, allegedly of aborted fetuses, though who even knows what they're actually pictures of. They have a panel van they drive to events, with one of those vehicle wraps—the pictures are plastered all over the sides and hood of it. That's why we call them the fetus-van people, but they're actually called Life Begins."

I nodded. Columbus had its own fringe contingent, which operated out of an office on Broad Street not far from my apartment. "You've had trouble with them before?"

"That's a word for it. Do you know how Nora Health works?"

"Only what I saw on the screen in your lobby."

Constance sat up slowly. "Basically, we figured out a way to eliminate barriers for women to receive low-cost reproductive health care. Doctors in private practice can sign up to see a limited number of patients through our platform without changing the entire structure of their practice. A woman buys a yearly membership to the service. After that, she gets access to Nora's patient portal, where she can go online and see which doctors in her area have availability that day, or at least that week, for various health services, not even limited to reproductive health."

"Nice."

Constance nodded. "It's a win for doctors because they can attract new patients this way, and it's a win for patients because they have access to a network of vetted medical professionals with a willingness to be flexible about payments. It sounds like an extremely simple concept, but it's been revolutionizing the landscape."

"So what do the fetus-van people object to? It doesn't sound like this is about abortion access at all."

"No! It's not. But everything is so reductive with these people. You can say, 'I don't think women should die from treatable bacterial infections,' and their response is, 'You're going to burn in hell, you baby-killing harlot.'" A flare of pink spread across her cheeks. "A staff member showed me this clickbait article about us after we got seed-round funding, published by the fine folks of Life Begins. The headline was something like, 'Toledo Abortion App Puts Babies At Risk.'"

"Abortion app."

"Yes."

"Wow."

"Right?"

"Could someone even get an abortion from a Nora Health doctor?"

Constance nodded. "Yes, if the doctor operates at a facility that is allowed to perform them. But like you said, Nora is about health care access, not abortion access."

"It's hard to imagine how anyone can be opposed to women receiving necessary medical care. I know that plenty of people are. It's just hard to understand."

"Oh, I know. But these wing nuts don't care. Plain and simple. A reproductive health clinic does so much for so many women. Here in Toledo, there is literally only one abortion provider left. One. Planned Parenthood doesn't even perform them here. So all of the work Planned Parenthood is doing is prevention and birth control. But because Planned Parenthood is linked to dead babies in the addled minds of these fetus-van people, that's it. All the good work doesn't matter."

"Have they ever shown up here at the office?"

"No, that's what I'm saying, they always stop just short of

crossing a line. On one hand, that's a good thing. On the other hand, I wish they'd cross it already so we could file charges."

I thought about the explosion at my office building. "Be careful what you wish for. Are you familiar with the Keystone Christian Fellowship?"

Her eyes narrowed slightly. "I feel like I've heard of them."

I showed her Aiden's picture on my phone. "I think this is the kid who's been calling you. He's the stepson of the group's pastor. It's ostensibly a church, of the fundamentalist flavor."

Constance looked at the image. "Wow, he's an actual kid."

"Sixteen."

She shook her head. "And why do you think he's the one who has been calling me?"

"The calls have been coming from a woman's house, in Perrysburg. She's dead—she fell while hiking in Columbus about a month ago. In the meantime, he's been hiding out at her house."

"What's your connection to him?"

"My client's mother is the woman in question," I said, "and mostly what I need is to find him to figure out what happened to her. In the process of that I came across your problem."

Constance's color paled a little. "This woman—she was murdered?"

"I don't know."

"Fuck. What's her name?"

"Rebecca Newsome. Know her?"

She shook her head. Her mind was elsewhere now, and I felt bad for making the situation seem worse. "I have another meeting at three. I'm sorry but can I give you a call if I remember anything else?"

I handed over a business card and said, "One more thing. Did you ever record the calls?"

"No. They never really last long enough for me to do that. It's more the volume—lots of hang-ups. No messages. I don't even know how he got my number, actually."

I wasn't sure either; I hadn't had any luck figuring out who the number belonged to when I first tried. But data warfare was the new black, so it probably wasn't all that much of a mystery.

CHAPTER 19

Neither Aiden nor his car were at Rebecca's house or the rental property. The back door to the latter was unlocked, though. The house was dark and dusty and cold, but enough light came in through the bare windows for me to see that a folding cot, Army green, stood along the back wall, heaped with quilts and a crocheted blanket in Bowling Green brown and orange in place of a pillow. There was a laundry basket at the foot of the bed, half full. I lifted the hem of a khaki jacket; its pockets were empty. Below the jacket was a white shirt—similar to the one he'd produced from his backseat at the St. Clair Club—embroidered with the Horizons Academy logo.

I looked through the rest of the basket at jeans and another uniform shirt and six identical black tees.

I also found an electric space heater, wrappers from activated-charcoal hand warmers, a puffy pair of gloves, three hats, a large trash bag half full of discarded fast-food bags, and half a dozen empty Mountain Dew two-liters.

So Aiden had been living here for who knew how long.

I wondered what had brought him to her house the other day? The temperature? It had gotten cold in a hurry, and the electric had been shut off recently here.

Or maybe he just really wanted to order a sub.

I checked out the rest of the house but found nothing other

than dust bunnies and an impressive cobweb stretching across the top of the stairs.

Aiden Brant was going to be difficult to find again.

It was early afternoon. I stopped by the Creedle house and rang the festive doorbell—it made more sense now that I knew about Joel's involvement in the church—but got no answer. Somewhere inside, the shaggy white dog whined. The blue Audi wasn't parked in the driveway, or in the garage. A red one was there, though, like a matching set. I had to jump to see through the decorative glass panel in the garage door, since it was attached to the house and had no separate entrance. The space looked orderly enough, no flashing lights that said "CLUE." Just power tools and athletic equipment.

I did a lap around the house. Through gauzy curtains I could see a nice place done up in a poor man's version of luxury—brocade furniture, faux Tiffany lamps, an enormous replica version of a medieval tapestry that I recognized from my one semester as an art history major as *The Knight*. It hung in what appeared to be the living room, which also contained cream-colored carpet and an enormous grand piano.

After I finished my fruitless tour of the house's exterior, I went back to the driveway and looked up and down the street. The neighborhood was quiet.

The house beside the Creedle place was a more angular version of the everystyle McMansion, with dark wood and dramatic front windows shaped vaguely like the blade of a guillotine. I rang the doorbell, which made a normal chiming sound, but got nothing in response.

I tried the house on the other side, a brick colonial with a HATE HAS NO HOME HERE sign between the hedges. The woman who opened the door had smudges of flour on her forearms.

"Sorry," I said, "I didn't mean to interrupt."

"It's okay, I'm sick of this anyway." She smiled. She was about forty with brown hair threaded with grey and a nice smile, warm. "Can I help you?"

"I'm trying to get in touch with your neighbor, Nadine. I was wondering if you've seen her today."

A furrow of concern creased the woman's forehead. "Come in, and let me wash my hands."

Her name was Danette Carrasco, and she was in the process of making six dozen cupcakes for her son's school Halloween party. "And he specifically requested *from scratch*. Like he even knows what that means. Those cupcake mixes from a box? They're designed to be just as delicious. He said he'd help me, but of course that's not happening." She finished washing her hands at her fancy no-touch sink and dried them on a dish towel. "To be clear, I don't know Nadine that well. She just moved here about a year ago, maybe a little less."

"I sense a but."

The corner of Danette's mouth bunched up. "I don't know Joel that well either. But I've always had a feeling about him. You know, the feeling you get when you meet someone who is just not for you, not your kind of person?"

I thought of the sign in her yard. I doubted she had purchased that from a Keystone Fellowship fund-raiser. "You mean the church stuff?"

She winced, just a little. "I was raised with Jesus. Don't get me wrong. A person's faith is nobody else's business. But the Keystone Fellowship is strange."

"How so?"

"They've been around since I was in college, at least. I went to UT and there was a group of students who were just, you know, everybody knew they were Keystones and unless you wanted to get involved with all of that, just stay away. Even if they invite you to do cool things, which they did, sometimes. But it was always guise for a Bible study. My roommate—sophomore year, I think—she was friends with one of them for a while. Very high-pressure tactics to get people to commit to the group and all that. Seemed kind of cultish to me. But when you're young, everything has the power to sweep you off your feet, doesn't it?"

I nodded. "Must be terrifying, then, having kids in this world."

"Oh, it is. I worry so much. And honestly, watching Joel next door with his boys—it's chilling."

I waited.

"There's something about the way he acts to those kids. It's like, they'll be running around after school, when nobody is home, whooping and hollering and being, well, boys. Then Joel will drive up and they just get so quiet and well-behaved. Like a switch flips."

"Is he abusive to them?"

"Not that I've ever seen or heard. But of course, that's only what I can see or hear across the yard. They've just always been like that, even when they were probably nine or ten. We moved in about five years ago, this was shortly before his first wife killed herself. Oh—you didn't know about that."

I shook my head. "No. Go on."

"Trish. I only met her once. Very much the same type as Nadine, to be honest."

"How so?"

"Haunted? I don't know. That doesn't make any sense."

"It kind of does."

"Well, anyway." She picked up a naked cupcake on a cooling rack and peeled off the crimped orange wrapper. "She drowned. In the pool, which Joel subsequently filled in."

"And it was a suicide?"

Danette nodded. "She'd taken a bunch of pills, there was a note, she apparently had a long history of problems."

At the mention of the note, I thought about Elise Hazlett.

Who's the mystery now?

I pointed at the cupcakes. Danette nodded, so I helped myself to one. "When did Nadine come into the picture?"

"Oh, much later. A year and a half ago maybe. At first I thought—good, someone can bring some life into that house." She shrugged. "I haven't seen her in a few weeks. She used to sit outside every morning with her coffee on the terrace. We'd chat a little when I was out there gardening. Then one day, she wasn't there, and I haven't seen her since. It was shortly after school started, I remember that."

"What about her kids," I said, "Aiden and Katie?"

Danette finished off her cupcake and chewed in silence for a few beats. "I assume they're with her, wherever she is. Katie goes to the same school as my sons."

"And she hasn't been in class?"

"No." Something dark passed through her expression. "Wait, do you think something, I don't know, bad happened over there?"

"I don't know. But when you say 'wherever she is,' where do you think that is?"

"I figured, maybe she left him. And went to stay with a relative or something."

"Did Joel say something to that effect?"

"I haven't spoken to him in a year, probably."

"Did Nadine say anything that indicated to you she was planning on leaving him?"

"No, we talked about the weather, mostly. The summer, gardening, whatever. I have a lot of veggies growing—my crops, I call them. But Nadine had a real touch for cultivating flowers. I guess she had a rose that won a Home and Garden Show competition once. I know she volunteers at the florist that their church runs.

But she just seemed, I don't know, unhappy. Pained. Deeply serious. I honestly don't think I ever heard the woman laugh. And the way she'd act around Joel? So quiet, always a step behind him, head down."

"What about his kids. They get along with the new family?"

Danette thought for a second before answering. "I barely ever see or hear Nadine's kids. They definitely don't hang out with the twins. And the twins, well, I don't know, it's no wonder they're weird, after what happened." She made a face. "Eh, that's not fair. They're just kids. I don't mean they're destined to be outcasts of society or anything. But Preston's like a used-car salesman, he'll talk to anyone, about anything—he once cornered my husband for forty-five minutes about the new riding lawnmower we got."

I laughed. "How much could a fifteen-year-old have to say about a riding lawnmower?"

"Right? That's what I thought, but it turns out, plenty. Pete—my husband—he came in after that and was like, I swear, nobody has even so much as looked at that poor kid recently."

"What about the other one?"

"Porter. Yeah, he's the opposite. So quiet, and always scribbling in a notebook. I tried talking to him a few times and he always just runs away."

"Do you happen to have a phone number for Nadine?"

Danette shook her head, then paused. "Well, actually, we have a school directory for the Science Academy. Let me check."

She opened a series of drawers of the desk built into her kitchen cabinets and brandished a small booklet. "Here. Creedle . . . no, it would be under Brant, I suppose." Her brow furrowed. "Oh. Well, that doesn't help much."

She showed me the page in the school directory. Next to Katie's name, it listed Joel's and Nadine's names, but only one email address and phone number—his.

left after asking Danette if she could try to find out anything about Katie Brant at her son's school. There was already a lot of information swirling around this family: Sharon Coombs's claim that Aiden transferred to a boarding school in Michigan and Danette's detail that all three of the Brants were conspicuously absent from the house in Ottawa Hills. Add to that Aiden hiding out on Rebecca's properties and we had one strange situation.

Danette told me that the Creedle twins would probably be home from school within the hour. I left for a while, wandered around the famous Franklin Park Mall, and called Shelby. "You'll never guess who I met today."

"Who?"

"Constance CAN."

"What? Where—how?"

I let myself smile at her excitement. "I'm back in Toledo for my case. It overlapped with her a bit."

"What was she like? This is so freaking cool."

"She was very helpful. And I can see why she's taking the state of Ohio by storm—she's a compelling speaker."

"Did you get her autograph?"

I laughed. "No, I did not think to do that. But I have her phone number, which might be cooler than an autograph."

"You got her number?"

"Not like *got* got," I said. "I'm pretty sure she's straight, isn't she?"

"I hope not! She has a husband but that doesn't mean anything."

"Well, if I talk to her again, I'll ask her."

"And for an autograph."

"You got it."

"Can I ask you a question?"

Teens were beginning to swarm into the mall, which probably meant that school was out. "Sure."

"So Miriam was over last night and we were watching a movie."

"Okay."

"And she put her head on my shoulder. And fell asleep."

"Aw, Shel, that's adorable."

"Well, I don't know, that's what I wanted to ask you. Do you think she was just, like, tired? Or were we, you know, snuggling?"

I sat on a wooden bench outside of a store called Zumiez, where many of the teens were trying on skater shoes. "Presumably she was tired, if she fell asleep. But if she put her head on your shoulder first, I think that definitely counts as snuggling."

"But what if she was just sitting beside me and fell asleep because I'm the most boring girl ever, and her head just happened to end up on my shoulder?"

"You're far from boring."

"That doesn't answer my question!"

"Okay, I think there's pretty much zero chance of her falling asleep and accidentally ending up with her head on your shoulder. Did you talk to her after?"

"No, I didn't want to wake her up, so I just sat there. And then eventually I fell asleep too and when I woke up it was morning and she had left for class."

"And texting no longer exists or anything."

"You're making fun of me."

"A little."

"Well, I don't know what I'm supposed to do!"

"Just talk to her. I definitely think she was sending you a message. I've been telling you she's into you for like a year, Shelby."

She made an agonized moan.

"No, this is the good part! Young queer love, Shel, it's everything."

"Okay. Maybe I'll text her later."

"Let me know how it goes."

"Why are you back in Toledo? You were just here, I thought."

"Such is the life of a detective," I said.

Back at the crazy-looking house, I rang the doorbell for a second time that day. Nobody cared, but I heard a teenage boy's machine-gun laughter and an outraged giggle, followed by footsteps clomping across the brick driveway. "Give it back, omigah!" the girl trilled.

The pair of them burst through the covered path between the garage and the house and froze when they saw me. The girl was pale and freckled, leaves caught in her long red hair. The boy was Preston, the one who looked like a jerk in his school picture, and he was holding hostage an iPad in a rhinestone case, arms above his head.

"Hi there, is Aiden at home?"

"Aiden still lives here?" the girl squeaked.

Preston Creedle sniffed loudly. He had a prominent widow's peak and a grown man's jaw despite the layer of baby fat he still sported. "No, he's not here."

"How about Nadine?"

The redhead had a lot of feelings about my questions. "Who's Nadine?"

"My dad's new wife, settle down," Preston told her before looking back at me. He still held the iPad aloft, his arms beginning to quiver. "She isn't here either."

"Katie?" I tried.

"This is my house." Preston lowered the iPad and the girl snatched it away. "What do you want with them?"

"Maybe they won something," the redhead offered.

That wasn't the worst idea. "Well, Aiden applied for a, a scholarship. At Zumiez," I said, recalling the name of the mall store I had sat in front of. "Half-Pipe with a Purpose? It's to highlight skaters who make a difference in the community."

Preston snorted, but his friend looked starstruck. "Do you, like, work for Zumiez the brand?"

"Yes." This was getting out of hand. "But I really need to speak to Aiden. It's just that he hasn't returned any calls about this so the company asked me to come check it out."

"What kind of scholarship? Like, for skating?" the girl said.

"There's no such thing as a skating scholarship," Preston said, but I could see the wheels beginning to turn. "But what does he win?"

"Oh," I said, "he hasn't won anything yet. But I do need to speak with him. Do you know when he'll be home?"

"He's in Michigan," Preston said, "at some camping school. They don't even have phone service there so that's probably why he didn't call back."

"A camping school in Michigan?"

The kid nodded, not offering any explanation as to what the hell that meant.

"And his mother and sister? Are they at the camping school too?"

"I guess. But, like, I'm his stepbrother. So if he can't accept it, maybe I can? Do you want to make a video of me skating or something? I have a sick board that I've barely even used yet."

Now the front door opened and the other kid, Porter, poked his head through. He was skinny and bespectacled and he looked deeply suspicious. I could tell that he had been listening from inside the house. "I'm calling Dad."

"Whatever, rat fink," Preston said.

The redhead dissolved into giggles again. "Rat fink, omigod, Preston, you're soooo funny."

Porter slammed the door and went back into the house.

Preston said, "So should I show you my tricks?"

"Sorry, kiddo," I said, "I'm just the messenger."

The florist shop, Bloom, seemed a bit like a trap designed to ensnare college girls with a certain Pinterest aesthetic, one of mason jar lights and tangly wildflowers and succulents in vintage planters. The location near the University of Toledo campus said that too. But you didn't have to look too closely before the church angle became apparent—psalms in the price-tag artwork, a whole collection of unironic gifty knickknacks sporting #BLESSED. There was music playing, a mildly catchy acoustic rock band singing about hope. And if you made it all the way to the back of the store without noticing, they cleared it up with a lightly colored but gigantic mural on the back cinder block wall that said,

> *The flowers appear on the earth, the time of singing has come, and the voice of the turtledove is heard in our land.*
> —SONG OF SOLOMON 2:12

I was one of two customers in the shop. I wandered among the succulents and listened to the music, thinking about Keir Metcalf and my client and their youth-band "disagreement." The only employee—or maybe volunteer, like Nadine—was young and blond with small, close-set brown eyes heavily lined with blue. She walked up to me and said, "What brings you in today?"

I picked up an anemic jade plant in a small ceramic pot. "I was wondering if Nadine was working today?"

"Nadine?" Her name tag said KYLA | FAVORITE BLOOM: HYA-CINTH. "I'm so sorry, but no, Nadine isn't in right now."

"Do you know when she might be by?"

"She isn't on the schedule for this week."

"Have you seen her recently?"

She blushed. "I don't—why are you asking me about her?"

"I know she spends time here and I'm just trying to track her down." I regretted the word choice—too harsh.

Kyla's expression closed off. "Maybe you should check with her husband."

"I'm checking with you, Kyla."

"Maybe I could help you with something else," she said brightly, opting to end the conversation with a change of subject. "I see you're holding one of our jade plants. Did you know that jade is also known as the friendship plant?"

I sighed. "No, I didn't."

"Succulents are very easy to care for, even for working moms."

I put the plant back down on the display. "Not today, thanks."

"We actually have a little workshop tomorrow night that's all about succulents, if you might be interested in that?"

"Great," I said, "I'll take it."

She led me up to the counter, which had one of those lazy-Susan-type iPads instead of a cash register. "Can I just get your phone number?"

"That's okay."

"I just need it for the transaction."

"I'd rather not."

Kyla tipped her head to the side. "Why?"

"What are you going to do with it?"

"Put it into the system."

"For?"

"I . . . for the transaction?"

I rattled off ten random digits, and she smiled with relief.

"Okay, and your email?"

I went three more rounds with her, giving my name, mailing address, and date of birth before she finally scanned my jade plant, which hovered ever closer to the grave, and said, "That'll be twenty-three oh six."

I handed over my debit card, annoyed. "Is it possible to get Nadine's contact info?"

Kyla smiled and thrust a small flyer into my hand. "This workshop is going to be great. Tomorrow night, absolutely free, and you'll leave with your very own soul-stirring planter."

"Soul-stirring?"

"It's so much fun. You can mingle with the gals, learn something new, I know you'll love it."

The flyer showed a group of ladies in matching neon shirts, all ecstatic over the succulents they held in their hands. *WOMEN'S CIRCLE*, it said. *Please join us for coffee, conversation, and crafts! This month we're playing in the dirt and arranging our own succulent planters. FREE EVENT! Bring a friend! All are welcome.*

In the tiniest print I'd ever seen, the flyer said, *Women's Bible Study Group to follow.*

I watered my bedraggled jade plant with a few cubes from the motel ice machine—a trick Shelby had taught me—and called Sharon Coombs.

"I would have to check, but I'm pretty sure it was Aiden's stepfather who came in to officially withdrawal him from the school."

"Did he provide the name of the new school?"

"I'm not sure I can answer that, legally. What's behind your questions about Aiden Brant?"

"Well," I said, "I don't think he's at a boarding school in Michigan. I encountered him in Rebecca's house the other day, and

I think he's also been staying at one of the rental properties she owned."

Sharon drew in a sharp breath.

"I'd love to talk to his mother about it, but I can't seem to find her, either."

"Oh, dear."

"So anything you can tell me about this family would be much appreciated. I just want to find Aiden and his mother, and make sure everything is all right."

"Aiden was with us for about two years. The Creedle twins have been students at Horizons since first grade. Aiden was from the public high school, I believe. I think he transferred to us when Nadine and Joel got married. There was always tension, which I chalked up to Aiden having some adjustment difficulties to life at a private school."

"When was the last time you spoke to Nadine Creedle?"

"I have no idea. I know I met her at one point, when Aiden first enrolled. But I'm not sure that I've seen her or talked to her since then. Joel is the one who handles the family affairs, I think." Her tone got a little defensive. "And him, I've known for a long time."

"Friends?"

"No, I wouldn't say we're friends. But we're friendly. He's on the PTA board of the school."

That was a bit of a concern. If Danette Carrasco thought his kids were terrified of him, the idea that he was involved in making decisions for an entire school seemed like a problem. I said, "Do you know anything about the church he leads, the Keystone Christian Fellowship?"

"Sure."

Sharon didn't seem to share my worry. "Any thoughts about it?"

"Thoughts?"

"I've heard that it's a little, I don't know, insular."

"We have a lot of Keystone students at Horizons. They're some of our highest achievers and most community-oriented, too." She cleared her throat. "All churches—all groups—look insular from the outside. That's what makes it a group."

I wasn't sure if this was true. But Sharon Coombs actually knew people from the church, whereas I did not.

After I hung up I returned to my browser tabs of Keystone research. On their website, I clicked a flashing button that said YOU BELONG HERE!, halfway wondering if I would be sucked into a portal through the computer screen.

It's important to us to avoid labels like conservative or liberal; instead, we try to focus on Jesus, discerning what he is doing in, and saying to, our community, and following him as faithfully as we can.

That didn't seem so terrible.

We're not here to put on a show or provide entertainment. We gather together to worship the living God who wants to speak to us, and who wants to be glorified through us. If you've never experienced the grace of God, or if it's been a long time since you have, then Keystone is the place for you. If you feel unworthy, unwanted, or unloved, like you don't belong anywhere, know that you do belong here. Come join us. We've been waiting for you.

Okay, the last part did sound a little creepy.

I opened a new tab and searched for Keystone Christian Fellowship, then clicked on the Images tab. Modern life had rendered all of our attention spans so short that this was a reasonable shortcut that I employed in moments of annoyance.

Scanning the top row of results, I saw images of gatherings that appeared to take place inside a theater of some kind. Sunday services? I kept looking until I found an image that looked out of place—an old guy holding a picture frame. The headline snippet said, FATHER STILL WANTS ANSWERS TWENTY-FIVE YEARS AFTER UT TRAGEDY.

Curiosity piqued, I clicked and skimmed the article text.

. . . Toledo residents of a certain age remember where they were when they heard about the Antama Society drowning . . .

"Fuck," I said, and read on.

. . . of Angela Wade, who died under suspicious circum-stances during a party at the Antama Society's "ministry house."

Farther down on the page, I found the photo of the old man, captioned with: *Roger Allen Wade now runs a website dedicated to eradicating all traces of the Antama Society in our community.*

I wasn't seeing how this fit together at all until I read to the bottom of the page:

The Antama Society has changed names and faces in the twenty-five years since, morphing from an insular group to a widespread Bible study called Keystone Christian Fellow-ship to a fundamentalist megachurch under the guidance of Pastor Joel Creedle.

Creedle was quoted in the article, saying, People who don't understand what it means to believe in something will always find fault with us. They are sinners. I would never judge a sinner who knows that he has sinned. I myself led a life of sin but I turned from it when I came to know Jesus. That's all I want for the sinners of our community. The sinners who self-medicate their soul pain with drugs, drinking, promiscuous sex, tattoos, abortions, immodest attire, homosexuality, pornography—I only want repentance for them, repentance in order to be resurrected to eternal life. Otherwise, they will receive eternal punishment in the Lake of Fire.

I had to stand up and walk away from the computer for a second, wigged out by the lake-of-fire business. So maybe Danette was right and this was on the culty side. I googled the name of the old man, Roger Allen Wade, hoping to find his website.

Easy enough.

It was called *Keystone Kult*.

Things didn't get any clearer than that.

CHAPTER 21

Roger Allen Wade lived in a brick ranch in the town of Curtice, some fifteen miles to the east of Toledo proper. For whatever reason I expected a Doc Brown type in a shambling farmhouse with no-trespassing signs mounted on the edges of the property, but instead the home was orderly and inviting, and Roger himself was a big, soft-spoken man with a thick silver beard and a shirt that said CAT DADDY in a purple typeface that could only be described as *zany*.

"Hope you aren't allergic," he said, moving a fluffy white cat off an armchair. "I have three, but you probably won't see but two."

"Not allergic, but they never seem to like me." As if on cue, the white cat batted my boot and ran away. "Thanks so much for seeing me on short notice." After staying up most of the night reading posts on his Keystone Kult website, I had messaged him in the wee hours and asked if he would meet up with me, something he was more than willing to do.

Roger puttered in the kitchen behind me. "My pleasure. *Scientia potentia est.*"

I mentally groped for some high school Latin. "Knowledge is power?"

"If only everyone felt the same. Do you take sugar in your tea?"

"No thanks."

"Is that preference, or discipline?"

"Preference."

"I personally prefer coffee, namely, a nice bold Ethiopian variety, but I can't have caffeine anymore. My heart. I'm disciplined enough to follow that particular suggestion of my doctor, but he can pry the sugar from my cold, dead fingers, as the saying goes."

"It's good to take a stand," I said, and Roger chuckled.

He shuffled out of the kitchen with a tray balanced with two mugs and a packet of shortbread cookies.

"Such hospitality."

Roger set the tray on the coffee table between us and slowly lowered himself into his recliner. "Don't get too many visitors, to be honest. These cookies might be rock-hard."

I took a mug and sipped. "Tell me about Keystone."

"I hope this isn't an elaborate ruse. To get me back into court. They've sued me, because of the website. Three times."

"I promise, no ruses here."

He studied me over the frames of his reading glasses. "I suppose this would be entrapment if it was." Then he nodded, like his mind was officially made up about me. "Stop me if you know any of this already. Keystone started at UT in 1989. It wasn't a church at all at first, but a newsletter that a couple of grad students put out. Roommates. It was called *Antama*, which is Greek for togetherness or some such thing. The goal was to introduce students to Jesus Christ. Not inherently a bad goal. Are you a believer?"

"I was raised Catholic. Now, I tend not to think about it much."

Roger nodded. "Fair enough. The *Antama* newsletter turned into a campus group that had monthly meetings, then weekly. Then people who came to the meeting started moving into the house. Then the house was full so they started another house. By 1993, they had three of them. That's when my daughter Angela fell in with them."

He was getting into his element now. "She had always been a bit troubled. We didn't have the language for it then, though.

Now we might say depression, bipolar disorder. And at first, her involvement with the group seemed like a good thing. Her grades improved. She started dressing like a normal young lady." Roger got to his feet and disappeared into the kitchen again. "Here's Angela pre- and post-Antama."

He handed me a pair of photos. In one, his daughter sported jet-black hair and a ratty leather jacket; in the other, she was blond and clad in a floral sundress, smiling vacantly. If a person's wardrobe were proof of anything, the transformation was complete.

Roger said, "Those pictures are a year apart."

"Wow."

"The point is, the group sparked a radical change in her. But what could have been a good thing turned into something else. She stopped coming home as much. She stopped calling. We went to her house and were told she didn't want to see us. Then eventually, that she'd moved. We never saw her again after that. There isn't some big, dramatic moment where she renounced us and everything we stood for. We just had less and less of her, until she was gone." He held out a hand for the photos. "Our poor girl drowned at a gathering at the house."

"What kind of gathering? A . . . ritual?"

"They're not Satanists, if that's what you're asking. She drowned in some kind of baptismal rededication. A thing like that—it does something horrible to you. I thought we had all the time in the world. That she would eventually come back to us. If I had known she wouldn't, I would have tried so much harder to get her back."

I nodded along at his words. I'd felt the same thing with my father, and still did—the sense that time had run out, stamping its finality on our relationship. I'd forever be the girl who had a shitty relationship with her dad. His last words to me would always be, *Be nice but not too fucking nice.* There wouldn't be a resolution. It just was what it was, forever.

"So anyway," Roger continued, "I made it my mission to keep

tabs on them, in all their incarnations. An obsession, if you'd asked my wife while she was alive. For all the good it's done—they have something like two thousand members now."

"Seriously?"

He nodded. "Something about his approach resonates with people, this ultramodern 'nondenominational' open-arms nonsense that's actually quite fundamentalist. Fire and brimstone. But people, young people, especially, get taken in by the glossy packaging. The hip logo, the fun gatherings."

"How do you know all of this?"

"When I created the website, survivors came out of the woodwork to tell me about how they escaped. Some tried for years before they finally managed. It's like the frog and the pot of water. You put a frog into a pot of boiling water and he'll jump right out. But you put a frog into a pot of cool water and slowly turn up the heat, he'll just sit there and let you cook him."

"You're saying Keystone turns up the heat gradually."

"Yes, until suddenly you have nothing and no one, and even if you did come to your senses and decide to leave, you wouldn't even know how."

"Bleak."

"It is, really. And the public doesn't get it. They know, oh, yes, the quirky little flower shop is owned by the Keystones. Oh, yes, the free legal clinic at the library on the first of the month is run by the Keystones. They're very visible, but on the surface, you can't see the manipulative tactics. You don't see that they only use church-owned cell phones and email addresses. That everything they do and say online is monitored. There's a software they use— UnityView. It allows members of home churches to see what other members look at on the internet. This is to discourage the use of pornography."

I shook my head. "But, why?"

"It's *sinful.* I've heard from survivors that if anyone slips up, forgets, or even accidentally clicks on a link somewhere, the home church group will publicly shame them, break them down even more. Like any cult, they're good at what they do."

I took a shortbread cookie and nibbled. A touch stale, but I'd had worse. "When you say cult, I think of David Koresh. Or Jonestown. This sounds deeply screwed up but not like Jonestown."

"No, you're right about that. It's more subtle. It's almost like how you walk into a store that sells candles. It smells great, it's got dreamy music. Then you see the woman working there is a hippie-witch-whatever. You yourself may be a hippie-witch, or maybe not. Either way, she's doing her thing and that's just fine with you. That's the stance the public takes with the Keystones. Kooky but harmless. Not even that kooky, not when you look at their core beliefs—not any kookier than any other evangelical Christian religion. But they're incredibly manipulative, systematically isolating members from their friends and families until they have no one except the others."

"Is Joel Creedle the Jim Jones figure here?"

"Oh, he's something, all right. They don't worship him, per se. He's the senior pastor but the Keystone Fellowship is a home church network. Their focus is on small groups. Something to do with the New Testament's description of early churches in the book of Acts."

"So no big, once-a-week sermon?"

"They do have a congregation-wide weekly gathering, yes. They're in the process of building this megachurch compound up north—while it's under construction, they have their meetings at a movie theater, if you can imagine."

I remembered the odd photos I'd seen. "Interesting environment for Bible study."

"Most of the actual Bible study takes place in what they call home churches, which are large groups that meet in members' homes on a weekly basis."

"I think I read about that. The people living together in fellowship?"

"No, that's something else. The ministry homes. People who don't have families are encouraged to live together, six or eight people in one house. The home churches are more like what you'd imagine a regular church service to be, with readings and homilies, but in groups of twenty to fifty people."

I sipped my tea. "So they get together twice a week."

"Oh no, that's just the beginning. They also have lifegroups, of fifteen people or so, and these meet on yet another day. There are women's groups, parents' groups, singles' groups. Their members are busy every night of the week with something church-related."

"Busy with what, though?"

Here his determination seemed to falter a little. "They do some good work in the community. I won't pretend that they don't. The legal clinic I mentioned—I'm sure that has helped a lot of people. They were running a CSA for a while and donating tons of fresh fruits and veggies to the food bank. But the good that they do is far outweighed by the harm."

"Have you ever heard about them being involved in antiabortion protests? You know, the big, graphic signs?"

"The Keystones? No, I wouldn't think so. Their beliefs are conservative and certainly antiabortion, anti-contraception, but protesting wouldn't be their approach. They aren't confrontational. I could see them opening up one of those pregnancy crisis centers, but not protesting. Unless things have changed."

Maybe they had. I sipped my tea, which had gone cold.

CHAPTER 22

called Maggie but she didn't answer. In light of what Roger Allen Wade had told me about church members' communications being monitored, I thought twice this time about leaving a detailed message, instead just saying, "Hi Maggie, it's Roxane, I'm calling to check on you and Bea. Give me a call when you have a minute."

I hung up wondering if she would listen to that and think I had lost my mind. If Roger's claim of church-owned cell phones wasn't true, she probably would. Maybe she would either way. Maybe I had. I wasn't able to see where all of this was going yet, but there were too many questions to assume that there was nothing here to see.

Back in my motel room, I tried to find an address for Life Begins and was only able to turn up a post office box. But their events page told me they would be performing outreach on the University of Toledo campus that afternoon, in front of the Lancelot Thompson Student Union. I remembered appearances of such groups on the Oval when I was in college at Ohio State—specifically, I recalled the use of a bullhorn and counterprotesters from the women's studies program. Shouting had probably never changed a single mind, but that only seemed to make the true believers shout even louder.

While I waited for the afternoon and a chance to find out if Aiden might be involved with the group, I tried to find out more about Nadine Brant Creedle. Yesterday, Danette had suggested that maybe she went to stay with family somewhere, but it seemed that her social network was scant—she had a sister in Indiana who told me over the phone that she hadn't spoken to her in six months, a few cousins who didn't answer my calls, and a father in a memory care facility in West Virginia. Then I reconsidered her deceased first husband's family, thinking maybe she would turn there. The obituary I'd read listed a slew of relatives, including a sister and two brothers. I made a few phone calls and left messages and then, newly reminded that obits were gold mines for familial data, I looked one up for Cynthia Weary Shafer, my father's sister.

> . . . survived by her children: Caroline Horton and her husband, Bill, of Pittsburgh; Albert Shafer of Erie; and Josephine Shafer of Cleveland, Ohio. She is also survived by a brother, Francis Weary of Columbus, Ohio; two grandsons, Caleb and Louis; and several nieces and nephews.

So the girl named Andy was not Cynthia's granddaughter.

My brothers and I counted as three of the *several* nieces and nephews—were there others?

A name would make all of this a lot easier. It wasn't my business, but that had never exactly stopped me before. I returned to my search for pictures of the police academy grads in case one had them labeled, but no dice.

I called Tom. "There's a brand-new patrol cop named Andy something who looks exactly like my dead aunt Cynthia. Do you know her?"

"Your aunt Cynthia?"

"Har, har."

"What is this about?"

"Zervos said something weird to me about her and now I want to know who she is."

I heard Tom sigh. "What does your aunt have to do with this, exactly?"

"Sorry, Zervos said this Andy person looks so much like my dad that she assumed she was his daughter. So I looked at a picture of the recent academy class and sure enough, the family resemblance is clear. Do you know who I'm talking about?"

"I can't say that I do."

"Is there a list of the graduating class that you could get for me?"

"Whoa," he said, and I heard him walking away from the maze of cubicles in the homicide unit to somewhere that was quieter. "I can't just look up personnel files."

"I don't need *files,* just names." As I said it, I realized how bonkers it must have sounded. I cleared my throat. "Never mind. I don't want to abuse your willingness to help me out by asking for something inappropriate. Even though I just did."

Tom sighed. "I'm sorry."

"No, I'm sorry. Let's begin again. How are you?"

He didn't answer right away, and I got the feeling that I had crossed a line. Then he said, "I was glad to see your number on my phone, but you just wanted to call about a favor."

I flopped backward on the motel bed. "I'm an asshole. I'm sorry."

"You're not an asshole. I just don't get why it's so hard for you."

"Why what's so hard?"

"It doesn't matter. Everything is fine."

"No, it does matter. What were you going to say?"

"Looking at this as something other than temporary. You and me."

That threw me. "Temporary?"

"Because nothing about this feels temporary to me, but it seems like an afterthought to you. You didn't mention you were going to Toledo the other day, then after somebody leaves *an explosive at your office,* you go right back to Toledo without mentioning it, again. Shelby told me that. When I went to your place last night, where I thought you still were." He sighed again. "And obviously the solution here is that I shouldn't assume I know what city and/or country you're in at any given time, and I should always call before I just show up. But, I mean, would I really have to do that, if this mattered to you at all?"

"Tom," I said, resting a hand over my eyes. "You're right. About all of it. Except the part about this not mattering to me. Because it does. It does. I just—I don't know, I get caught up in things. Obsessive. I feel like it's been worse lately, this hypervigilance. That's my garbage though, and not anything to do with you. Sometimes I want you so much it freaks me out. I don't just mean *want.* But that too."

"Freaks you out why?"

The conversation had gotten serious fast. "When you want something," I said, my voice coming out small, "when you really want something and you say that you want it—" But I stopped. What did I want to say? That the power shifts, that you might not get it, that wanting out loud had never worked out for me before? "I don't know. You're right. It is hard for me. But I'm trying. I really am."

"I have to go."

"Tom, wait."

"Yes?"

"I'm trying. But I'll try harder."

"Okay."

"And, Tom?"

"Yes?" he said again.

"I'm in Toledo."

Finally, a smile came through in his voice. "Thanks for the update."

It was damp and grey on the grounds in front of the student union, which dulled the enthusiasm for the college students who crossed to and fro but not for the matching shirts of Life Begins, who'd set up a portable white gazebo to protect the giant digital screen they'd brought with them to show a constant loop of propaganda—the twenty-first-century version of the big posters that I remembered.

A young woman in a UT sweatshirt was chatting with a trio of skater boys who looked bored and confused. Her counterpart, a kid with glasses and red hair, thrust a brochure at me. "Have you received this information yet?"

I took the brochure from him. I didn't look at it; I didn't want to look. The graphic images were upsetting, which was exactly why they used them. I said, "I'm actually hoping to chat with someone in your organization who's in charge."

The boy said, "Talk about what?"

A woman was sitting behind the two young people, older and slightly more bedraggled in a grey rain jacket with too-long sleeves, and she stood up from her spot at the table and looked at me. "Do you want to talk about getting involved?"

"I do not." I set the brochure down on her table. "I'm a private investigator. I've heard that your group has had some run-ins with Nora Health—and," I said, interrupting an attempt to launch into something, "I'm not going to debate your stance, I just want to know if a kid named Aiden Brant is a part of that."

"Why, so you can harass him too?"

"Harass?" I spread my arms to indicate their booth. "I don't know that I'm the one doing the harassing. But the kid is missing. I just want to piece together what his life is like. So I can find him."

Her expression softened, just a touch. "Missing?"

"Missing. You know him?"

"No."

I put my hands on my hips.

"His stepdad, though. He used to be involved."

"Joel."

A nod.

"Used to be involved?"

"Yes."

"How so?"

The woman looked at her counterparts under the booth, who were ignoring the students who walked by in favor of listening to our conversation. "Let's talk elsewhere."

I got us each a cup of tea inside the student union and we sat at a table near a wide bay window. The timing was right; the rain had picked up already.

"Life Begins is a nonprofit with a board of directors. Joel Creedle was one of them some years back. He was elected, technically, that's how the board positions work. But he wasn't a good fit for us, not at all." Her name was Marcia, and she'd been involved with the group herself for a decade.

"How so?"

"He had very strange ideas. We're relentless defenders of the rights of the preborn. But we aren't criminals."

I felt my eyes widen. "Criminals?"

"He thought, why spend money on printing brochures and sending people to college campuses when we could make a real difference. He kept talking about how we could leverage surveillance to find out everything we could about the people who staff Planned Parenthood. He even suggested that we blackmail someone on the city council to get permits revoked for groups protesting the president."

"Blackmail?"

"I'm all for getting permits revoked for those snowflakes, but *blackmail*? Come on."

"What other crimes did he suggest?"

"Oh," Marcia said, "it's not that he was constantly suggesting stuff like that. But he wanted to argue everything we did. He obviously wanted to be a part of a different organization. We confront, but we don't coerce. We don't threaten or manipulate. Our tactics are straightforward. The truth works. We don't need to rely on shady backroom dealings to make a difference. We don't seek to punish women who have committed preborn murder—we counsel them. He was asked—firmly—not to seek reelection."

"And he went without a fight?"

"He was pretty disillusioned by the response that he'd gotten from us by then. And he'd been working his way up in the church he's a part of. So yes."

"What about Nora Health?"

"What about them?"

"They've been getting phone calls, and they think Life Begins is behind it."

Marcia shook her head so quickly that a damp tendril of hair stuck to her cheek. "We don't make phone calls. This is what we do." She pointed out through the window, where the redheaded kid was hugging a young woman in the rain. "We connect with people. We try to heal those who have faltered. Spread the word that anyone can become a defender. We aren't out here trying to make enemies. And we definitely don't make harassing phone calls. That sounds like some teenager nonsense."

I didn't agree with Life Begins, and even if I did, I wouldn't like their approach. But I had to admit that Marcia was right. It did sound like teenage nonsense, to call and hang up, to threaten vaguely. What was Aiden's goal, to unsettle Constance

Archer-Nash so much that she decided to just shut the whole thing down?

I went back to the motel and lay on the bed. With the low, grey light outside and the heavy curtains closed against it, the room was near dark. Disorienting. Up here I was disconnected, a satellite arm of myself. I didn't understand why it was always so easy for me to put cards on the table with Catherine, and so hard with Tom. Maybe because with Catherine I knew deep down that the stakes *were* low, that it didn't matter how clear I was about my feelings since she'd disregard them anyway. Things with Catherine were always temporary. She was always on the brink of leaving, even when she acted like she wanted to stay. It was the opposite with Tom. I could count on him to stay just as sure as I could count on Catherine to leave, and there was pressure in that somehow.

The phone rang. I half expected it to be Catherine, because she had a knack for calling at the exact moment I was thinking about her. But that was a parlor trick, not love. And anyway, it wasn't her. "Hi, this is Elliott Brant, returning your phone call from earlier."

I sat up, pity party concluded. "Hi," I said, "Geoffrey's brother, right?"

"That's right. Your message said that you wanted to know if I was still in touch with Geoff's wife, Nadine?"

"Are you?"

"No, I'm not, other than a card at Christmas or what have you. But my ex-wife was pretty good friends with her, when we were together. I'm not sure if they still talk. But maybe."

"Do you think she'd be willing to speak with me?"

"I bet she would," Elliott Brant said, "she actually works for a private investigator, so she'd probably get a kick out of it. Her name is Lindy Brant."

was hoping Keir Metcalf would leave the AA Security office first, but it didn't work out that way.

At four fifteen, the fashion-plate receptionist emerged from the tinted glass door and got into a dark purple Honda Fit and drove away, me following three cars behind. While I'd been waiting for Metcalf to leave so I could talk with her in semiprivate, I'd learned all about Lindy Brant, née Lindora Pletko. She'd lived in Perrysburg most of her life, attended Perrysburg High School, went to Owens Community College, and worked as a receptionist or office manager for half a dozen small businesses in the intervening twenty-five years before winding up at AA Security.

Lindy drove to a boxing gym on Boundary Street and went inside with a duffel bag. Assuming she was there to work out and not hold up the place, I stayed in the Range Rover and pulled more background on her: house in Lemoyne, two kids, a girl and a boy, public school students both. Lindy had a dating profile on Plenty of Fish—the thought gave me chills—and appeared to sell Pampered Chef, Tupperware, and Jamberry in her spare time. Facebook listed her religious views as Presbyterian, which seemed like a good sign. She'd never been arrested in Ohio. On paper she seemed a little boring in contrast to her loud sense of style, but I remembered the farming magazine on her desk; she was a woman of contradictions.

She came out of the gym after forty minutes, having traded

her denim jumpsuit and matching jacket for basic-black leggings and an electric-blue sports bra. Her blond hair was pulled up in a high ponytail and I was surprised to see that she was ripped, her shoulders sculpted like antique furniture legs.

She got back in the car and drove on.

We went to a small white house on a big, fenced lot off of Route 23. A girl about Aiden's age was in the side yard, kicking a soccer ball against the house, ears in headphones. She looked up as Lindy went inside, but neither said anything. A few minutes after that the girl went inside too.

I rang the doorbell; the soccer player answered. "Hi, is Lindy at home?" I said.

The girl glanced over her shoulder. "She's in the shower."

"You're not supposed to say that," an unseen youth called.

"Oh, okay—"

"Sorry," the girl said, and then she shut the door.

A certain demeanor ran in the family.

I went back to the car and waited, wondering how long a woman like Lindy Brant would take in the shower. But before I could make up my mind about that, she came out of the house—re-dressed in her denim getup, her wet hair restyled into a braid—and got behind the wheel of her car again.

We got on I-90 and then took 75 North for a while. After a few miles she threw on her turn signal and merged to the left, and I thought for a moment that she was settling in for a long ride and would be heading to the St. Clair Club too. But in reality, she was just passing a truck emitting a noxious cloud of fumes from its tailpipe, and we exited the freeway near the university, where I'd just been earlier.

She parked on a side street, got a stack of catalogs out of her hatchback, and hurried down the sidewalk. I drove past her and parked farther up, realizing that I was also near Rebecca Newsome's rental properties. Where were we going? I didn't know the Toledo area well enough to hazard any more guesses.

Then Lindy's denim form turned a corner, and I saw the neon Bloom sign from two blocks away.

Everyone in the area was apparently in need of soul-stirring. As I walked up the block to the flower shop, I saw almost a dozen other women go through its front door. Some were college-age, like the hyacinth-loving Kyla who had sold me the sickly jade plant. Some were my age, businesswomen in business-casual workwear. And some were in their sixties and seventies in billowy art-museum shawls.

The common denominator? Everyone went in alone.

I was greeted at the door by a blond young woman—not Kyla, but basically a clone—who welcomed me effusively and thrust a name tag at me. "I'm so glad you're here! We have sparkling water, coffee, tea, snacks, so feel free to make a little plate for yourself and mingle! We'll get started in a few minutes. Oh, and we ask that you refrain from using your phone until the end, when it's picture time. To foster a sense of community and togetherness for the next ninety minutes."

I filled in the name tag with a purple marker; for Favorite Bloom I wrote daisy and hoped nobody would ask me what kind.

Things had been moved around on the sales floor since I was here the other day, with most of the shelves rolled out of the way to make space for two long tables with picnic-style benches attached. Each place setting was delineated by a white place mat emblazoned with the Bloom logo, and an empty ceramic pot. Barrels of dark, loamy potting soil stood at the ends of each table and made the space smell a bit like rain.

I didn't see Lindy right away, but her stack of catalogs was on the end of one of the tables. The rest of the women attending the gathering appeared to be bad at mingling—those who had taken seats at the table did so with several spaces between each other, and the rest were paying close attention to the snack table. I got in line behind a woman who was surreptitiously checking her phone from within the confines of her large burgundy handbag.

"What about fostering a sense of community and togetherness?" I whispered.

She looked stricken and dropped the phone into the depths of the bag. "I was just checking on my daughter. She was home sick today."

"That was a joke. Not a very good one."

"Oh." A blush crept along her cheekbones. Her name tag said MAURA | FAVORITE BLOOM: LILY. "Sorry. Haha."

We moved up in the line. I saw a cheese tray and some very nice-looking cheesecake brownie bites in little crimped foil cups.

"Have you been to one of these before?" I tried.

Maura nodded. "Last month we made autumn wreaths. It's really a very nice group. I like how they aren't pushy."

I wasn't so sure that was true, based on her expression when I called her out for using her phone. I said, playing dumb, "Pushy about what?"

"Oh, um, the worship aspect. This isn't a prayer group if that's not what you're here for. It can be just about taking time for yourself."

"Prayer group?"

But Maura saw someone else she knew and scuttled away, apparently uninterested in fostering a sense of anything with me.

I put a few cubes of Colby-Jack on a clear plastic plate. The tray for the brownie bites contained a plastic serving knife, which had been used in a performative slice-off to see who could cut the smallest possible piece of dessert—someone had actually cut one of them into quarters and left three segments behind.

I ignored the knife and took two of the foil cups, and the woman in line behind me raised her eyebrows.

A few minutes after seven, one of the Kyla look-alikes went to the front of the room and clapped her hands. "Okay, we're going to get started pretty soon here! I see a lot of you still standing around in the back—please, come on over, take a seat, there's room for everybody, I assure you."

I was one of the lurkers, and I preferred to keep it that way. The small store was full enough that Lindy might not notice me at first, and I wanted to figure out how involved with this group she was before I let her know that I'd made this connection. But Not-Kyla locked eyes with me and called me out. "There's space right here, come on over, you can sit right next to Lindy."

Lindy glared at both of us. "This seat is taken."

"We don't save seats, everyone is welcome here."

I squeezed in beside her. "What are the odds?"

"I'm saving this seat for a friend."

"Well, if your friend comes, I'll get up."

"What are you even doing here?"

"Fellowship and community?"

She narrowed her eyes at me but said nothing, just calmly chewed a piece of celery, keeping her eyes on the door like she was looking for someone.

I noticed that the rest of the attendees were giving us a wide berth. At first I thought it was me, but then I realized that it was Lindy. She was seated on the end of a row, next to the snack table. Rather than line up beside her, people started going around the opposite side of the table and reaching across. I saw Maura, the phone criminal, go up to one of the Not-Kylas and whisper something, pointing.

Lindy folded her arms over her chest. "Here we go," she muttered.

Not-Kyla came over, smiling hugely. "Lindy, could I chat with you for just a sec?"

"Go for it."

"I meant, over there, maybe." The young woman pointed toward the back of the shop.

"I'm quite comfortable here, thanks. What would you like to chat about?"

"Well, it's just, um." Not-Kyla struggled, glanced at me, at the floor. I pointedly looked away and listened carefully as she dropped her voice to a whisper. "Some of the women aren't comfortable having you here. After last time."

"I'm just sitting here, minding my own business."

"Yes, well, this environment is about community, and you're not even trying, Lindy, is the thing. So it's hard to accept that you genuinely want to be here."

"Would I be here if I didn't want to be?"

Not-Kyla sighed. "You know I can't tell you to leave."

"I know that."

They had reached an impasse.

"Well, okay, then." She clapped her hands again to get everyone's attention. "Welcome to October's women's crafting circle meeting! As always, we want to thank you for showing up as your best self today in the spirit of Christ's love. Let's take the next few minutes to get to know the person you're seated beside."

I turned to Lindy, but she shook her head. "No."

I tried the woman on my right, a kind, grandmotherly woman named Edith. "Don't mind her, it's not personal. What part of town do you live in?"

"I heard that," Lindy snapped. "And yes, it is personal."

Edith's eyes widened. "Oh my."

Lindy let out an exasperated sigh. Then she bolted up out of her seat, kicking me in the side in the process. "You people make me sick," she announced. "Nadine has been the heart and soul of this place and you don't even care."

She slung her handbag over her shoulder and hit the back of my head with it.

To a chorus of alarmed cries, I followed Lindy out of the shop and called her name. "Wait."

"Fuck off."

That wasn't very churchly of her. "Please."

She was almost a block ahead of me, even though her shoes clearly weren't built for speed. "You're talking about Nadine Brant," I said.

That got her to stop. She had enough forward momentum that she stumbled slightly. "Do you know something?"

"I know she's your former sister-in-law."

Finally, Lindy turned around. Her eyes were still flashing mad. "Yes."

"And you're worried about her."

Some of the anger in her face softened under the streetlights. "How could you possibly know that?"

"Because you haven't seen her in a while."

Now Lindy just nodded.

"Can we go somewhere to talk?" I glanced over my shoulder, where the large windows of Bloom's storefront were patchworked with faces watching us.

introduced Nadine to Joel," she told me a half an hour later, after we relocated to the bar at the Tin Can. "I didn't know he was a psycho. Keir isn't like that, you know. After I started working for him, I went to one church event and it wasn't for me, and I said so. He never brought it up again. But Joel. Wow. I had no idea."

I sipped my whiskey, glad that Lindy wasn't a psycho too. "When did you introduce them?"

She had an Amstel Light in front of her and she spun the bottle around on the waxy surface of the bar, a thick coat of resin encasing a collage of crushed beer cans. "The Brant brothers didn't make the best husbands. Their marriage was over long before Geoff got sick, to be perfectly honest. Nadine didn't want to turn any heads. But when she was ready to start seeing someone seriously, Joel was the first person I thought of. I think it was about two years ago."

"You know him through Keir?"

"Double A does security for the church," she said, nodding. "So Joel is a client. I always thought he was charming, likable. And he'd lost his wife too. It just seemed to make sense."

"He's so charming but you didn't want him for yourself?"

"Please. I have two brat kids of my own. I don't want any more."

I laughed. "Okay, so you introduced them."

"They hit it off, big-time. I think they were engaged by the six-month mark. I started seeing less and less of her, but I didn't really understand at the time that it was a sign of something being wrong. I just thought she was spending more time with her man." Lindy rolled her eyes on the last word there, or maybe at herself.

"When did you figure out that wasn't the case?"

"Well, when she got serious about Joel, she invited me to the women's circle and I got in the habit of going. At some point I realized that those nights were literally the only times I saw her. Or even heard from her, really. I sent her an email that mentioned it, and I got a response back. From Joel." She played with the end of her jumpsuit's fabric belt. "I don't know how long he had been reading her emails. Hell, maybe he'd even been responding as her. Maybe I'm the biggest idiot in the world. But he wrote that I was upsetting her with my insolent questions."

"Insolent?"

Lindy shook her head, her mouth pressed into a thin line. "After that, emails to her came back as undeliverable. Her cell phone got turned off. So at that point, I was, you know, very concerned. I mentioned it to Keir and his response was kind of like, oh, Joel's a good guy, it's not our place to interfere between a man and his wife."

"Ew."

"Ew is right. I was shocked. I did a little digging about the church and I ended up finding this blog, it's called Keystone Kult."

I nodded and let her talk.

"I learned so much from this site. About the way they prey on people who are lonely—away at college for the first time, fresh out of a breakup, people who are looking to find meaning and community. They overwhelm new recruits with love and companionship. Sometimes it takes a few gatherings before the recruit even realizes it's a religious group. Like the women's circle. Free craft supplies, cool! No. Not cool." Lindy finished her beer and motioned to the bartender for another. "Then, once they have you hooked, they isolate you from the people you know until you're doing nothing but spending time with them."

"Why?" I said. "I mean, what's the point of this?"

She frowned at me. "You can't ask a true believer what the point is. The point is that they believe, and they want everyone else to believe."

"And Nadine—she believes?"

"Not long after I read all this stuff, I went to the women's circle and I tried to talk to her about it and she said that it wasn't the right time. She said she'd call me later and we could chat then. But of course she never did, and that was the last time I saw her. She didn't come to the next women's circle, and she didn't come tonight."

I remembered what Not-Kyla had whispered to Lindy earlier in the evening about *last time*. "Did something happen last month?"

Lindy's nostrils flared. "I was just trying to help."

I waited.

"I'm a sales consultant on the side," she said. "Tupperware, Jamberry, Longaberger, although not so much of that anymore. Recently I started selling Damsel in Defense. I tried to get clever by handing out Tupperware stuff to the women with Damsel catalogs tucked inside."

"Damsel in Defense," I said, "which is what exactly?"

Lindy hoisted her purse onto the bar and produced a digital camera. "It only looks like a camera. It's actually a stun gun."

I took it from her and studied it. "Really?"

She reached over and flicked a switch, and a terrifying crackle issued from the thing along with a burst of light, much to the alarm of the bartender.

"They also make pepper sprays, tactical pens, concealed-carry bags like this one. Self-defense, girlified. This model is my favorite. I actually gave Nadine one as a gift a while ago. I can give you a catalog if you want."

"That's okay. But I take it this didn't go over well at the meeting?"

She tucked the stun-gun camera back into the purse. "It really hit a nerve, no pun intended. I just wanted them to know that there were options. But instead it turned into a shouting match. Tense stuff. They didn't tell me not to come back but I think it was implied."

"Did you ask anyone there about Nadine?"

"Sure, and everyone repeated the same line about her kids, some emergency with her kids. But I'm telling you, I saw real fear in her eyes, that last time. I asked Keir about her, he said the same thing. Aiden was having some behavioral problems, whatever whatever."

Based on what I knew of Aiden so far, it did seem like he was having such problems. But he was hiding out under a dead woman's guest bed, and Nadine was nowhere to be found. So problems or not, somebody was lying. "Did you know Keir's ex-wife?"

Lindy shook her head. "They were already separated when I got hired."

"Did you know she's dead?"

A nod this time, confused. "Why?"

"That's how I got involved. Her daughter hired me to look into her death, and one of the first things I uncovered was Aiden Brant hiding out at her house."

Her eyebrows knit together. "What? Why?"

"I don't know, and he ran off before I could find out."

"I knew something messed-up was going on. I knew it. That sunovabitch."

"Do you know anything about the church's involvement in protesting against reproductive health care?"

Lindy cocked her head to the side. "I know they did some Right to Life march a while ago. And I've heard Joel ranting about how birth control is ruining America or whatever it is that he believes—I try to ignore him when he gets like that."

"What about Nora Health?"

"The abortion app?"

Lindy said it unironically; Constance Archer-Nash wouldn't be happy to hear it. I nodded.

"I mean, I'm sure the church people don't *like* it, but I never heard anything in particular about Nora Health."

dreamed about church, about being an altar server in the sixth grade. I was trailing after Monsignor McFarland on Palm Sunday with a bucket of holy water while he dowsed the congregation in a shower from the aspergillium. As we walked down the center aisle, he dunked it into the bucket I carried again and again, water splashing up my sleeve, the linen fabric of my robe cold on my skin. With each splash, I grew more and more waterlogged, unable to breathe. And then Elise Hazlett was there, in the blues and pinks of every stained-glass window.

In this way, it was the same as all the dreams I had lately.

I woke up gasping, sputtering, as if I were submerged in water for real. The digital clock told me it was four in the morning but I got out of bed and turned on all the lights and double-checked the dead bolt on the door.

I didn't want to be here anymore. Here, as in Toledo. But also as in this same dream, the stuck feeling. I could leave the area, but I couldn't leave my own head.

Annoying, the way that worked.

I wondered if the new Keystone Christian Fellowship campus would be a formidable place like the churches of my youth, dark wood and stained glass, or if it would be modern and cheery to belie the dark undercurrent of manipulation that its members employed.

You could get away with a lot by putting a modern spin on

things. Young people and slick marketing materials did wonders for Keystone, and for groups like Life Begins. But from what I'd learned yesterday at the college campus, it didn't sound like they'd welcome Joel's particular flair for marketing.

Aiden expected some kind of help from Rebecca, which seemed to imply that he couldn't get, or didn't want, that help from Joel. But what kind of help could involve both Nadine Creedle and Constance Archer-Nash?

Constance had five minutes to meet with me before she had to leave for the airport. "Literally five minutes," she said as she stuffed items in her computer bag. "So talk fast. Dean, get me a coffee for in the car, please?"

Dean was her security guy, or one of them. His broad shoulders made an inverted triangle to his narrow hips and he was dressed in all black. If he resented being treated like a personal assistant, he gave no sign, just nodded curtly and left the room as I said, "So the kid who has been calling you—he has nothing to do with Life Begins."

Constance, clutching a tangled earbud cord, looked puzzled. "What?"

"I'm saying Life Begins isn't behind the harassment."

"Then who is? Other than this random kid."

"Well, I mentioned the Keystone Christian Fellowship to you the last time we talked."

She put the earbuds into the bag and sat down behind her desk. "Yes."

"It sounds like the guy in charge over there has some strange ideas about the way to get things done." I flipped through my notebook until I found the exact quote. "'Blackmailing city council to get protest permits revoked, leveraging surveillance on Planned Parenthood staff.'"

"Surveillance?"

"Not a far cry from surveillance and blackmail to trying to hack your systems, is it?"

"No one has hacked our systems. It's our CRM. A company that lots of campaigns and businesses use."

"So now you're not concerned?"

Constance sighed. "I just don't see how I can help you. Not that I mind your company. I'm just saying, as far as sharing information goes, I don't know why this kid has been calling me and I don't know what this random church wants from me."

"Okay, well, suppose the attempted hack has been successful."

"Perish the thought."

"What information could they get about Nora users?"

"Oh, wow, everything—names, addresses, Social Security numbers, phone, email, all that."

"Confidential medical data?"

She paused a second before answering. "Like what?"

"I don't know, pregnancy-test results? Blood type? Prescriptions?"

"No, we don't store that information. Our medical providers are the ones who'd keep that. We're just a middleman."

"Not even for the users who get contraception by mail?"

"No, we store their Nora account information, but their medical data is housed via our—you know, I probably shouldn't be telling you all of this. Our service model is unique. But suffice it to say that the attack on the CRM wouldn't have medical data even if it had been successful."

"Humph," I said.

"I thought that was good news."

"It is."

Dean the security guy reappeared in the doorway of her office with the coffee she had requested. "The car's here, ma'am."

Constance slung the computer bag over her shoulder, earbud cord dangling. "Roxane, stay, Dean can help you more than I can."

She took the coffee and disappeared.

Dean looked at me flatly. "What is it that I'm supposed to help you with?"

"How come you don't get to go to Chicago?"

"Is that really what you want to know?"

"Among other things."

He sat down on the low, modern sofa where Constance had been sprawled out yesterday. He was so tall that his knees practically reached his ears. "Someone has to make sure things are secure here, too. Her body man travels with her." He looked at his watch. "I have a meeting in five minutes."

Everyone only had five minutes in this joint. "Okay. The attempted data breaches."

"Security and IT security are two completely different things."

"Okay, can you introduce me to someone in IT security?"

"He's with Ms. Archer-Nash, heading to Chicago."

I sighed. "Okay. Let's talk security-security. Ever see this kid?" I showed him Aiden's picture.

Dean shook his head.

"How about this guy?"

The security man looked at Creedle's picture on my phone and narrowed his eyes. "Him, yeah. Ohhh yeah."

I waited.

"There was a rally a while back, pretty early in the campaign. Everything was going fine until this guy and two or three other guys start making noise, going on about how Constance wants birth control to be mandatory or something—nonsense stuff. They were filming it, I remember that. I got the impression that the whole thing was designed to provoke someone into throwing a punch, or maybe they wanted to get arrested—I don't know. Constance shut them down pretty quick—she has a knack for it—and we tossed them out and that was the end of it, but I got the sense that they were hoping for some big scene."

"Had to be disappointing."

Dean shrugged. Then he smirked and said, "For them, or for us?"

I went back to my motel room and found a record of the event on YouTube: *PROTESTERS GET OWNED BY CONSTANCE CAN!* The video had a quarter of a million views and it showed Constance at a podium with people packed in behind her, nodding along to what she was saying. Then the faces that formed her backdrop started to turn to the right, the whoops and cheers fading until a disembodied voice could be heard: "Constance CAN'T make our women murder our babies!"

I recognized Joel Creedle's rich baritone as he repeated the phrase again. The camera was still on Constance and she made a face, almost bemused. She said, "I hear you, but I can't see you—the lights." The crowd pointed him out and the camera panned around the room until it found him. Constance held a hand above her eyes like a visor. "Hi. We haven't met, have we?"

The crowd tittered nervously. I could see tension in their expressions, ones that said *This might go south in a hurry.*

"Just in case some of you didn't hear, this man is saying, what was it? 'Constance CAN'T make our women murder our babies'?"

The camera went back to Constance as she said, "You're right, I can't—and won't—do that. I'm glad we agree. Is there anything else on your mind, new friend?"

Creedle stammered indistinctly. Even though I couldn't hear what he said, it was obvious that Constance had complete control of the moment.

The crowd clapped politely as security people escorted Creedle away.

"I'll tell you a little story, while our new friend is leaving," Constance said in the final seconds of the video. "When I was in grade school, I was such a nerd. Total teacher's pet. This kid in my class started a rumor that I read the dictionary for fun." She grinned, eyes sparkling. "I don't know why he thought that was such an insult, or why I did. But I went home crying and told my mother all about it and she asked me, Constance, how did you respond? I told her, Well, I said nuh-uh no I don't, et cetera, et cetera." Constance paused here, and the crowd was silent again but this time it was with rapt attention rather than ill ease. "Then my mother said, He just wanted to get a rise out of you, which he got. The next time someone does that, don't give him—and it's always a him, right?—the next time that happens, no matter what it is that someone has said about you, put him on the spot. Any idiot can think up a line or start a rumor. But not everyone can think on their feet. And smart girls know better than to bother arguing with someone who isn't a worthy opponent."

The crowd went crazy.

few hours later, I resurfaced from a YouTube rabbit hole of Constance-rally videos—the security guy was right, she was a master of getting control back from a rowdy crowd member. She had a chill, solid confidence that seemed unshakable, even though the woman I had encountered in her office the other day had been distinctly *shaken*. Grace under fire when it counted was a good quality in a leader, though. I was starting to understand what the big fuss about her was.

I left the motel in search of food. I unlocked the doors of the Range Rover with the remote but as I went to pull the car door open, a big hand slammed against it.

I whirled around and came face-to-face with Joel Creedle.

The other night, his charm had been easy to see. But now it was apparent why Nadine or his kids might be afraid of him. The wide jaw looked stony and the dark eyes flashed something volatile.

I ducked under his arm to avoid being trapped between the car and his body.

He said, "You're not an honest person."

An interesting intro. I said, "Are you?"

"We're not talking about me. What are you doing up here, really?"

"That's none of your business, and I'd suggest that you step away from me and my vehicle unless you want me to start screaming."

He actually lowered his hand and backed up a bit. "You lied to Keir, you lied to the elders, and you lied to my face again when you showed up with that yearbook."

"How did you find me here?"

Something—I wasn't sure what—flashed through his face. "I've been tailing you all week."

"Bullshit," I said, but a chill snaked down my spine. I doubted Creedle's surveillance skills were good enough to pull it off. I knew his vehicle, after all, and he himself had not noticed both Aiden and me on his tail to Detroit the other day.

But I didn't know how else he could've found my motel.

"Why are you snooping around the Fellowship?"

"For a group that recruits so heavily, you aren't being very welcoming, Joel."

"What do you want?"

"I want to know who killed Rebecca Newsome."

An eyebrow went up, just a hair. "Rebecca?"

I watched him carefully. "Yeah."

"She disconnected from the Fellowship. But she was a good woman."

"Even though she was helping your stepson hide from you?"

It was a wild guess, but the punch landed squarely. "Aiden doesn't need to hide from anyone except his God."

"What about your wife?"

"What about her?" A note of desperation had come into his voice. "Where is she?"

"You don't know," I said.

Creedle took a step closer to me. "So help me, if you know where Nadine is, I'll—" He cleared his throat, maybe remembering the whole thou-shalt-not-kill thing. "Tell me where my wife is. She can't be on her own like this. She doesn't know how to do anything on her own."

"Wow, thank goodness she found you then."

He didn't pick up on the sarcasm, instead nodding solemnly. "Where is she?"

"I don't know, Joel. Where's Aiden?"

"At school."

"We both know that isn't true."

"If he's not at school, then I don't know where he is. He resists my efforts to shepherd him. In the time of Jesus, he'd be an adult."

"In case you didn't notice, this is not the time of Jesus. This is the time of parents going to jail for truancy when their kids skip school."

"He's not my kid."

We stared at each other for a while.

"If what you want is something to do with Rebecca or with Nadine's son, you have no business harassing the Fellowship. We have nothing to do with them any longer. The women's circle was very shaken up last night."

"I'll decide what's my business and what's not. What's your big plan, Joel? What are you doing to do?"

The eyes flashed again. "My plan? My plan is to pray. I might suggest it for your own heavy soul."

The chilly air whipped around us, catching Creedle's tie in a brief dance. Then he decided he was done talking to me and turned to go. He glanced over his shoulder and said, "It's the devil in people that makes them cynical and mistrustful of man."

I wondered where on earth in the Bible *that* was.

CHAPTER 27

drove aimlessly through the late-afternoon sun, unsettled. The paranoia I felt was like an aspirin on an empty stomach, a vague slithering sensation.

Maybe Creedle had someone else tailing me.

Maybe he'd LoJacked my vehicle.

That made a strange kind of sense, I realized. He said he'd been tailing me all week, but if he was doing it digitally, he might not know exactly where I was going.

And it could explain why he was so proud of himself, announcing it like that, when the smarter thing to do would've been to continue following me, not self-report that he was doing it since that would make me hyperaware of someone on my tail.

I turned on a side street and drove slowly past a row of small houses with long driveways, eyes on my rearview mirror.

No one was following me right now.

I pulled in at a gas station and grabbed a flashlight from the backseat.

It was close to dark now and the pavement was oily and grey as I dropped to my knees next to the rear driver's-side tire and shined the flashlight up into the wheel wheel. I didn't see anything, so I reached in and felt around. I came up empty, save for road dust and grease smeared on my fingers.

"Ugh," I muttered.

I checked the other tires; nothing.

Then I balanced one hand on the bumper and used the other to shine the flashlight into the undercarriage, squinting in the dark for anything that looked out of place. There were tons of GPS trackers on the market, so I didn't even know what I was looking for, just that I'd know it when I saw it.

A pair of work boots appeared next to the vehicle.

"You need some help there, honey?"

"No, I'm good," I said, my eye catching on something small and rectangular stuck behind the valance panel near the passenger-side rear tire. I dropped down to an elbow and tried to reach the thing, but I couldn't quite get my hand on it.

"You sure about that?"

I extricated myself from under the car and stood up. The owner of the work boots was a guy in a trucker hat and a grease-spotted blue shirt, a cinnamon toothpick in the corner of his mouth. He was tall, and his arms were long, so I explained the problem.

The guy's eyes widened. "Who put it there? You on the lam or something?"

"Yes, I am on the lam. Can you help me or should I go buy a yardstick?"

"A yardstick, heh," he said. He eased himself down to the pavement and reached under the car and patted around. "Holy mother, you weren't kidding."

"I never kid about being on the lam," I said.

"Well, here you go."

He handed the thing to me: about the size of an old flip phone, dirty, a length of duct tape stuck to it. A little green light blinked from the side.

I took a few pictures of it and inspected the thing for details. But it offered nothing but dirt.

My helper stood up. "What are you gonna do with it?"

If I destroyed it or left it at the gas station, Creedle would figure out that I'd cottoned on sooner rather than later. I said, "Where are you heading?"

"Indiana."

I held up the tracker. "Mind if this thing hitches a ride for a while?"

The guy chuckled. "I s'pose not."

"Keir takes a kind of libertarian view of most things," Lindy Brant told me later. "Hands off, no questions asked. There's no way he'd put a GPS tracker on someone's car."

"And yet he's a member of a church that monitors members' phone calls?"

Lindy frowned. We were in her kitchen, a homey wood-paneled affair that looked like the inside of a log cabin. She had recently baked zucchini bread, which we were eating now. "Really?"

"I don't know. I'm hearing all kinds of crazy things."

"Well, why don't we go ask him?"

I shook my head. "Sorry, but I don't trust him."

"He's a good guy. Honestly, he is."

"Your former sister-in-law disappeared, and when you asked him about it, he said it was between a man and his wife. That's your definition of a good guy?"

She ran a hand through her blond hair. "Maybe I didn't push it enough. I didn't want to piss him off—I need the job."

That was fair enough.

"And anyway," she added, "it's been months and months since Joel came by the office. I have wondered if they had some kind of falling-out."

"About?"

Lindy crimped a sheet of foil around the edges of the plate that contained her zucchini bread. "I don't know. I'm just saying, if Keir knew that Joel was doing crazy stuff like putting trackers on people's cars, he wouldn't be happy."

I thought about it. When Keir Metcalf saw me inside Mancy's Steakhouse, he could've ignored me, and he also could've told the elders he was with exactly what I was up to. But he hadn't. Did that mean something?

If someone wished to lure me to my death, zucchini bread might be a decent way to do it. Fortunately, Lindy Brant had no ulterior motives, and it turned out that she might have been right about her boss.

"You found this where?" he said, squinting at the photo of the GPS tracker.

"Up under the rear bumper. I don't know how long it's been there. But I do know that Joel Creedle put it there—he showed up at my motel and bragged that he'd been tailing me all day. Or maybe longer."

Metcalf's house was a creaky old place with so many deer heads mounted to the walls that I felt like I was in a hunting lodge.

"If he thought there was a security concern," Metcalf said, "he should have told me."

Lindy nodded. "That's what I said."

"He's lost his way. I don't know when, exactly, but Joel has gotten . . . grandiose."

"How so?"

"The Fellowship doesn't need a massive house of worship and social hall. It was Joel's idea, all of it. Everything feels out of control now though." Metcalf sat down heavily at his kitchen table.

"He wants to reach more people. That's what we all want. Joel is persuasive, and our board of directors keeps voting yes. But what does any of this have to do with Rebecca?"

"Joel's stepson was hiding out in Rebecca's house. He was using her phone to make harassing calls to a local women's health organization. And now he—and his mother and sister—are nowhere to be found."

"What, you think Joel . . . ? No."

"I don't know what to think. But something's going on."

"A women's health organization?"

"Nora Health."

"Ah."

"Does the Fellowship have a stance?"

"Birth control is contrary to our nature. It's wrong."

"What about cancer screenings for low-income women? Is that against nature too?"

Metcalf frowned at me. "I know Joel has been involved in the preborn-defender movement. The Fellowship is firmly antiabortion, of course, but we don't take an active role. We try more to effect change through example. Lindy, why didn't you tell me about Nadine?"

Lindy piped up with, "I asked you about her. Weeks ago. Remember?"

"She's been gone for *weeks*?"

"He never said anything?"

Metcalf shook his head. "He knows that I'm not a fan of the direction he's trying to take things, so maybe that's why. But this is definitely strange. Lindora, I'm sorry that I didn't take what you said seriously the first time around."

Lindy patted his hand. I wondered about the closeness between them, if there was more to it than the employer-employee relationship. "What should we do?"

Metcalf looked at her, then at me. "Can you give me a few days? To talk to him, and see what I can figure out?"

"He's not going to tell me anything," I said, "so okay."

I was just leaving Lindy's house after dropping her off when Danette Carrasco called me. "Would you be able to stop by tonight? I have someone I think you need to talk to."

She sounded if not nervous, then at least pensive. "Sure, I can be there in thirty minutes."

Unlike the other day, her house was literally vibrating with life this evening. Her husband was cutting the grass with his famous riding mower, one kid was playing a first-person-shooter game in the den, another was hammering away on a piano, and someone else was blaring trap music from the second floor. "I'm sorry," she said, leading me into her kitchen for the second time that week, "but if I don't let them be noisy, they won't leave me alone. Here, Rivky, say hello."

The other woman in the kitchen wore her hair under a *tichel*, twisted into a large bun at the back of her head. She gave me a shy smile. "Rivkah Andai."

Danette said, "Roxane Weary, the private investigator."

"Only in your kitchen would I hear such a thing."

"I take that as a point of pride. Roxane, Rivky's kids go to school with mine at the Great Lakes Science Academy. I was asking about Katie Brant in the school office this week, like I told you I would. Rivky overheard. Tell her what you told me."

"My daughter, Emma, is in class with Katie. The two of them are friends."

I nodded, trying to encourage her along.

"Katie stopped being allowed to come over to our house after her mother married that man. We're Jewish, obviously." She pointed to her head covering. "And he doesn't like that. I thought that the girls had a falling-out at school because I stopped hearing about her—I didn't realize she hadn't been in class. Until, well, my husband came to me with the phone bill and he showed me all these calls, late into the night, to a number with a 519 area code. That's Windsor. Neither of us had made the calls, but we talked to the kids and Emma admitted that she had been calling. Because Katie had moved there. I didn't think anything of it until I heard Danette talking about her."

Danette opened the fridge and pulled out a Coke, which she offered to me. I shook my head. "The woman in the office said that Katie had been enrolled at some girls' school in Michigan," she said. "And I looked up and Rivky was staring at us."

"I just thought, so which is it, Windsor or Michigan? And I went home and I, well, I dialed the number that my daughter had been calling." Rivkah looked a little nervous. "It was a casino."

Rivkah's daughter was the one playing the piano, the *Moonlight Sonata* at double time. She looked at me shyly without lifting her fingers from the keys. "Am I in trouble?" she whispered.

"No, honey," Rivkah said, smoothing Emma's hair. "Just tell her what you told me. About Katie."

Emma stopped playing but kept her foot on the pedal, a minor seventh chord lingering in the air. "I wasn't supposed to tell anybody, that's what she said."

I made my voice as gentle as I could. "How come?"

"Because of her mom. She said her mom would be mad if she knew Katie was using the phone. But we're doing the rain forest right now and she's missing it!"

Rivkah murmured, "In fifth grade they turn the classroom into a rain forest and everyone makes different animals and plants. It's really cute."

"How often does she call?"

"On Mondays, because Mom has class and I'm alone with Zevi and he doesn't pay attention to me."

"My son," Rivkah supplied.

Emma said, "And sometimes I call her too."

"She gave you the phone number?"

A nod.

I was pushing my luck but I tried anyway. "Did she tell you her room number?"

"What's a room number?"

"When you call her, does she answer the phone or does the front desk answer?"

Emma didn't say anything. I realized a nine-year-old would have no reason to know what a *front desk* was.

"What happens when you call the number?"

"She told me press the zero then say 'Miss Newsome in six one five.'"

Things had come full circle, or at least something vaguely oblong. The cashout ticket among Rebecca's possessions turned out to be a blockbuster clue, and I could only assume now that Barry Newsome was lying to me when he said he had a brief catch-up coffee with his ex and nothing more.

But why? What wasn't I seeing?

I resisted the urge to head back up there tonight, wanting time to come up with some kind of plan.

The plan I came up with was a trip to the liquor store near the motel for another handful of tiny Jim Beams, which I lined up along the edge of the desk once back in my room and thought about the fact that Maggie still hadn't called me back.

The best-case scenario was that she was ignoring me.

Going with that, I tried her from the motel phone—maybe she could be tricked into talking to me—but my client didn't answer.

I turned on the television and caught a snippet of Constance Archer-Nash giving an interview at the Toledo airport. "We're so close," she was saying, "this is the home stretch. We just need to stay focused and not give in to bullies."

A sign that I needed to go home: The television seemed like it was speaking directly to me. I uncapped one of the bottles and poured it into a plastic cup from the bathroom and tossed it back. I'd been thinking about this moment all day, and now that it was here, it was almost a letdown. Not the taste but what I wanted to feel, and didn't. I was still in the motel room, a hundred miles from home, and I was still me.

CHAPTER 28

For the second time in as many days, I made the drive north into Michigan. But this time I went straight for the tunnel beneath the Detroit River and paid my five bucks and made it into Windsor by eleven in the morning. I'd been trying to come up with a plan since last night and had ruled out a number of options.

Idea #1: Call the room.

Idea #2: Call Barry Newsome.

Idea #3: Bribe the housekeeping staff to let me into the room in question, thereby taking everyone by surprise.

Ultimately, I decided to go with knocking on the door.

After riding up and down in the elevator a few times waiting for someone with a room on the same floor, I found myself in a tan and bronze carpeted hallway in front of room 615.

My thinking was this: if Nadine and Katie were staying here of their own accord, having ditched the problematic husband and troubled son, I had no desire to interfere and could be on my way. But if something else was going on, maybe I could help.

I knocked.

A vague rustling came from inside but no one answered the door.

I said, "Nadine?"

Rustle rustle.

Then, "Who is it?"

The voice was female, quavering, but almost comically upbeat—a sitcom character caught in some embarrassing act.

"My name's Roxane. I'm a private investigator from Columbus, and I just want to chat with you about your son."

The door opened a few inches and stopped.

I felt my forehead crease, confused, when nothing else happened.

I pushed on the door with my fingertips, gently. It slammed against the safety bar and before I could grasp what was happening, a hand darted through the gap and my rib cage exploded in pain.

There was carpet on the floor, tan and textured. I was flattened against it, palms pressing into its looped fibers. My ears were ringing and the inside of my mouth tasted like wet pennies. I tried to sit up but nothing happened.

Three pairs of feet were in the room with me: Silver ballet flats, pacing. Wing tips. White canvas sneakers, kicking back and forth against a damask stripe bedspread.

". . . did the right thing," a man was saying.

"Is she dead?"

"No, she'll be fine."

"She looks dead."

I guessed they were talking about me. I tried to sit up again, this time making it onto one elbow before the room righted itself and I had to close my eyes against a sharp pulse of nausea. I wiped my mouth and my hand came away slick with spit.

The wing tips came closer to me, then disappeared beneath knees in charcoal-grey trousers. I blinked and Barry Newsome's face appeared. "She got you with a stun gun. Not a quick li'l zap either, the full five seconds. Your nervous system is probably going haywire right now but give it a minute and you'll be okay."

I struggled into a sitting position, perspiration popping along my upper lip. With shaking hands I lifted up the hem of my shirt and saw a large red welt, tinged purple at the edges, with two dark-colored dots at the center as if from the fangs of a snake. I felt my head lolling to the side but I couldn't quite manage to lift it.

Behind Barry, the canvas shoes hopped down from the bed, disappeared, and came back a beat later with an offering of a small bottle of orange juice.

"That's probably a good idea," the man said. "The stun gun converts sugar in the blood to lactic acid and all that." He opened the bottle and held it out to me but I was using all of my energy to keep myself from flopping back onto the carpet.

Finally, I was able to tip my head back against something hard—the wall, or a dresser. I saw that the canvas sneakers belonged to Katie Brant, a skinny, nerdy kid with a messy dun-colored ponytail and wide eyes staring at me from behind translucent pink-framed glasses.

The ballet flats, then, belonged to her mother. Nadine was still pacing, arms crisscrossing her midsection. Her dark hair had a grey stripe at the roots where the natural shade had grown in over the last month. She didn't look at me.

I reached for the orange juice and managed to grasp it and move it to my lap without spilling it.

Barry Newsome stood up, knees crackling. I saw that he was holding my wallet in one hand, my laminated investigator's license in the other. He went on, "How did you find them here?"

I hadn't noticed it the other day, but he looked like an investment banker.

I cleared my throat and said, "Give me back my ID."

My jaw wasn't working properly and it came out strained and tight. But he did as I asked, which made me feel the tiniest bit better.

"I checked you out," he said. "You're not one of them. At least I don't think so."

"Can someone please tell me what the fuck is going on?"

Nadine gasped a little.

I added, "Rebecca asked you for help."

"And I thought I was doing a damn good job. How did you find this room?"

I took a small sip of juice and lifted my eyes to Katie's wide ones. "Your friend Emma."

Nadine stopped her laps across the room. "What? Katie, I told you you could not contact anybody—"

The kid burst into tears. "I just miss everybody, we've been here for so long."

"Please," I said. I was able to breathe properly now, though my side throbbed with even the tiniest movement. "I didn't come here to get anyone in trouble or to stress you out. And certainly not to get tased. I'm trying to help you."

Nadine sat down at the foot of the bed. "I'm sorry. I panicked."

"I gathered that."

"Do you know where my son is?"

"No. I was hoping you could tell me that."

She pulled on the ends of her hair. "He's been using his phone card to call us. But then last week, he stopped. I never should have let him talk me into this. Coming here."

"Why *are* you here?"

"Because Joel isn't." She nodded like that explained it. "Because he can't be. He doesn't have a passport. Neither does Aiden, which is why he's not with us. But Katie and I do, she went to this science program in Toronto a few years ago."

Barry Newsome said, "Why don't you get off the floor, have a seat, and we can tell you the whole thing."

Barry and Katie left the room in search of food so that Nadine and I could talk in private. "I know that Rebecca is dead," she said. "Barry told me. After we didn't hear from her, he did some digging. But I haven't told my daughter. I don't want to scare her. She just lost her dad a few years ago."

I was sitting upright in a desk chair, doing my best not to move the left side of my body. Nadine sat cross-legged on the bed. "You didn't tell Aiden either."

"No. I thought he might do something stupid."

"Such as?"

Nadine ran a hand over her face. "Joel," she said, and it looked like she was going to continue, but she didn't.

"He hurt you."

She nodded. "Aiden never liked him. Katie didn't at first either, but then she started to. But Aiden, he begged me not to marry him. I thought it was because of his dad. Like he didn't want me to replace his dad. I wasn't trying to, though. I just—I wanted to make sure they were taken care of. My kids. Geoff wasn't a saint. He never hurt me, not physically, but he was no saint. He left me with a lot of things to deal with. Debt. Joel didn't care about any of that." She folded her arms over her chest as if she was freezing cold. "And the people at Keystone were so welcoming. I wanted—needed—that so much. It happens so gradually, the way it takes over. And when they take away all that love-bombing, it just makes you feel so cold and small, like you'd do anything to get it back. Put up with anything."

Nadine looked up at me with bright eyes. "Aiden kept trying to tell me and I didn't get it. It made more sense to me to wear long sleeves to cover the bruises than to listen to my child."

"How did Rebecca get involved?"

"He told me that she saw one of the Keystone tracts in his backpack at school. She was familiar with our—with the Fellowship. She'd been a member some time ago and had to fight to get out. I told her I didn't want out of anything. At first I really thought that this woman was crazy. But then Joel was pressuring me to take Katie out of the Science Academy—because Keystone has plans to open its own school in the future. My girl is exceptional, and she needs to be with other gifted kids. I told him no, I wasn't going to take her out of school. It was so much easier for me to draw a line where it came to her, than it ever was about myself. That was the night that I truly realized what a monster he is."

I waited for her to elaborate, but she seemed to withdraw into herself for a long moment. Then she said, "Rebecca told me about Barry, who'd helped her out when she left the Fellowship. She'd been in touch with him and he offered to let us all stay here until we figured out a plan. But Aiden doesn't have a passport. I said we could apply for one for him and just wait until it came, but he was afraid for me. So afraid. Rebecca said that Katie and I could leave now, and Aiden could stay with her until his passport came. She was so helpful. Supportive. She even let my son drive an old car she had so he could get to the homeless shelter where he volunteers. And I just—it's an idiotic plan. I realize that now. But it was only supposed to be for a few weeks."

"When did all of this happen?"

"Around the middle of September."

About a week or so before Rebecca's fall.

"Aiden was so brave," Nadine added. "He even said he was working on something to make sure Joel could never bother us again."

"Like what?"

She shook her head.

"Do you know anything about Nora Health?"

"Who?"

"Is Joel still involved in antiabortion protesting?"

She sighed. "He's very dedicated to the cause."

"What does that mean?"

"His first wife. She never told him that she was pregnant, and she ended it. This was shortly before she passed. Joel is haunted by it. By the child that could have been. It's so sad."

"That she felt like she had no other choice?"

Nadine's eyes widened in horror, but then fluttered closed as she realized that she could relate to the feeling. She said, "He's on a mission to make people see."

"And how does he go about doing that? I know he's no longer involved with Life Begins."

"He's forming his own coalition."

"Of?"

"I don't know."

"With other people from the Fellowship?"

"Everything he does is with people from the Fellowship."

"Do you know what people?"

"No."

"Do you know what he intends to do?"

"No. What does this have to do with my son?"

Now I shook my head. "I'm not sure, but there's something going on here that I can't see yet."

Barry and Katie returned to the room with a large pepperoni pizza in a grease-spotted cardboard box. I was hungry, but my jaw hurt too much to chew. While Nadine and her daughter ate, I went down to the security office with Barry.

"She got you good with that thing, huh?"

At some point, it would probably strike me as funny—that time I got zapped by a stun gun shaped like a digital camera—but I wasn't there yet. "What's the deal with you and Rebecca?"

"There's no *deal*."

"You know what I mean."

Barry sighed. "I was a terrible husband and father the first time around. I abandoned her and Maggie. It was wrong of me. It's no wonder that Rebecca turned to a community like the Keystones in the aftermath."

"So Maggie was brought up in the group."

Barry nodded. "Rebecca and I had a major falling-out over it. Over Maggie getting brainwashed by those nuts. But she told me, and rightfully so, that I wasn't a part of their family anymore, that I gave up the right to have an opinion when I left them to start a new family. It was pretty ugly. I hadn't heard from Rebecca in, oh, ten years, maybe more. I got divorced, remarried, divorced again. Then one day I got a call from her, here at the casino. There'd been this profile of me in some security newsletter her new husband subscribed to and she happened to see it."

"So ten years after a knock-down, drag-out fight about her church, she just calls you up."

"She told me that I was right. About the Fellowship."

"And you were her hero who swooped in to save the day."

His expression tightened. "Not her. She was already well on her way to save herself. She was calling about Maggie."

"Oh."

"She and Maggie'd had a version of the same conversation I tried to have with her all those years ago, with more or less the same result. Maggie wasn't speaking to her. She wanted me to try."

"Did you?"

"I tried. She wouldn't return my calls. But after that, Rebecca and I kept in touch here and there. Six weeks or so ago, she reached out and told me about Nadine. Of course I was willing to help."

"What changed between Rebecca and Maggie?"

"Oh, I think Maggie getting pregnant made her realize a few things."

That echoed what Sharon Coombs at Horizons had said, too.

Barry added, "Rebecca wasn't going to question it too much. She was just happy."

"Did Maggie reach out to you after Rebecca died?"

"No, and I tried getting ahold of her, but again, she wouldn't talk to me."

"So what's the plan now?"

He rubbed a hand over his jaw. "Rebecca's plan made sense at the time. I swear it did. But now I don't know what to do, because Nadine's son is out there somewhere. She doesn't want to leave the hotel because this is the only place he knows to look for her. But if he doesn't have the passport by now, I don't know what's going on."

I wondered if Aiden's passport was sitting in a pile of mail at Arlene French's house.

"A few days ago, he was still at Rebecca's," I said. "I talked to him there. He was very freaked out to learn that she wasn't coming back."

Barry nodded. "Where is he now?"

"I don't know. I followed him to Detroit—while he was following Joel."

"Joel was in Detroit?"

"Yes."

"Where?"

"Downtown. The St. Clair Club."

He leaned back in his chair and shook his head. "I'm not familiar with it. Is he still in Detroit?"

"When last I saw him, he was threatening me in Toledo. Do you really think this whole cloak-and-dagger bit is necessary?"

"I thought Rebecca was being a bit dramatic, but she's dead. So who was right?"

I sighed. That was a good point, though Joel Creedle had seemed surprised when I mentioned that my interest here was finding out what had happened to her. I said, "If she hears from Aiden, will you give me a call?"

As I walked out of the casino, I dialed Lindy Brant's number. I hadn't clued her in on my lead about Nadine because I wanted to make sure all was well first, relatively speaking. Now it seemed safe to let her know.

I could tell something was wrong as soon as she answered. "I was just getting ready to call you," she whispered, voice thick with emotion—fear or anger. "I think something terrible's happened."

CHAPTER 29

Keir Metcalf's Escalade was parked just outside his closed garage, its driver's-side door hanging open. The keys were in the ignition and the rhythmic chime of its warning alert punctuated Lindy's footsteps. "Keir?" I heard her say in the video, which wobbled in her shaky hand. "Something isn't right here."

In person, in her homey kitchen, she said to me, "I don't know what made me start the video. I just thought, there needs to be a record. In case things get weird."

It wasn't like Keir not to come in to the office without telling Lindy he'd be late, she'd explained already, so she had gone over to his house to make sure he hadn't thrown his back out or something. She found his vehicle with the door open but the house locked up tight, and Keir nowhere to be found. On closer inspection she saw his phone in the SUV's console and his concealed-carry holster on the passenger seat, empty.

She called Eddie, a young guy who worked for AA Security. She also called me, but of course I hadn't answered. No one called Joel Creedle but he showed up in short order anyway, and that was when things had gotten weird.

"Put that away," he snapped at her, pointing into her camera. "What do you think you're doing?"

"I don't want anyone to say everything's fine. This is not fine."

Creedle tried to snatch Lindy's phone away. "This is your boss's private property. What gives you the right?"

"What gives you the right to tell me what to do? I'm concerned about Keir, which you don't seem to be, even though you showed up here like you were expecting some kind of trouble. Do you have a GPS tracker on my vehicle too? Huh?"

From off-camera, Eddie said, "Joel, what's she talking about?"

"She's being hysterical. I have no idea what she's talking about."

Lindy went on, "Or maybe on both of our cars, me and Eddie? Keir was going to confront you about all this. Today. And now, suddenly, he's gone?"

"He probably saw something and went into the woods after it."

Eddie said, "Like what?"

Now Creedle was scrambling. "A wounded deer, maybe. I'm gonna go look for him. You two want to come?"

"I am not going into the woods with you, Joel," Lindy snapped.

Eddie walked behind Creedle on the video. "I think we ought to call the police."

"Do you have any idea how mad Keir is going to be if you do that?" Creedle made another move for Lindy's phone, but she moved out of his reach. "If anybody can take care of himself, it's Keir. He has a piece on him. He'll be fine."

Back in Lindy's kitchen, she wiped her eyes with a tissue and said, "I can't believe this."

"So what happened, did Eddie call the police?"

She snorted. "Yeah, he called Keir's buddy, Scooter. Also a member of the Keystone Fellowship."

"Fuck," I said.

"I feel sick. I'm such an idiot. It never crossed my mind that Joel would've put a tracker on my car." But he had; the tracker was currently in her trash can, smashed to bits. "So all those times I went to the flower shop, thinking this was the one safe place where I could talk to Nadine—I was wrong."

"Can I make you some tea?" I said gently, and Lindy nodded.

I filled a teakettle with water from the sink and put it on what I assumed was the burner of her glass-top stove.

"I do have some good news, about Nadine. She's okay."

"What do you mean? Did you talk to her?"

I found a store of tea bags in a kitchen cabinet and selected Moroccan Mint. "I saw her. This morning."

Lindy drew in a sharp breath. "Where? Where is she? Is she all right? And Katie?"

"Yes. They're in Canada. Safe. The whole situation is pretty delicate, but it seems like Keir's ex-wife helped them get away from Joel. Aiden's supposed to join them but there's an issue with a passport. So I'm not entirely sure where he is."

She began to cry again. "Does she hate me?"

"Lindy, no, why would you think that?"

"She could've asked me for help—I just—I wanted nothing more than to help her get away from him. She must not trust me at all."

A thin stream of steam came from the teakettle, and I lifted it off the burner just before it began to whistle. "No, it isn't like that. Rebecca used to be a member of the Fellowship. She understood it in a different way than either of us could. And, besides. She used the fake camera you gave her on me," I said. I lifted the hem of my shirt to show her the stun gun's bite.

Lindy let a small laugh escape. "Ouch."

"Yes."

"What did it feel like?"

"Terrible. But the point is, she kept that, and she wasn't afraid to use it. I don't know if that makes you feel any better or not."

She wiped her eyes with the tissue again. "What do we do now?"

I poured hot water over tea bags in two mugs. "I don't know. I honestly don't."

"Do you think Joel did something to him? To Keir?"

"I don't know. After talking to Nadine, I definitely believe that she believes he's capable of it. But there's still something here that I'm not seeing yet and I feel like Aiden is at the center of it."

Lindy sipped her tea. "If Joel did hurt Keir, what's to stop him from trying to come here? Or my kids—" She stopped, her face seizing up in fear.

Lindy's kids, Molly and Finn, were delighted to be pulled out of school with no apparent warning, then alarmed to see their mother in public without makeup. "Jeez, what happened? Is it Grandma?" Molly said, sliding into my backseat.

"No, honey," Lindy said. She reached backward to clasp her daughter's knee. "It's kind of a long story, and maybe it's nothing. But we're going to stay with Uncle Connor."

"Yes!" Finn said. He was the younger of the two, a high school freshman with curly hair that he wore a little too long. "Do you think he'll let me go on the pole?"

Lindy glanced at me. "Finn wants to be a fireman someday too."

"There's nothing to do at his house though," Molly said. "He doesn't even have internet!"

"No, but he's exactly who you'd want to be with if you're scared."

"I'm not scared."

"Well, I am."

"Of what?"

"Nothing you have to worry about, baby."

I saw Molly's eyes narrow at me in my rearview mirror. She clearly believed that her internet-less future was all my doing. "She's that lady who came to the door the other day."

"Yes."

"Who is she and why are we going to Connor's house?"

"This is my friend Roxane," her mother explained.

"Since when do you have a friend?"

Lindy sighed. "It doesn't matter. Have either of you talked to your cousin Aiden lately?"

Both kids shook their heads. Molly said, "This is the weirdest day."

I said, "Tell me about it."

After Lindy and her kids were safely ensconced at her brother's place, I drove out to Keir Metcalf's house. The Escalade was still in the driveway, but the door was closed now. Most interestingly, an unmarked car sat at the end of the driveway and I could see Scooter's silvery, gelled-up hair in the beams of my headlights as I drove by.

I drove by the Keystone Fellowship compound and found a similar sight—a tan unmarked car just outside the gates.

Joel Creedle's house was dark, no vehicle in the driveway.

Rebecca Newsome's place had a vehicle out front, but I didn't pay it any mind because I was on her street for Arlene French's house.

I still chose to pull a baseball cap low over my eyes before I got out of my SUV.

"Oh yes, dear, here's everything," Arlene said, using a slippered foot to nudge a milk crate out from under a plastic bench in her enclosed side porch. "I've been going over once every few days to get it since she passed—I just don't think it's right to let it pile up like that."

"That's kind of you." I lifted the crate onto a hip and tried not to wince. "But you know what, I think you should leave it from now on. Until you talk to Maggie about what she wants to do with it."

You're going to be feeling that for a few days," Tom said after I'd told him about the stun-gun camera. "Those are no joke. Well, I mean, a camera-shaped Taser might be, but I'm sure the pain from it isn't."

"You ever use a Taser on someone?" I was on the motel bed, a makeshift compress of ice wrapped in a washcloth on my side while I sorted through the mountain of Rebecca's mail.

"Not on duty. But at the academy, we all had to take turns getting stunned, getting maced. Oh, and shot by a rubber bullet. I'm not sure if this will make you feel better or worse, but I'd prefer the rubber bullet or the Mace."

"That does not make me feel any better." Much of the mail was sheets of those crumpled-up Arby's coupons that nobody wants, and bulk-mail postcards for carpet cleaning.

"Happy to help," Tom said, and I smiled.

"If you happened upon a car with the door open and the keys inside, but no driver—what would you think?"

"That the driver fled the scene of the accident."

"No accident. It's in the driveway of the owner's house."

"That's different, then."

"So?"

"Is the owner a little old lady or some big, burly guy?"

"Not that it strictly matters, I don't think, but more along the lines of a burly guy."

"Evidence of a struggle?"

"No."

"And I take it the guy can't be reached by phone, and isn't in the house?"

"Correct. His phone is actually in the car, too. So he left his phone and his keys. But—he took his gun."

"Or someone did."

I swept a stack of expired coupons back into the milk crate. "That's a good point. The owner might not have been the one that left the car like that. But who did?"

"I'm guessing we're not talking hypotheticals here."

"I want to come home."

"So do it."

"I can't. My case isn't solved. It's actually getting progressively more unsolved the longer I work on it."

"You always think that at some point. Usually right before you figure it out."

"I don't think that's true at all."

"Come home. Tomorrow."

"Maybe."

"Your client's mother died here, not up there. Maybe there's something left unexplored in this neck of the woods."

Speaking of my client, I realized that she'd ignored my attempts to reach her for another full day. "Yeah, maybe."

"Listen, Roxane."

"Uh-oh."

"What?"

"If you're going to say *about the other day* I'm not sure I can take it right now, post-tasing. I know that this is all me. I know. I'm sorry."

"Just come home. Okay?"

"Okay."

I'd gone through about half of the mail and was sick of it already, so I hastily shoved some of it onto the floor with enough force to fan it out.

I immediately saw a flat Priority Mail envelope addressed to Aiden Brant, c/o Rebecca Newsome.

If I had known that would work, I would've tried it first.

I tore the envelope open—what's a bit of mail fraud between

friends—and pulled out Aiden's passport and two pamphlets about international travel.

The date on the postage sticker indicated that the package had been shipped two days before Rebecca fell.

So the passport had probably been sitting in Arlene's porch since even before Rebecca had died, and Aiden had been waiting for it for no reason.

I set the small blue booklet on the nightstand and decided to go through the rest of the mail while I was at it, energized by the small success. What if Rebecca had gotten a letter marked "CLUE" or something? If not, at least I could organize her bills into some semblance of order for Maggie to deal with whenever she felt up to it. Then I separated the remaining envelopes into three piles: bills, junk, and miscellaneous. I avoided the urge to commit additional mail fraud until I came across an envelope from Motor City Towing, postmarked a few days earlier.

> This letter is to inform you, your CHEVY LUMINA, License number EV55YJ (OH), has been impounded and towed from 104 LAFAYETTE ST by MOTOR CITY TOWING to 156 DAVISON STREET. The cost of the Tow is $125; administration fee $50, and storage accumulates on the vehicle at $15 a day until claimed . . .

I had a sinking feeling in my gut. When I'd realized that Aiden's car was no longer parked at the St. Clair Club, I had assumed that it was because he'd left. That was why I checked in Rebecca's garage for him multiple times—I figured he would come back here eventually. But this told me that the car had actually been towed, leaving Aiden stranded in Detroit without a vehicle.

Hiding out in Rebecca's garage had seemed like a bad situation for him to be in, but now it looked like a best-case scenario.

left another voice mail for my client while I had a breakfast of yogurt and toast in the cramped motel lobby—I'd slept too late to get any mini muffins, apparently. With a lidless cup of tea sloshing around in my cupholder, I drove up to Detroit again to see about the car.

The tow pound was on a corner lot of Davison Street on a block that also offered a decrepit railroad track and the citywide juvenile detention center. The sign advertised TOWING • AUTO PARTS • USED CARS, which made me wonder if all of their business came from the same unlucky vehicle owners. It was a dirty place outside and in; the small office smelled like motor oil and burned coffee and hungover, angry people, two of whom were currently arguing with the impassive man behind the counter.

"We parked right beside the sign," a woman was saying, her eyes hidden behind mirrored aviators. "The sign that said the parking-zone number. Why would there be a sign right there if you can't park there?"

"Look, lady," the employee said, "I don't decide who gets towed. I just tell you, it's one twenty-five, cash only."

The woman's companion flung out his arms in disgust. "And I just tell you, we don't have any cash."

The employee pointed at an ATM in one corner. "Cash."

"The transaction fee is fifteen dollars!"

It seemed that the two of them were arguing two separate

points, both of which did appear to be valid. But I needed the employee's help, so I paid the fee and put the cash in my pocket while the hungover couple continued to argue with him for a while.

"Come on, I'd rather spend fifteen dollars on another Uber to go to a normal ATM machine than pay that fucking fee."

The couple stomped out of the office, the door slamming shut behind them with a cheerful chime.

"You wanna fight too?" the employee said. He was at least a foot taller than me, muscular under grease-stained grey coveralls with a name embroidered above the chest pocket: TAD. He spoke with an accent of a distant Eastern European variety.

"I just want to get this car."

I handed over the letter.

Tad took the paper between two massive fingers. "You got ID?"

I thought for a second about how to get around that particular detail. "It's not my car," I said, "I'm just here to pick it up."

He pointed to a sign. ID MATCHING REGISTRATION IS REQUIRED BEFORE VEHICLE WILL BE RELEASED TO YOU.

"Unfortunately, that won't be possible," I said, "you see, the owner of the car passed away."

"And you are, what, the daughter of this Rebecca Newsome?"

"Yes."

"Then you have some ID with this name."

"No, my ID has my married name."

Tad's eyes flicked to my naked ring finger. He was pretty good. "Nice try."

"Look," I said, "if you don't release this car to me, no one else is going to come get it. Then you'll just end up storing it forever without seeing a penny. And if you think you'll sell it at auction at some point, nobody's going to want an almost twenty-year-old beater. Nor the parts from one."

Tad ran a hand through his hair, thick and longish in a didn't-bother-to-get-it-cut way rather than a sartorial choice. "Nah."

"Nah?"

"I will not release the car to you."

I sighed. "Not even after I pay the towing fee of, what did you say it was, two twenty-five?"

He scrunched up his nose. "One twenty-five, and, no."

"I'm trying to help you out here."

"I don't think that's what you doing."

"I'm a private investigator, and I work for Rebecca's daughter. How about that?" I flashed my license.

"And where is she?"

"Ohio," I said. "Columbus. She has a new baby. She can't drive all the way up here over this."

"Let's call her then."

"Jesus, I had no idea tow pounds were so concerned with ethics."

"The world is a messy place. I just try to keep my part nice and clean."

I rattled off Maggie's number as Tad dialed. But my client didn't answer for him, either.

He replaced the grimy handset into the cradle. "Sorry, too bad."

"Could I just *look* in the car?"

"Why?"

"My client's, um, passport might be in the glove box. That's all this is about. I just need the passport."

Tad shook his head. "Honesty is the best policy."

I sighed again. "When this car was towed, a sixteen-year-old kid from Toledo had been driving it. Now I don't know where he is, only that he's now without a car. I'm hoping something in the car can clue me in as to where he went."

Tad thought about this, then nodded. "Okay. You can look. Five minutes."

The Lumina was parked at the far edge of the lot, its rear bumper smushed against the rusty chain-link fence. The vehicles on either side of it were parked so close I couldn't get either front-side door open and had to reach in to crank the window down. My new friend Tad escorted me to the back of the lot and stood in a muddy aisle with his arms crossed over his chest, watching with amusement as I contorted myself into the vehicle through the passenger-side window.

"Four minutes," Tad said, tapping his wristwatch.

I opened the glove box first: paperwork, manual, a bottle of Tylenol.

The footwell of the passenger seat contained another of the embroidered shirts from the school, some fast-food wrappers, and a skateboard.

The backseat offered a black hoodie and a pair of Chuck Taylors that were held together with duct tape. I pushed down the armrest, hoping this particular GM allowed access to the trunk through the backseat like a car my father had.

It did.

I shifted my body so that one foot was on the floor and one knee balanced on the seat. Then I shined the flashlight from my phone into the trunk.

It was mostly empty, save for a case of Mountain Dew cans and a Walmart bag.

I stuck my arm through the gap and reached for it.

The Walmart bag contained six brand-new flash drives still in their packaging, and the empty package from a seventh.

I spread them out on the backseat.

Different brands, different storage capacities, but they were all red.

"Two minutes."

I found the receipt from the purchase balled up in the hoodie pocket.

Ten days ago, Aiden had bought the twenty-four pack of Mountain Dew, a package of teriyaki beef jerky, and fifty bucks' worth of flash drives at a Walmart near Ottawa Hills. The time stamp said 3:14 in the morning.

"What the fuck," I muttered.

Tad said, "Okay, time's up."

After snapping photos of the flash-drive packages and the receipt, I leveraged my body through the window again—more difficult to do in reverse—and returned to the tow yard's office with Tad.

The St. Clair Club was the last place I'd seen Aiden. I doubted he was just hanging out there, but I hoped someone inside might know something. However, I was wearing jeans. I stopped at the Madewell on Woodward Avenue and grabbed a pair of olive-green wide-leg trousers, a striped shirt, and some oxblood loafers off the sale rack. In the small fitting room, I undressed quickly, then paused to examine the place where the stun gun had gotten me. The red welt had turned into a proper bruise overnight, and I could tell I was going to be feeling this particular kiss for a while. But there wasn't time to feel sorry for myself at the moment.

I balled up my jeans and T-shirt and went back out into the store, transformed. "I need all of this," I said. I lifted my hair off my neck and felt for the tag in my shirt and yanked it out.

The sales clerk widened her eyes and nodded as she scanned the tags I unearthed from my new clothes. She was very confused. "Do you need a bag, for the, your, um?"

"No, I'm good." I transferred my wallet to the new pants, which had dumb, tiny pockets but fit like a dream. Just before she swiped my card I grabbed a tortoiseshell hair clip from a last-chance display next to the register. "This too."

I twisted a section of my hair up and secured it to the back of my head with the clip and hoped the strigine security guard who'd escorted me out of the St. Clair Club wouldn't recognize me now.

My new loafers were a bit stiff but made a satisfying sound on the terrazzo flooring as I breezed past the hostess stand and through the curtain and into the dim, crowded restaurant.

I took a seat at the bar and ordered a whiskey and Coke from the same caterpillar-eyebrowed bartender who had served me the other night. "A repeat customer already."

"Yes, I'm hooked. Hey, can I ask you a question?"

"Shoot."

"I'm trying to find this kid. Have you seen him here?" I showed the bartender a photo of Aiden on my phone.

"In the bar?"

"Anywhere in the club."

The bartender busied himself with slicing lemons. "It's not exactly a kid-friendly place anymore."

"Anymore?"

Without looking up from the lemons, he said, "My family used to belong to this place. Half of my childhood was spent running around this restaurant."

I waited.

"Now I work here. I can't eat here, but I work here. Got it?"

"So things have changed."

"Old money, new money, it's a whole thing. You know? My family, whatever money we used to have, it's so old it's been gone for two generations. My dad could barely rub together two nickels but he was always a member here. We were that kind of family, and it was that kind of place."

"What kind of place is it now?"

"Mostly new money. People make money from all kinds of things now. You've got the shale-ionaires, you know, they made money from fracking or whatever. Petroleum companies. Then there's tech money, app developers. Corporations. It's all very different. But to answer your question, no, I haven't seen the kid. Your kid?"

"Heavens, no. One more question?"

He nodded.

"What's the deal with the penthouse suites? Do people live there?"

The bartender shook his head. "It's like a meeting room, a member perk. You're going to get me in trouble. Members never want to talk to the staff here."

"If you see or hear anything about this kid," I said. I folded a business card inside two twenties and tossed it on the bar.

Too smart for his own good, Sharon Coombs from Horizons Academy had said about Aiden. Certainly too smart for me, at any rate—I had no idea what he'd been doing at the St. Clair Club in the first place. The white shirt that he pulled on as he had walked up the sidewalk told me he'd been at the club before, maybe multiple times. Maybe he'd followed Joel Creedle to multiple meetings there. Meetings with whom? Aiden knew—I was sure of that— and I'd do anything to find out for myself. But now he was who knew where, stuck without a car in Detroit—what would he do in that situation? Where would he turn? A bus ticket back to Toledo probably ran fifteen bucks; if Aiden could afford a bag full of flash drives, he could probably afford that. But what if he'd never made it out of the club in the first place?

As I drove back to Toledo, I flipped through radio stations, searching for I had no idea what—something to solve my case or fix my mood. Instead, I caught a snippet of a gloomy news story that made my stomach hurt:

In Lucas County this morning, a man was found shot to death in the woods in Sylvania. Identified as Keiran Metcalf, the victim was the owner of Double A Security . . .

I couldn't hear the rest—I swallowed bile and saw red for a second and forgot to make my brain listen. By the time I remembered, the news anchor had moved on and was talking about traffic on I-90. "Fuck," I said, and snapped the radio off.

Some ten miles of silence later, the phone rang—finally, Maggie calling me back. "Hi," I said, "I'm glad to hear from you. I want to ask you a few questions about the Key—"

"I'm really sorry to have wasted your time," she interrupted, "but I've changed my mind about all of this."

I blinked in the half sun. "What?"

"I can't be doing this right now. I need to focus on my baby."

"Maggie, I know it's hard to think about, but you were right—"

"No, you aren't listening to me. I thought this would be, I don't know, cathartic. But instead it's just upsetting me more."

I was struck dumb for a second. "But I think I'm making real progress here."

I could hear Bea crying in the background. "If I owe you more money, you can send me a bill."

"Maggie."

"I told you I didn't want anything to do with Barry and what did you do? You talked to him again? You asked him to call me?"

"No, that's not what happened—"

"Please, let it go."

"I don't know if I can do that now, Maggie, it's bigger than just you."

She bit off a sharp laugh. "You sound just like her."

"Maybe that's because she was right about something—"

"Stop. Just stop it."

She hung up.

I tossed the phone at the dashboard—it hit the AC vent and flicked upward, smashing into the windshield before bouncing off the dash and sliding down to the floor. A small dimple appeared in the glass of the windshield.

"Fuck," I snapped at no one. I leaned forward and ran an index finger over the chip. It was tiny, no bigger than the head of a pin. You might not even notice it if you didn't know it was there. But I knew it was there, and I could already tell that every time I looked at it I was going to think of this shitty moment and feel annoyed all over again.

I retrieved the phone from the floor. It, at least, appeared no worse for wear.

Aiden Brant was still missing, and if it hadn't been for me, he'd still be safe-ish under Rebecca's guest bed instead of on the lam somewhere. I decided that it was time to have a real heart-to-heart with Joel Creedle—now that I knew his wife was out of his range, I didn't see the harm in pissing him off.

But when I parked on his street, I saw that a cream-colored Beetle was in his driveway where he usually parked his Audi.

Preston and the redheaded girl were playing a game that could only be described as Flirty Keepaway with a partially deflated basketball. "Oh, you're the Zumiez lady!" Preston said, apparently having grown fonder of me in my absence. "Did you reconsider? Do we get the prize now?"

"So you haven't seen your stepbrother, then," I said.

"I told you, he's at school."

"Right, the camping school. Do you remember the name, by chance?"

The front door of the house opened and the white dog bounded out, followed by a young blond woman that I recognized as a member of the Bloom staff, a Not-Kyla.

The dog ran over to me and jammed its nose into my crotch.

"This is the Zumiez lady, remember, I was telling you about her?"

Not-Kyla looked at me, profoundly confused. She was holding a cordless phone in one hand, or maybe another cleverly disguised stun gun.

"I'm hoping to chat with with Mr. or Mrs. Creedle," I said. "About this awesome scholarship opportunity that Aiden qualified for . . ."

"Oooh, oooh," Preston said, "can we pretend she's my stepmom and then we can get the prize?"

"I think we should all go inside now," Not-Kyla said. Then she looked at me again. "I don't know what you're doing but lying to children is so wrong. So wrong. Preston, come on. Inside. And you—if you don't leave now, I'm calling the police." She brandished the phone at me.

I held up my hands and walked away, but not so fast that I couldn't hear her place a phone call behind me.

"Did Pastor Creedle leave town yet?"

I saw no reason to stick around, but the clerk at the motel told me that even if I checked out now, I'd still be on the hook for tonight and tomorrow night because their policy required a full twenty-four hours of notice.

"And twenty-four hours from now is after our check-in time, so."

"It's fine," I said, again, "I just need the zeroed-out invoice."

"I can't zero it out yet, because you still have to pay for tonight. And tomorrow night."

"You have my card on file. Can you just charge me and then give me the invoice?"

He shook his head sadly. "I can't do that."

"So there's literally no way for me to get an invoice."

"No, you can."

I waited.

"Not tomorrow morning, but the morning after that, you can come back and I will print it for you."

"But I am checking out of this motel right now. That means I'm leaving town. Can you fax me the invoice?"

"Fax it? No, I don't think we have a fax."

"Can you mail it to me?"

"Mail it?" He scratched his jaw. "Man, I don't know about all this. Maybe you should just stay, that would honestly be the easiest thing . . ."

I went back out to the car empty-handed and placed my phone in the center console so that I wouldn't fling it angrily at the windshield again. I could tell that this case was something big. I never got frustrated like this about the cases that weren't big, even the tedious ones, the cases that involved staring at the same house for six days straight or digging through an unheated shipping container full of identical documents or—the worst of the worst—looking at a spreadsheet for any amount of time. The frustration that came from boredom or inconvenience or a medium-bad tension headache was different.

So I would have known this case was something big, even if my phone hadn't started buzzing under my elbow at that moment.

CHAPTER 31

This is Helen Pickett calling from the Franklin County Juvenile Detention Center. Am I speaking with a Roxane Weary?"

"You are."

"Great. Ms. Weary, I'm calling because we found your business card among the personal effects of a young man in our care—"

"Aiden," I murmured.

"Excuse me?"

"Go on."

"He was arrested downtown a few nights ago and placed with our facility today. He wouldn't give his name so we aren't sure who he is—"

"Arrested? For what?"

Helen Pickett gave an immense sigh. "If you'll let me finish."

"Of course. I apologize."

"He's currently being treated by our medical staff—it's quite serious. I'm just trying to find out who the young man is and get in touch with his parents or legal guardian."

My first thought was that this was another trick—a ploy to get me to rush out of the city. I said, "Can I call you back?"

"Um, I suppose?" She gave me her phone number.

I hung up and googled the Franklin County JDC—the numbers matched.

Not a trick.

I dialed and asked the receptionist to connect me to Helen Pickett. "Me again," I said.

"Well, okay then. As I was saying, I was hoping you might know who this young man is."

"Is he okay?"

"Like I said, his injuries are pretty serious. He's stable at the moment but I really need to speak to his parents or legal guardian."

"What happened?"

This woman had no time for my bullshit. "Unless you're his guardian, which I can tell you're not, I can't and won't give you medical information. Can you tell me how I can get in touch with his family?"

"I'll do you one better," I said.

Barry Newsome drove Nadine and Katie Brant down to the first rest stop inside the Ohio line. Katie climbed into my backseat without even looking up from her iPad, her ears encased in bright pink headphones. Nadine was swaddled in a wool coat several sizes too big for her, eyes puffy and red following her phone conversation with Helen Pickett. The bits and pieces I'd heard didn't sound great—internal bruising, fractured ribs. But he was alive, and Nadine would be in the same city as him in the space of a few hours.

Once she was tucked into my front seat, Barry came around to the back of the car to talk to me. "You're sure you can handle this," he said.

"I'm sure."

"Because I can bring her down in a few days. I can't get away for long enough tonight, but tomorrow afternoon, if that would be better?"

"Why, because you're a man?"

"No," he said. "Yes?"

I shook my head. "She'll be fine with me. I'm armed. I'm very pissed off at these people."

Barry studied me for a while. "I read about you online."

"Fortunately for all of us, they don't write news articles about my abject failures. Now," I said, "I want to get back before it's dark. I'll call you if anything comes up. Okay?"

He gave me an uncertain smile. "Okay."

I got behind the wheel beside Nadine. She was staring at nothing, working at the cuticle of one thumb with the nail of the other. She didn't look at me. She didn't say anything. I decided I wouldn't say anything either, hoping she'd open up first.

By the time we hit 23—at which point we'd been riding in silence for an hour—I finally spoke.

"It's fine if you don't want to talk. But if you do, you can."

Nothing. She was clearly an expert at the quiet game.

"I think your son is a very smart kid, for what it's worth."

I saw Nadine look over at me in my peripheral. She said, "He is. Too smart. Katie too, but she's so young. She still thinks the grown-ups have it figured out."

I glanced in my rearview mirror and saw that Katie was asleep against the doorframe, her headphones askew. "Did the woman on the phone tell you why he'd been arrested?"

Nadine shook her head. "What's he even doing in Columbus? He doesn't know anyone."

"What matters now is that you'll get to see him. Soon."

"What if Joel finds him first?"

That was a vague possibility, though I was hoping that Joel's out-of-town trip was to Detroit instead.

She added, "He's Aiden's stepfather, and he can be very persuasive."

I wanted to tell her not to think about it that way. That worrying herself sick now wasn't going to help her son and it wasn't going to keep Joel Creedle at bay. But I also knew that statements like these never made anyone feel better and sometimes only made things worse.

"You probably think I'm a ridiculous person."

I stole a glance at her. "No, not at all."

"You think I'm some silly woman who wasn't even bright enough to see what was so clear to a sixteen-year-old boy and wasn't strong enough to do anything about it."

"But you did do something. You decided to leave."

"I hid. I let my son tell me that he could take care of himself better than I could, and I hid."

"You had a plan. An unconventional one, but I think it could've worked. Then Rebecca died, and everything changed. That's what happened."

"Why are you helping me?"

I felt her eyes on me. I said, "Because I believe that you're right about your husband. I think he's a bad guy who's been hiding behind the church for a really long time. In my world, you help the ones who are up against people like him. And, because I like to think I can be pretty tough when I need to be, but I was no match for you and your little stun-gun camera. So I figure we can make a good team."

For the first time in my presence, she smiled.

Aiden Brant had a small cut above his eye, but otherwise he looked fine—except for the various tubes and wires connected to his lanky teenage body. He was unconscious and had been since puking blood and passing out in the intake office of the juvenile detention center. He had a perforated liver, a collapsed lung, and a slew of other internal injuries. But his surgeon, Dr. Chan, seemed optimistic about his eventual recovery.

"We were able to repair the liver," she was telling Nadine inside Aiden's hospital room. "We had to put a tube in the lung, which will help with drainage . . ."

I was in the hallway with Katie, to whom I did not know how to speak. I could deal with teenagers all day long, but the nine-year-old had me stumped.

"What do you like to watch on TV?" I tried.

"Joel doesn't let us watch TV."

"What about music?"

"We don't listen to music."

"Then what are you listening to in those headphones?" I tried to give her a playful nudge but she recoiled.

"I'm trying to learn Japanese." She glared at me and showed me the language-learning app on her iPad.

The caseworker from the JDC came out into the hall with a clipboard and a coffee in a small Styrofoam cup. She rested the clipboard on the forearm above the hand holding the coffee, which seemed like a bad idea to me, but she obviously had some practice. "I appreciate you helping me out," she said. "Sorry if I gave you a hard time on the phone. It's just that this was an unusual situation and the boy needed emergency medical care."

"No worries." I watched as Helen Pickett scribbled something on the clipboard. "I'm impressed that you can do that without spilling."

"What— Oh, this." She gave me a smile. She was fifty or so, with pale, freckled skin and curly red hair streaked with white. "Social work is powered by coffee and clipboards."

"Can you tell me about his arrest?"

She stuck her pen in her mouth and flipped a few pages. "Not really," she said around the pen. Then she took it out of her mouth and repeated herself. "Not really. Says here he was brought in for disorderly conduct." She looked at me over the rims of her glasses. "Which could mean pretty much anything. But apparently once they took him to the substation, he refused to give his name and continued to be argumentative. That's when they shipped him to us."

"His injuries, I hope those were sustained prior to the arrest?"

"That's what the officer said. I know it seems hard to believe that he was walking around like that, but I can tell you that I had him in my office and I didn't have a clue anything was wrong until he threw up on my desk."

"So now what's going to happen, as far as his arrest goes?"

Helen Pickett glanced into Aiden's room, where Nadine was now sitting quietly in a bedside chair, face pressed against praying hands. "Now that we know who he is, I'm sure he can be released to his mother. Disorderly conduct isn't exactly worth a stint in juvie."

It wasn't, but I very much wanted to know the circumstances around the arrest.

"I know it's not exactly the Ritz, but it's free and it's safe."

Kez stood in the middle of a suite at the East Side Motor Lodge with her arms spread wide. She lived in the room next door as a part of her arrangement with the management of the place—room and board in exchange for providing security for the place. It was a bit of an upgrade for her; when we'd met, earlier in the year, she was working twelve-hour shifts at the front desk. Generally, the visits people made to the East Side Motor Lodge were of the short-stay variety and nobody wanted any trouble, but every now and then she got to threaten someone with a metal baseball bat and/or a gun.

"Is it?" Nadine kept looking furtively through the curtains that flanked the motel room door.

"Is somebody out there or are you just low-key racist?"

"Excuse me?"

"Black people live in this neighborhood. Get used to it."

Nadine flushed bright red and paced into the adjoining living room, where her daughter was eating Boston Market carryout in front of the television.

Kez perched on the edge of the desk. "So what's the plan?"

"The plan is, she needs a place to stay until her kid is out of the hospital. After that, we'll have to see what she wants to do."

"I meant more in an immediate way. Tonight."

"Oh." I looked at my phone, surprised that it said seven o'clock. It felt like at least midnight tomorrow by that point. "I want to find out what her son was doing when he got arrested. And I want you to keep her company. Peter Novotny will come over and take a shift in the morning."

The three of us—Kez, Petey, and me—made a very unlikely law enforcement trio. The age gap alone was some fifty years. But we worked well together.

"Why's she need a babysitter again?"

"Because the little girl already blew her cover once—and it was lucky for them both that I'm the one who found them."

"You sound mad paranoid right now."

"Yeah, well," I said, but I didn't have a comeback for that. "Can you just do it?"

Kez nodded. "It's your dime, so whatever."

I sighed. My lack of a paying client didn't mean I could avoid paying my team. I said, "It might cheer her up to hear your story. You can fantasize about neutering your exes together. Maybe do an even trade."

"I like the sound of that."

"I figured you would."

The officer who'd arrested Aiden was one Greg O'Neil, and he was no longer on duty. The sergeant at the substation on West Town

Street wouldn't tell me anything else, not even the guy's phone number, and I didn't have it in me to argue.

So I went over to my office to stare at the ceiling and try to relax. But really, I doubted I could ever relax in the office again. Someone had intended to slip an explosive under my door here. This did not create a soothing ambience. What I actually needed was to keep this office as a decoy office, and get a new working space elsewhere.

I wondered if it was too late to go back to school to become a dental hygienist.

After I poured a shot of whiskey and drank it and poured another and drank that too, I committed to the full glass and curled up on the love seat and called Tom. "Please tell me you're on your way to my office with Chinese food today."

"Are you currently in the office, or is this Chinese food for someone else?"

"My printer-scanner is lonely."

"What's going on?"

"Nothing. A lot. I got fired, I guess. Before I even had the chance to fail."

"I hate it when that happens."

"That's not what you're supposed to say."

"I'm sorry. But not that sorry, if it means Toledo is over."

"So over."

"Chicken with garlic sauce, extra green peppers?"

"Please and thank you."

Tom got to the office a half hour later with Ho Toy carryout in hand. "I heard there's a printer-scanner looking for love in here."

He put the bag of food on the coffee table and sat down next to me. He was still dressed for work in a pale grey button-down and tie, loosened slightly. I shifted so that I was leaning into him instead of into the arm of the love seat, managing to spill only a few drops of my drink on the ugly upholstery.

"Detective work is powered by whiskey and thrift-store furniture," I said, burying my face in Tom's collar.

"It sounds like you had a day." He gently took the whiskey glass from me and took a sip. "But I'm glad you're back. I missed you."

"Ew."

"Especially the profound sincerity. The way you embrace feelings. The emotional maturity."

"Tell me more."

"I don't want you to get full of yourself."

The heater rattled on and off and on, and we went quiet for so long I wasn't sure if he was asleep, or if I was.

Finally he said, "Do you want to eat or was all this talk about your printer just a ruse?"

I unfolded myself from the love seat and ripped open the bag. It was impossible to be in a bad mood in the face of Chinese takeout and its cheery little white paper containers. I got paper plates out of the filing cabinet and sat down cross-legged on the floor on the other side of the coffee table. "I missed you too," I said. "Now let us never speak of it again."

CHAPTER 32

P eter Novotny was teaching Katie to play blackjack over orange juice and Egg McMuffins when I got to the East Side
Motor Lodge in the morning. "She's a natural," he said, "got
a brain for probabilities like you wouldn't believe."

"She's nine."

"Eh, she has an old soul."

Katie beamed.

Nadine was still asleep in the bedroom, the door closed tightly.
Kez had gone back to her own room after Novotny had arrived
with breakfast. He said, "So what's on the agenda for today?"

"Why is everyone always asking me what the plan is?"

"Because you're the boss, boss."

"Fuck. I mean, fudge."

Katie glared at me. "I know the f-word."

I had to fight the urge to put my hands on my hips and tell
her *well, good for you.*

"Call me when Nadine's up, okay? I'm going to follow up on a
few things unless you need anything from me here."

Katie's expression said it all.

Aiden was still out of it when I dropped by Nationwide Children's
Hospital, so the explanation for what had happened to him would
have to come from Officer Greg O'Neil. I'd never met him, but he

knew my father, like just about everyone had. At some point all the cops in the city who'd known Frank Weary would be long re-tired and I wouldn't have to deal with their comments about how I looked just like him, but I sure as hell hoped I wouldn't still be doing this by then. I caught up with O'Neil outside the Roosevelt Coffee House on Long Street, where the aftermath of a three-car accident was just getting swept away.

I offered to buy him a coffee in exchange for information, but he shook his head. "Not hipster coffee."

"You'd turn down free coffee just because it's made by millennials?"

"I'm a man of principles."

I could respect that, so I didn't press the issue. "You arrested a kid yesterday," I said. "Sixteen, dirty blond, disorderly conduct, he wouldn't give you his name?"

O'Neil nodded. He had a thin, whitish mustache like a layer of cappuccino foam on his upper lip. "What about him?"

"He's in Children's right now with internal injuries and sepsis."

The cop's expression turned stony. "Internal injuries."

"I'm not saying—"

"Good, because I didn't touch the kid. What's he saying?"

"Nothing, he's still unconscious. Can you tell me what happened?"

His eyebrows knit together. "It was really kind of strange. Mid-dle of the day, I'm headed back to the station for my meal break, sitting over on Third and Broad. The kid pops out of an alley and runs right over to me, bangs on the hood of the cruiser."

"Seriously?"

"The weirdest fuckin' thing."

"Okay, then what?"

"Well, it startled me, to be perfectly honest. First thing I thought, there's something in progress that he's trying to alert me to—you know there was just that explosion up the street the other day, right?"

I frowned. "Yes, I heard about that."

"But the kid is just standing there, banging on the hood and yelling."

"Yelling what?"

"Hey you, asshole, look at me, that kind of thing."

This wasn't making much sense to me. "What did you do?"

"Well, I got out and asked him to step away from the car. Which he did, and he went to the car in front of me and started kicking the fender and banging on the trunk. In the middle of the damn street! I told him he needed to settle the fuck down and he spit at me. So I said, Okay, kid, that's enough, you're going to go cool your heels in the precinct lockup."

I waited.

"That's pretty much it. He settled down in the car and when I put him in the holding cell he was just sort of quiet. He wouldn't give us a name or anything. Didn't want a phone call. Just sat there. I was starting to wonder if something was wrong with him."

"Starting to?"

O'Neil shrugged.

"Was he on drugs?"

"He didn't seem like it. I mean, the erratic behavior, sure. But I got a look at his eyes, pupils were normal."

"Any visible injuries?"

He touched his eyebrow. "A small cut, here. It wasn't even bleeding."

"Okay, so you put him in the holding cell and he won't give you his name."

"That's basically that. He sat in there for a couple hours. Eventually my sergeant said we should ship him over to the JDC and they could figure out who he belonged to. I told you, the whole thing was strange. It was almost like he wanted to get arrested."

I thought about that. Why would you get arrested on purpose? To escape someone or something, maybe; if you have a tail on you, a holding cell is a pretty good place to shake it. Similarly, being locked up is a failproof alibi. "And you didn't see anything out of the ordinary on the street? Nobody following him, or some kind of scene he was trying to get away from?"

"The only thing out of the ordinary I saw was him."

"And where were you, exactly?"

He rubbed at his mustache. I almost expected it to smear off. "Third and Broad, but you know how it backs up there sometimes. I think I was by the hotel, the Renaissance."

"So Third and Gay?" My office was a half a block from that intersection.

"No, must have been Lynn, where he came from. One-way street. I was right about there."

"Okay, thanks."

The security man named Darren was on medical leave; he'd been working the evening of the explosion and had subsequently had a minor nervous breakdown. His replacement was a rent-a-cop from a security service and he didn't bat an eye at the idea of showing me the security cameras from yesterday morning. He even let me sit behind the desk; he walked a post across the tiled lobby.

"Just don't delete anything. I'm not allowed to delete anything!"

"Okay, I won't delete anything."

I clicked around the jerky old closed-circuit system, which took several seconds to refresh between frames. I could tell I was going to be here for a while. But I hadn't been at it too long when the doors of the building opened and Detective Mariella Zervos came in.

"Um, hello," she said to me. "New career?"

"Yes, that's it exactly."

"Tom said you were back in town. Mind chatting for a few minutes?"

I pulled myself away from the security camera and we went up to my office. I said, "Are you any closer to figuring out who left the Tanzanite or whatever?"

"Tannerite. And, no. Not really. I wanted to talk about something else."

"Shoot."

"I said something the other day. That I shouldn't have. It's been driving me crazy ever since. About Andover. Andy."

I saw the police academy picture in my mind, the young woman who looked just like my dead aunt. "Tell me."

"Your dad liked to drink."

"No shit."

"He liked to drink, and when he drank, he liked to talk."

That hadn't been my experience of him, but whatever. "Okay."

"There was a woman in the narcotics bureau a long time ago, a very attractive gal named Lenore Chisholm. People used to speculate about her, you know, a lot."

I didn't specifically know what she was hinting at, but I got the gist and motioned for her to continue.

"Frank told a few of us one night that he'd slept with her. Nobody believed him. He said she's pregnant, isn't she?"

"That's an awfully fucked-up thing to brag about. How do you even know it was true?"

"Well, I saw Lenore at Frank's funeral and she said something. And then this past year, my son became friends with this girl, Lenore's daughter, at the police academy. So I met her a couple times and it's just, wow. Just like you. The eyes, you know? Anyway, her name is Blair Andover. I just figured you should know."

"Does *she* know? About Frank?"

"I don't know. So please don't go, you know."

"Please don't go dumping this shit on her like you did to me?"

"Hey, you said *tell me*. You could've let it go."

Nothing was funny, but I laughed. "Let it go?"

"Not everything is your business. I wish it hadn't been mine. And I am sorry about bringing it up in the first place. But I didn't want you to be wondering, you know?"

"Well, thanks. Thanks so very much. I certainly wouldn't want you to feel uncomfortable about spilling the beans, not when *I* could feel uncomfortable instead."

"You aren't mad at me. You're mad at Frank."

I stood up and pointed at the door. "Are you done?"

"I'm sorry."

"Fine, I'll leave."

I stalked out into the hallway and stabbed the elevator call button. To my chagrin, Zervos joined me there a beat later and we were forced to ride down four floors in the most awkward silence imaginable.

I could feel my pulse pounding at my temples as I sat back down at the security desk. I refused to look at Zervos. Eventually she left and I called Andrew while I looked, unseeing, at the split-screen view shown by the cameras—lobby, front entrance, rear entrance, first-floor elevators.

"Are you calling to say you changed your mind about the tea?"

"What? No. Remember how I told you the other day about cop who kinda-sorta implied that we have a half sister out there?"

"Yes." There was the tiniest pause, maybe a hitch in his voice.

"What does that mean?"

"It means yes, as in, an answer to your question."

"Andrew, what is going on?"

"Nothing—"

"Don't lie to me."

"I'm not—"

"I can tell when you're lying and I know you know that."

He let out a tortured sigh. "This is a conversation that should be happening in person."

"No, Andrew, spill."

"You know Dad had affairs, plural."

"Yes, I know that."

"Mom told me about this earlier in the year. I was going to tell you."

I leaned my elbows on the desk and covered my eyes with a hand.

"I have no idea what the fuck is wrong with this chick that she would just say something like that, I mean, who does that?"

"What did Mom tell you?"

"Well, I had asked her, back in February or March, I guess, I asked her about Dad's estate. It just seemed like, okay, it's been two years, is this ever going to be done? I told you about how I was thinking of going into business, legit business. Even before what happened with Addison, I'd been thinking about that. So anyway, I asked Mom about the holdup and she said that Dad had a lot of complicated debts."

"Complicated how?"

"The long and short of it is, he got some woman pregnant. This would've been when we were in high school, or when I was. Mom knew."

"She knew when it happened?"

"Yes."

"How?"

"He told her." Andrew cleared his throat. "He always told her, apparently. When he, you know."

"When he fucked some random woman."

The rent-a-guard looked over at me. This was no doubt the most interesting temp assignment he'd ever gotten.

"I was going to tell you. I've hated having this secret from you, honestly, but I feel like things have been weird between us the last few months."

"So you just . . . didn't."

"I was going to."

"When?"

"I don't know."

"Does Matt know?"

"No. I don't think so. I didn't tell him. I doubt Mom would've. You know he never shuts up about anything so I'm sure he would have brought it up already, probably to gloat about him taking the high road."

"Have you met her?"

"Don't do this."

"Andrew."

"None of this is her fault."

"Have you met her?"

"No."

"Have you communicated with her?"

My brother said nothing.

"I can't believe this," I muttered.

"We've emailed a little bit. She seems nice."

Nice. My eyes inexplicably filled with tears. "Good, I'm glad Frank got the nice daughter he always wanted. What else do you know about her?"

"She's a cop. She has a dog named Orville."

"I feel really fucking blindsided by this information, Andrew."

"I know. I'm sorry. I can't believe someone would just blurt it out like that."

"Unless everybody already knows," I said, "everybody but me." As I said it, I wondered if Tom knew, and my stomach turned itself inside out. I wiped my eyes and turned my attention back to the security system. "I can't talk about this right now."

"Are you okay?"

"I'm fine. Great. Really, really great."

"Rox."

I hung up and stared at the grainy grey images on the screen. Orville. The flight brother, or the popcorn company? I shook my head as if I could send this new development out of my brain that way. Andrew was right—it wasn't this Blair Andover's fault that my father was a pig and my family was living a lie.

That was no one's fault, and also all of our fault.

I finally got back to yesterday morning on the tape and found, at 10:43 a.m., a figure that could've been Aiden—baggy pants and hoodie, head tucked into his chest. He waited at the elevator, went in, then reappeared less than five minutes later and walked out.

I clicked forward a bit to see if he returned but nothing else happened.

I went backward to watch Aiden walking through the lobby again. I couldn't see the side of his face, so there was no way to tell if he had the cut above his eye at this point. But I noticed that when he reached out to push the elevator-summoning button, he paused for a second and touched his rib cage with his other hand.

I took pictures of the screen, more out of habit than anything else, and pulled my coat on. "I'll get out of your hair now," I said.

"I didn't mean to eavesdrop." The security guard leaned over the counter to look down at me. "But I couldn't help but overhear. I just wanted to say, you deserve better, girl. Okay?" He held up a fist for me to bump. I wasn't sure what else to do so I rapped my knuckles lightly against his.

wanted a drink, or several. But it wasn't smart to roll up to the police headquarters reeking of whiskey, so I held off until later when I could really make it count. "I need to ask you something," I said when I got to Tom's cubicle. "Please don't lie to me."

"I would never lie to you."

"Yeah, well, lies of omission count. Blair Andover."

To his credit, he didn't feign confusion this time. He closed his eyes for a beat. "Yes."

"You know."

"I do," he said slowly. "But—"

"And you never thought to tell me?"

"Let's go in a room. Okay?"

I nodded and followed him out of his cube and into a conference room. He closed the door behind us and locked it.

"First of all," he started again, but I shook my head.

"No, first of all, I brought this up to you the other day. And you picked a fight about what an asshole *I* was being."

"You're right."

"Why didn't you tell me then?"

"I was surprised. I didn't know what to say. Especially not over the phone. So I hedged. That was wrong. Roxane, I'm sorry. I'm so sorry. Until then, I didn't know that you didn't know."

"What are you talking about?"

He ran a hand through his hair. "Frank told me that your mother knew, that she'd always known. I guess I just assumed that the whole family knew."

"Even though I literally never mentioned it, ever."

"You think that I should have been like, hey, is this thing I know a family secret or just something you don't want to talk about?"

"Yeah, I do."

"And when would I have done that? The night Frank died? The night of the funeral?"

"Some other day in the two-plus years since would've been good. Just thinking out loud here."

"You never told Shelby what you know about her father."

I winced; he was right. "That's different. Shelby would be devastated if she knew Joshua isn't her real father. I'm doing her a favor by keeping that secret. I'm not devastated, Tom, I'm just mad, and here you are saying that not telling me makes perfect fucking sense."

Tom leaned against the wall, smudging someone's blue dry-erase marker. "I—I don't know. I honestly thought you might know."

"You thought I might." I paced to the opposite corner of the small conference room and stared at the dingy white wall.

"I *thought* you might, and I *knew* it wasn't my place to bring it up."

"How's that?"

"Frank told me in confidence."

"I swear to god if you mention how you promised—"

"I'm not going to do that. Roxane, look at me."

"No."

"I'm sorry. I understand how this feels from your perspective."

"You can't possibly. Trust me."

"I'm trying."

"Frank's dead." I spun around. "I'm right here."

"I know that."

We stared at each other. His warm brown eyes were worried and sad and a little angry all at once.

I said, "Are there any other Weary family secrets that he told you?"

"No."

"How can I believe that?"

He didn't say anything. Maybe I was being unfair to him, or maybe I wasn't. I couldn't tell anymore what a normal relationship was like. A normal job, a normal life. "I feel betrayed, and I never would have expected that from you. But I guess that's why it's called a betrayal. If you saw it coming, it wouldn't hurt."

"What can I do?" He closed the gap between us and took my hand.

I shook my head. "Nothing."

"Don't say that."

He brought my hand to his mouth and now I closed my eyes, remembering the night of my father's funeral, the two of us sitting in the car, the raw conversation slit open between us, everything out on the table. Or so I thought.

Maybe I was wrong about everything.

Maybe I had always been wrong about everything.

"I need to go."

"Don't, please."

"Tom."

"Please." He held my forearm to his chest. "If you need to be angry at me, be angry. But please don't use this as an excuse to blow everything up."

"An excuse?"

"Not an excuse. A reason. I know you're always looking for a reason."

I yanked my hand away and opened the door. "I have to go."

I was already out on the sidewalk when I realized that I had left my jacket somewhere inside. Maybe in the conference room, or maybe on Tom's desk. I couldn't bear the thought of going back for it now. Besides, righteous indignation had warmed my blood and even though the wind gusted along the river, I wasn't cold. The coat would keep. Even the hundred-odd bucks in cash from the tow pound were safe enough, there in police possession.

Besides, I had an idea.

"I don't know if I can do this," Nadine said on the way over to the juvenile detention center.

"You can. All you have to do is go in and ask for his belongings."

"What if they ask why?"

"They won't."

"What if they do?"

I hit my turn signal so hard I was surprised that it didn't snap off in my hand. "You just say that you're his mother and show your ID. That's all."

I'd already tried doing it myself, but not even my new friend Helen Pickett could help me get past the rule that possessions could only be released to a legal guardian. So here we were.

"What do you think he has?"

"I don't know. But I think he got himself arrested in order to hide something in a safe place."

I'd gone a few mental rounds about this between the police station, the JDC, and the motel. Maybe Aiden was trying to get away from whoever had beat the crap out of him—which is what I had thought originally—but if that were the case, why clam up as soon as he got arrested? Why not tell someone that he needed help? I supposed he could have decided that Greg O'Neil was untrustworthy, but by the time he got to Helen Pickett's office, he could have fessed up, given his name. He had to be incredibly uncomfortable, all that time he spent in the squad car and holding cell. Instead, he kept quiet until the moment he officially entered the system and his possessions were secured before he gave in to the pain.

"I don't want to go in there by myself."

I nodded. "Okay. We'll go in together."

Thirty minutes later, we were back in the car with an envelope. I ripped it open to reveal a piece of cardboard, the contents of Aiden's pockets suspended under shrink wrap. "Why do they do it this way?"

I pointed at Aiden's name scrawled in the corner. "So no one can say something was stolen later."

There wasn't much to see—just my business card, its edges dirty, and a five-gigabyte red flash drive.

I sat at the small table in Nadine's motel room with Kez and Novotny, staring at the contents of the flash drive: a single .csv file that contained some fourteen thousand phone numbers.

That was it.

"Now what?" Novotny said.

I rubbed the place between my eyebrows. "I have no idea."

Kez reached into the bag of Cheetos on the table behind my MacBook. "We could call them? Not all of them. But like a random sample. See what they have in common."

"That's a good idea. Except people can have lots of different things in common. We might call a hundred people who drive Fords, but that doesn't mean it has anything to do with Fords."

"Maybe it has to do with Fords." Novotny poured another round of grocery-store whiskey into our plastic motel cups. "Detroit, and all."

"They don't make anything in Detroit anymore."

"Let's look at these area codes," I said. "I see a lot of 614s. But there are also a lot of 330—that's the Cleveland area."

Kez pointed at my screen, leaving an orange residue behind. "So is 440."

"317, that's Indianapolis," Novotny said. "Watch it, Cheeto Hands."

I got out a sheet of paper and started making a list while the two of them bickered. The contrast between them was amusing—Kez with her labret piercing and her green and purple hair pulled back into severe French-braid pigtails, Novotny with his shock of white hair and old-man cardigan—but they were deeply fond of each other. I liked to think it had something to do with me, but it probably didn't.

I sorted the data in ascending order, a task my old computer needed a moment to parse.

"Okay. We have 312, which is Chicago." I wrote this down and scrolled. "A lot in Chicago. 313 is Detroit. 317, Indy. 330, Cleveland. 412 is Pittsburgh. 419, that's northwest Ohio. 440, Cleveland. 502 is what, Kez?"

Kez turned her Cheeto hands to her phone. "Louisville."

"Loo-a-ville," Novotny corrected.

"What'd I say?"

"Louie-ville."

I ignored them and kept going. "513, Cincinnati. 614 is here. 615, what is that?"

"Nashville."

I wrote that down too. "And 740 and 937 are kind of the rest of Ohio. Did we miss any?"

"Probably, that's a long fuckin' list."

"But, these are, what, all cities in the Midwest. Ish."

The three of us looked at each other.

"How long would it take to make fourteen thousand phone calls?" I said.

Kez picked up her phone again. "Average of maybe fifteen seconds per call?"

"That's speedy, but sure."

She tapped at the screen. "Fifty-eight hours."

I finished my whiskey and nudged my cup forward. "Hit me."

Novotny poured.

Nobody said anything for a while, because there was nothing to say.

Finally, Kez stood up and went over to the sink and washed her hands. "Maybe it doesn't matter. Maybe there's nothing to figure out. Nadine and Katie are safe here. Aiden's getting medical care. We don't have a client. For all we know Rebecca tripped over her shoelaces." Kez caught my eye. "Something's wrong. Do you want to talk about it or nah?"

"I thought I was hiding it so well."

"You're lingering over the actual worst whiskey I've ever tasted. Clearly something is wrong."

I looked at the swill in my cup. "It is pretty bad. Where'd it even come from?"

"The office," she said, "the motel office, not yours. I know your liquor cabinet does not contain, what is this." She squinted in the dark at the label. "Bird Dog?"

"Orville," I muttered. "Christ, what a mess."

"What's a mess?"

"Everything."

Kez raised her plastic cup in a toast. "Chin, chin. But look, we're trying to solve for *y* here. Maybe there is no why."

"There's always a why."

I sighed. "That can't be true. Creedle was planning something, and Aiden was onto it. It has something to do with Nora, with passports."

"Birth control and international travel?"

I didn't have an answer to that, but I pointed at the endless spreadsheet on my screen. "Maybe these are members' phone numbers."

Kez and Novotny looked at me like I'd lost my mind.

"Hear me out," I said. "These numbers are all in major metropolitan areas in the Midwest. Nora's service area is the Midwest. There's bound to be a higher concentration of women using an app to order birth control in metropolitan areas, right?"

"Okay, I see where you're going with this." Kez came back over to the table and stood with her hands on her hips. "But suppose you're right. What's the plan? A bunch of phone numbers without names doesn't really do much."

"Well, it would be a pretty big data breach. I know they've had some attempts recently."

Kez plopped down in her chair. "I'll be mad if it's about a damn data breach, Roxane."

I tried Constance Archer-Nash's cell phone and was glad when she picked up. "How sure are you, really. About the data breach."

"*Attempted* data breach."

"I take that as, *very sure.*"

"Yes."

"Then again, would you tell me otherwise?"

A pause. "You sound serious now."

"I am."

"Are you still in Toledo?"

"No, I'm back at home."

"Really? I'm in Columbus for the night. We could have that drink and talk about what's on your mind."

I made a copy of the list and put the flash drive in my pocket and asked Novotny for a ride to the Short North, since he was heading north anyway and I intended to continue drowning my sorrows at the Hilton.

"Anything I can do, honey?" he said once we were in his car, a big, dark red Caddy.

"You knew my dad," I said. "Ever hear about him and some intelligence bureau woman named Lenore?"

"What?"

"Is that a genuine no, or are you playing with me?"

"I don't know a Lenore anybody. Now, I remember Frank and various women, sure. Is that what you're upset about?"

There was something weirdly reassuring about the fact that he just said it, a statement of fact. "I'm fine. Really."

"You're not going to do anything crazy, are you?"

"Like what?"

"*Like what,* she says, all innocent, like she's never done anything crazy in her life."

I smiled in the dark as Novotny slowed to a stop across the street from the hotel. "I know you hate doing this, but—text me when you get home safe, okay?"

"Sure thing."

The first floor of the Hilton was crowded with people in pink T-shirts that said WOW VOLUNTEERS. I avoided them and headed for the enclosed spiral staircase that led up to the bar on the second floor, but Constance flagged me down from her perch on one of the low, silvery couches in the lobby. "It's overrun by this group, whatever it is," she said. "There's a bar up the street, divey little place?"

"Char Bar?"

"That's the one. Do you mind chatting there?"

As we walked the short block south, I noticed a serious guy in all black trailing about ten feet behind us—the body man, I assumed.

Constance caught me looking. "I know it's ridiculous, I know I'm not Hillary Clinton—nor do I want to be. But people are unpredictable, you know?"

We went into the bar and sat at a small round table at the back. "Two whiskeys, rocks," Constance told the security guy, and he nodded and perched on a barstool to wait for the drinks.

"So listen," I said. I put the flash drive on the table. "The kid who's been calling your office had this on him. It contains thousands and thousands of phone numbers, and I have this feeling that this might be related to Nora Health."

Constance picked up the flash drive, her eyes narrowing. "What are you talking about?"

"I don't know, exactly. But Aiden's calls to you—he was saying that he had some kind of information that you needed. A warning, right?"

"What, you think warning me about a data breach? Even though the CRM swore up and down yesterday that there's no way anything happened."

"Maybe."

The security guy brought over our drinks and returned to the bar, watching the room in the mirror behind it just like I had at the St. Clair Club. I felt a little bad that he was left out of the fun.

"So you found the kid, then," Constance said.

"Sort of. He's in the hospital. Someone beat the shit out of him. And I think he might have been trying to protect this." I took the flash drive off the table and put it back into my pocket.

"But all that's on it is phone numbers?"

"I think so."

"You can't do much with just a phone number."

"No, but think about how distressing it was to you that he found your number in the first place. Maybe there's another file, a companion document that contains names. Put this information on the dark net and who knows what could happen."

Constance sipped her drink and looked at me like I was a little bit nuts, which was probably true. I added, "Aiden's still unconscious. So I can't talk to him about what the hell happened. Without that piece of the puzzle, everything just looks random. But you're telling me there's been no data breach at Nora Health."

"No."

"And you'd for sure know if there had been."

"Yes."

"On pain of death?"

"That's a little morbid, but sure." She lifted two fingers. "Girl Scout's honor."

"The Girl Scouts do three fingers."

She flicked up a third finger. "I was a terrible Girl Scout. I stapled my badges to my sash thing because I hated threading needles. Still do."

"Same. Not the staples, but the sewing thing. Hey, can I ask you a question?"

"Hit me."

"I have a friend—she's obsessed with you. In a good way. She's young and has never been excited about voting for anyone before."

Constance's eyes lit up. "Aw, yeah, that's the stuff I love hearing about."

"So this question is from her."

"Okay."

"She wanted to know if you're straight."

She laughed. "What on earth?"

"Well?"

"*Your friend* wants to know, or you want to know?"

"Would the answer be the same?"

She rattled the melting ice in her glass, eyes still bright. "You are a fascinating person, Roxane Weary."

"Just nosy and slightly reckless."

"Yes, I can tell. So who exactly wants to know if I'm straight?"

Tension fissured across the air between us. Along the edge of her dress's scooped neckline, her collarbones moved up and down as she took in shallow breaths, and I was suddenly aware of how little space was between my hand and her knee. It would be easy to close that gap. I suddenly realized that I wanted to, but I didn't. "My friend."

Constance arched her neck and swallowed carefully. "I'm really sorry I can't help you more. With the data breach. *Attempted* data breach."

She didn't seem to be upset by the question, but the tone of the conversation had somehow changed—it had ended. I finished my drink and stood up. "Well, good luck at your event tomorrow. Raise those funds."

Constance lifted her glass and nodded.

woke up to Nadine's thin silhouette sitting at the table, drinking coffee in the near dark. In my half-awake, fully hungover state, there was something ghostly about her and for a second I was afraid that she was dead, or I was. Then I realized she was cast in the diffuse glow of my phone on the table in front of her.

"What time is it?" I murmured.

"Four thirty. Someone keeps calling."

I dragged myself to my feet. At first I didn't remember choosing to come here last night instead of home. Then it all came back at once—Tom, Blair Andover, Orville, Catherine. Fuck. "Why didn't you wake me up?"

Nadine sipped her coffee. "What if it's the hospital?"

"That's exactly why you should've woken me up."

I grabbed the phone off the table and realized she was crying. Scrolling through the phone, I saw I'd missed three calls from the same local number.

When I called the number back, I realized she was right.

There was good news and bad news. The good news was that Aiden had been awake and aware of his surroundings. The bad news was that he freaked out, hence the phone calls. By the time we got to the hospital, he'd been sedated and was unconscious again.

"I should have been here," Nadine kept saying. "In the waiting room, if not right there beside him. I think I should stay from now on. Can you take Katie back to the motel?"

"Sure." I glanced down at her daughter, who was sleeping awkwardly on a chair in the small waiting area, and terror seized my heart. It was one thing to be alone with this child when her mother was just in the next room, but quite another to be entirely responsible for her care. But it struck me as a good sign that Nadine was willing to be on her own here at the hospital. Nationwide Children's had good security; each unit had its own access code set by the parent, meaning no one but Nadine or the medical staff would be able to get in. "You'll call me when he wakes up? Or if you need anything, anything at all?"

She nodded, then surprised me by giving me a quick hug. "Thank you for everything."

Katie and I walked out to my car in silence. She was clutching a ratty stuffed orca whose name was Lynna. I opened the passenger-side door for her and she rolled her eyes at me.

"I'm too small to sit in the front seat. Do you want the airbag to decapitate me?"

She climbed in behind me instead.

"Why do I have to go with you?"

I navigated the Range Rover through the maze of the parking garage. "Your mom wants to stay with your brother."

"But why can't I stay with her too?"

"Like you said, you're too small. They don't allow kids under twelve to visit."

"That's stupid."

"Hey, I don't make the rules."

"Where are we going?"

"Back to the motel."

"I don't like it there. It smells like cigarillos."

I laughed. "What do you know about cigarillos?"

"I know they stink. Can we go to your house?"

"No."

"Why?"

The city streets at this hour were empty. I rubbed my eyes at the traffic signal at Broad and Washington and held back a yawn. "It's not kid-friendly there."

"I don't think that stinky motel is kid-friendly either. I heard people doing it through the wall."

"Doing what— Oh," I said. "Um, they were probably just watching TV."

"They were doing it. TV doesn't sound like that. Unless it's the sex kind. But even that sounds different. My dad used to watch porns in our basement. So I know."

I looked at her in the rearview mirror. "I'm really sorry you had to hear that, Katie."

She had moved on already. "Do you have a husband?"

"No."

"What about your dad?"

"He died."

"My dad died too."

"I know."

"What happened to your dad?"

"He was a policeman. He got hurt while he was working and he died."

"Wow."

We sat in silence at Broad and Gould, two fatherless girls in the middle of the night.

"What about your mom?"

"What about her?"

"Can we go to her house?"

"What? No, she's sleeping."

"I bet she isn't. Moms always get up early."

"No."

"I don't want to go back to that place. Please?"

I looked at her in the mirror again. She was hamming it up now, leaning forward with her hands clasped. "Pleeeeease."

I sighed. "If you promise not to tell Nadine I almost let you get decapitated."

The little girl was right; my mother was awake. She answered the door in a long cotton housecoat printed with a vaguely global pattern of golds and reds and blues. "This is Katie," I said. "Katie, this is my mom, Genevieve."

"Hi Katie, it's nice to meet you."

"Do you have any blueberry muffins? Because I love to have blueberry muffins for breakfast."

"I bet I could make some, honey, come on in."

My mother went into the kitchen and Katie curled up on the sofa and immediately fell asleep.

"I'm really sorry about this," I said to my mother. "I put her and her mom up at a motel and she told me she heard people having sex through the wall and I just, I don't know."

"Sit." She pointed at the small dining room table. "I'll make some tea to go with these muffins."

"You don't have to make muffins. She's fast asleep already."

"From what I recall, she's not the only little girl who likes a blueberry muffin for breakfast, right?"

She had her back to me, bustling around the kitchen in that efficient, soundless way she always had. I slouched down in my chair and looked up at the ceiling, at the peaks of its smudged-paint texture. The ceiling fan above the table that hadn't worked in twenty years. In so many ways the house was stuck in time. I felt like a teenager whenever I came here, both defiant and also not in control of my own life.

Was adult me really any different?

The microwave dinged and my mother retrieved a mug of hot water. "I have Lipton or Tetley."

"Surprise me."

She freed a tea bag from its little paper sleeve and dunked it in the water. "Andrew told me you already got a surprise this week."

I looked up. My mother's face was open, honest. She wasn't wearing any makeup, and her hair, icy blond and usually hair-sprayed into an impenetrable shield, was soft and fluffy and held back from her face with a wide headband. She added, "He said you were pretty upset."

The tea wasn't done steeping yet, but I took a long sip for something to do. "We don't have to talk about this right now."

"If not now, when? I never have you in this house, alone, all sleepy like this, with your walls down."

"Walls?"

My mother went at the muffin batter with a wooden spoon and kept her eyes on mine.

I said, "We don't have to talk about it ever. Clearly you didn't want me to know. So let's pretend I don't."

"Is that really what you want?"

"What I want is to not bring up something that's painful or embarrassing."

"Embarrassing? Roxie, I'm not embarrassed. Your father, he's the one who maybe could've been embarrassed. He wasn't, though. Nothing he did could ever embarrass him."

It was the harshest thing I'd ever heard my mother say about Frank. "Why did you stay?"

She began pouring the batter into an old muffin pan. "I had what I wanted. My three children."

"But you could have found someone else. A better husband. You could have found a Rafe twenty years ago."

"I loved your father. Screwups and all. I had what I wanted, and I was not about to give it up. I grew up without a father. I didn't want that for you and your brothers."

"But he could be so awful sometimes," I whispered.

"He was who he was."

"He got worse as time went on. Meaner. Drunker."

"I loved your father," she said again. "Is that so hard to believe?"

I supposed it wasn't. I'd played Catherine's little games for years, always willing to overlook the problems because when it was good, it was really good, and each time it got bad, the good times erased my memory.

"For a long time I decided that it had nothing to do with me," she continued. "His other women, this child."

"Did he spend time with them?"

"No. He provided, financially. I made him do that. And he saw them occasionally, Lenore and Blair."

The way she said the names, they sounded so normal.

"Once or twice a year. Lenore had a whole life of her own."

"Did you know her?"

My mother nodded. "I met her. Back when your father worked in narcotics. She was there too."

"Did you ever meet the girl?"

"No."

"Did you ever want to?"

"No, goodness, no. I can see why you kids might want to connect with her now—I never really thought about that before, but now that Frank's gone, she's pretty much the only part of his family you have left."

"I don't want to connect with her."

"Then don't."

"But," I said, and then I wasn't sure what else to say.

My mother slid the muffin pan into the oven and set the timer. "I'm not saying that I didn't make mistakes. With your father. With you kids, especially with you, honey. I know he made things hard for you. But you don't have to let any of it make things hard for you now."

She sat down at the table with me, in the place where my father used to sit, and she reached out and smoothed my hair away from my face. "You look so tired."

I closed my eyes. I was tired, but lack of sleep had nothing to do with it. "Yeah."

"Why don't you go lie down upstairs for a little bit? While it's quiet—your brothers are coming over later to work on the sidewalk for me."

"Are you sure?"

"Of course. I can handle a single sleeping child."

I slept like the dead in my childhood bedroom and woke up to my phone vibrating against my hipbone. "He's been in and out," Nadine said in a voice thick with tears. "He's very agitated. He keeps saying something about a can."

"A can?"

"Yes, I don't know what it means."

I had an idea about that. "Constance Can."

"What?"

"I'll be right over." I sat up and looked through the blinds on the window next to the bed; outside, there was full daylight. "I'm at my mother's house with Katie. Do you want me to bring her, or can she stay here?"

"How is she?"

I went halfway down the steps and found Katie and my mother in front of the television, watching *The Little Mermaid* with rapt attention.

"I think she'll have a better time here than sitting in a hospital waiting room."

"Please thank your mother for me."

I told her I would.

In the bathroom I splashed cold water on my face and combed

my hair with my fingers and thought about why Aiden would be agitated about Constance right now. Why he would have a list of phone numbers on a flash drive that he must've felt duty-bound to protect. I called her but—unsurprisingly—she didn't answer.

I found a bottle of Listerine under the sink, and while I was swishing, I pulled up Constance Archer-Nash's website to see about her event today. *Columbus Young Democrats, 12pm, Columbus Athenaeum.*

"It's a two-thousand-dollar-a-head fundraiser," Mariella Zervos said to me on the phone. "Not a public event. And besides, she has her own security detail. I am not worried about this."

I was stuck on 71, which was a midday parking lot. "But isn't this exactly the kind of thing you're supposed to worry about?"

"The threat being the delirious mutterings of a kid who was recently arrested for, what was it again? Assaulting a police officer?"

I inhaled slowly and shot lasers from my eyes into the rear window of the car in front of me, though they were in the same boat as I was. At least as far as the traffic jam was concerned. "Disorderly conduct," I said, "but you're not listening to me. What if all of this is connected? The explosion at my office building, the Keystone Fellowship. The pastor, Joel Creedle, has tried to make a scene at her events before. There's a video of it on YouTube if you need proof. And it's not out of the question that right-to-lifers would resort to murder. It's happened before."

It was clear that Zervos had stopped listening as soon as I said YouTube. "I know you don't think much of hunches, but maybe you could make an exception to avoid blowing up a few hundred people?"

"Would you please stop saying that?"

"Would you please listen to me? I know you aren't one for wild hunches but this could be serious."

"The Athenaeum is secure. You can count on it. I'm looking at this list you sent me right now and it just looks like a bunch of phone numbers."

I resisted the urge to punch the steering wheel. "Yes, and I think that's exactly what I wrote in my email. I know it's a list of phone numbers. But why would Aiden be so desperate to protect it?"

"That's your extrapolation, that he was trying to protect it. For all you know, he's the one who was planning something, and it's our good luck that you have the list, not him." Then she cleared her throat. "I'll look into it, okay?"

"When, on the first of never?"

"Funny," Zervos said.

"I hope you're right and I'm not."

I didn't think she found me funny at all.

Traffic crept past North Broadway before stopping dead just north of Weber Road. I turned on the radio seeking an update; it advised that traffic was all snarled up on 71 owing to an overturned semi and a confluence of big afternoon events around the city. The car in front of me was a ratty silver Tercel with a Columbus State parking pass that had expired in 2012. After a while of not moving, the owner got out and sat on the stubby little trunk and kept looking up at me, which I did not appreciate. But what could anybody do about anything? I plugged my phone into the charger and called Constance again, and this time she answered.

"Look, I'm sorry to bother you when you're getting ready for an event," I started, but she wasn't having it.

"What are you doing? What the hell are you up to?"

"Excuse me?"

"Pretty coincidental," she snapped, "that you keep asking and asking about data breaches."

I gripped the steering wheel. "What happened? Why is that a coincidence?"

She laughed, though nothing was funny. "Because my laptop was stolen from my hotel room, early this morning. Everything was on that computer, literally everything."

The traffic suddenly began to move, and the Tercel guy hopped back into his vehicle and squealed away. "Customer info?"

"Yes, everything. My speech for today, all of our financials, all of the company's data, social media logins. We've gotten those under control now but not before they already did some damage."

I was driving almost thirty miles an hour before the long line of taillights in front of me lit up red along the wide curve around the ghost of the Crew stadium and I had to slam on my own brakes. "What do you mean, damage?"

Her anger no longer seemed directed at me. "They posted something, um, it doesn't even make any sense. Let me find it." I heard her tap on her phone's screen. "There's this women's wellness expo at the Ohio State Fair grounds? They posted that I'm going to be there—which isn't even true. Fuck, this already has a few thousand retweets. You know what, I remember this event. The organizer was really pushy, asking us to sponsor it. What if this is, like, payback? For not sponsoring their stupid event?"

She kept talking, but I was no longer listening, just staring at the cars in front of me.

Zervos had been right about one thing—the Athanaeum was safe, far too safe for Creedle to be able to try anything. Constance herself was likely untouchable. But her enthusiastic supporters weren't, and they were all about to show up at a small, badly run event that probably had zero security.

"That's not what this is, Constance," I said, and I pulled a sharp right and drove over the triangle of grass that separated the freeway from the Hudson exit ramp.

CHAPTER 35

Peter Novotny beat me to the fairgrounds—he lived in Linden, just on the other side of 71, but even so, it had taken him ten minutes to make it a few blocks. "How many cars do you think this can fit?"

We were standing in the long parking lot that stretched behind the Celeste Center, which was almost full already. Ten rows by at least the length of a football field. "A lot. There are a lot of people here. You wait here for Kez. I'm going inside."

As I jogged toward the building, the entrance of which was on the opposite side of the parking lot and facing the front of a massive brick structure aptly called the Bricker Building, I glanced at Seventeenth Avenue behind me and saw cars backed up all the way to the top of the exit ramp from the freeway.

People were going to keep coming.

The doors to the Celeste Center were festooned with cheery pink and purple balloons and an upbeat ticket taker who informed me that it would cost ten dollars to get into the expo.

"Here, keep the change," I said as I thrust a twenty at her, craning my neck to get a look at the scene inside.

But the young woman caught my arm. "I need to stamp your hand so you can get back in if you have to go outside."

I swallowed my irritation and let her ink a purple flower onto the back of my hand and then tried to get past her.

"Your admission gets you this tote bag, which was donated by the Wexner Medical Center."

I waved her off. "It's okay, I don't need it."

"Oh, but you do! There are so many good freebies here, plus a raffle ticket inside . . ."

Why was the world like this? I let her finish the spiel while trying to see what was through the double doors behind her. The Celeste Center, which I knew I'd been in lots of times for different events, had a chameleonlike quality. I saw lots of pink and purple and green and heard a meditative tinkling sound from somewhere.

And voices, lots of voices.

After assuring her that I would participate fully in the myriad activities at my disposal, I finally escaped her and made my way into the room.

It was much too crowded. The type of jam-packed space that made you want to stick close to the walls or grab on to the person you were with so you didn't lose sight of them in the melee. Exhibitor tables formed a giant U-shape that terminated in a small stage, where a woman in a voluminous skirt was leading a group of giggling young women in a dreamy sort of dance. The outer ring of tables appeared to be occupied by legit services—health screenings, therapists, yoga studios, cooking demos—while the middle of the giant room featured people hawking dubious nutritional supplements, seven-day cleanses, silent retreats, copper bracelets to purify the blood, cosmetic surgery.

And everywhere that wasn't already occupied by those things were attendees with their tote bags and raffle tickets, spirits high because they all thought they were soon going to hear Constance Archer-Nash speak.

The white-painted cinder block walls of the entryway flickered purple from the decorative lights along the floor, and I noticed a

sign posted there that said, MAXIMUM OCCUPANCY FOR THIS FACIL-
ITY SHALL NOT EXCEED 10,377.

I went back to the woman with the stamp, who was continuing
to serve a long line of guests.

"I think you have to stop letting people in," I said, pointing
over her head at the sign FIRE CODE.

"Oh no, we've been keeping track," she said, and offered me a
manual counter.

It said 293. "Yeah, I don't think this is right."

The woman in front of us, hand outstretched for a stamp, said,
"When is Constance going to get here?"

I touched the stamper's shoulder. "Who is in charge? It's an
emergency."

The on-site coordinator for the event was a lady named Mave
Darcy and she had the whole look—headset, smart watch, a tablet
strapped to one hand and a walkie-talkie clipped to her belt—and
the first thing she said to me was that she was calling security. "I
know it's crowded but honestly, you can't just run around telling
people they're violating the fire code."

It was a bit of a relief to hear that there *was* security. "You very
well might be."

"No, with all these tables, we definitely have fewer people than
the fire code capacity."

"How do you know there isn't a different fire code for events
with tables?"

That stumped her for a second, but she regained her compo-
sure and spoke into the walkie-talkie. "Bill," she said, "over."

Nothing happened.

Mave pressed the button a few more times. "Bill, I need you.
Over." She looked at me. "I don't know why he isn't answering.
Wait here."

Someone touched the small of my back and I whirled around, my hand flying to the gun at my hip. But it was just Kez, looking on edge. "There are a fuck-ton of people in here. What are we going to do?"

I shook my head. I truly didn't know.

"Roxane?"

I heard Shelby's voice from behind me and the muscles of my core tightened.

She was there with Miriam, not for Constance Archer-Nash, but because Miriam's roommate was doing manicures in the "spa corner." She waggled her nails—neon yellow—at me and said, "I'm sure he could hook you up."

I wanted to tell Shelby to get as far away from this place as she could, but I also knew she wouldn't do it. And the more eyes we had until the police got here, the better. I said, "I need your help. Both of you."

Andrew walked in a few minutes after I sent out my SOS text. "We were at Lowe's on Hudson," he said, "so that worked out."

"We?"

He jerked a thumb behind him at my oldest brother, and I groaned. "Why'd you bring him?"

"We were in his truck. It was either that or not come."

Matt glowered at me from within his beard. "Great to see you too, sis."

I made a quick round of introductions among my motley crew and explained the situation. We divided the room into sections based on the rows that spanned the center. "Since almost everybody here is a woman, if you see any guys, let me know. There's allegedly a security person or people somewhere here though I have yet to see them. If you find such a person, grab them. Anything that seems weird or suspicious, keep eyes on them and let me know."

"I have a question," Shelby said. "It might be a stupid question."

"There are no stupid questions."

"Why don't we just, like, pull the fire alarm? So everyone goes outside?"

Kez cackled. "That is a stupid question."

"You are such an asshole. Shelby, it's not a stupid question. But that could actually make things worse in a giant crowd like this."

"Oh." She blushed bright red even in the faintly purple light.

"Where's your boyfriend?" Matt said. "Isn't this more his territory than a bunch of randos?"

"He'll be here soon." As I said it, I hoped it was true.

We split up, a six-way group audio call set up in FaceTime. Matt didn't have an iPhone and Novotny didn't have a phone at all, so I put him with Shelby and gave Matt the task of wandering around looking like he was up to no good in the hope of attracting someone's notice, whether it was the security team or Creedle himself. The Celeste Center had continued to fill up during our planning session, such as it was, but at some point, the staff came to their senses and stopped letting new people in; as a result, a crowd was forming outside the glass doors on the front of the building. As one person left, one person was allowed in.

So the crowd was never going to get any smaller.

I pushed and shoved through my row of the exhibitors' tables, scanning faces. Happy faces—the turnout was beyond amazing from their point of view. I pushed up my sleeves as the temperature in the crowded room climbed up and up.

In my ear, Kez said, "Maybe they weren't here yet, and now they can't get in. Like maybe the plan was just too good."

I didn't respond, just kept walking and watching. The room was noisy with happy voices, the plastic friction of credit cards being stuck into chip readers, the crinkle of paper bags.

Near the end of the row, a girl in a pair of those sweatpants with PINK written across the butt appeared to be arguing with one of the exhibitors. "I'm telling you, it charged me twice, look, right here."

She waved her phone around. Behind the table was a blond woman in a purple polo shirt. Something about her was vaguely familiar. "I'm so sorry, but could I take down your number and we can discuss it later? There are so many people waiting . . ."

I kept walking but turned back when I saw the wares that Polo Shirt was peddling: green succulents in little cement planters.

I tugged some of my hair in front of my face in case Not-Kyla extracted herself from her argument, and I grabbed one of the planters off the table. Sure enough, the modern Bloom logo was printed on a flag that was stuck in the soil.

"Plants," I said into the phone. "They're selling succulents." I turned away from the table so that I could speak more freely. "They have a table—"

"There are succulents everywhere," Shelby said. "Over in the last row by the food stalls, they have tables set up and they all have centerpieces."

The six of us on the line all let out a sigh.

Shelby added, "But they're actually just plants. Not, like, plant-bombs."

Then Novotny came on the line. "Just plants, dirt, and tiny decorative rocks. I dumped one out in the garbage."

Not-Kyla was still arguing with Pink over the double charge and hadn't noticed me. I walked away and pretended to look at the chakra candles for sale at the stand next to the plants. "Purple polo shirts," I added. "Look for purple polo shirts. I don't know why they'd wear uniforms to go enact a secret plan, but there she is, so."

Kez said, "Are these people suicidal?"

"Not that I know of."

"Then maybe it's a good sign that they're in here. Whatever's going to happen might not be inside the building as long as they're here."

That was a chilling thought, especially with the line of people snaking around the building.

Mave was still stomping around with her walkie-talkie, and when she saw me lingering near the chakra candles she stopped with her hands on her hips. "I told you to wait right there."

"Did you ever find your security people?" I said hopefully.

"Not yet. But what are you doing? I can tell you're not going to buy a chakra candle."

The person behind the table had been trying to make eye contact with me while I was standing there but now just gave up. I led Mave away from the table, my eyes still on Not-Kyla. "Who's behind this event?"

"Well, we have many generous donors—"

"Right, right, but who is *in charge* in charge? Not that I don't respect your authority."

Her eyes narrowed at me. "Well, Ms. Spinnaker is outside with Channel Four right now, if you must know."

"Of fucking course," I muttered. I had half wondered if Gail Spinnaker would be here, so it made perfect sense that the whole event was her brainchild. She was a former client of mine, and one of the few I'd ever fired—usually I just let them go ahead and do that to me. But Gail had hired me back in January to find out who was producing counterfeit athletic leggings under her successful brand name. It turned out that no one was, and actually she was simply trying to save face after a bad marketing move.

"Well?" Mave demanded, expectant.

"Well, what?"

"I asked you what the heck you think is going on?"

"Oh, um, how many security people do you have again?"

"We had three, but then Bill called some other guys in. I'm not sure how many."

"Do they have a break room or something?"

"Bill had everything set up in the office, up in the front. But he's not in there now."

"And where did you say Gail was?"

"Outside by the Bricker Building entrance, I think?"

I left her there by the chakra candles before she noticed that while I hadn't answered any of her questions, she had answered several of mine.

"Kez, you seeing anything where you are?"

"There's a chick selling concealed-carry purses, you want I should get you one?"

Damsel in Defense was apparently everywhere. "When have you ever seen me carry a purse?"

"Nothing else to see over here."

"Come over to the northeast corner and take over for me."

When Kez approached the Bloom table, she nodded at me and resumed watch.

I paused at a booth selling bejeweled earbuds with a built-in mic and bought a pair to free up my hands. I waved off the offer of a gift bag and plugged my new purchase into my phone and stuck the phone in my pocket.

I headed through the dense crowd over toward the main entrance. I could no longer see the woman with the stamp or the admission table with its stacks of tote bags. But I could see potential hazards, everywhere. The drop ceiling with its fiberboard panels, so easily moved out of the way to reveal who knew what. The stairs leading up to the mezzanine and its two-thousand-some permanent seats. As I pushed my way through the throngs of attendees and into the office, my forehead beaded in cold sweat.

The office, through a dingy door to the right of the entrance, was empty.

An elbow-height counter offered a stack of papers—a floor plan of the Celeste Center with the rows of tables sketched in. I flipped through five identical copies. I grabbed a highlighter off the desk and quickly drew a bold circle around the area of the Bloom table on all five and left one on the desk, taking the others with me just in case.

In my ear, Andrew said, "Two polo shirts with a dolly just came in from the loading dock. It looks like more plants."

"Going where?"

"Towards the north side of the building."

That was where the Bloom table was. Kez said, "I see them. They're redoing the display. They have the same hairdo and everything, Christ."

"Andrew, where did you see the loading docks?"

"Next to the big stage. Three o'clock."

The languid dance lesson was still happening up on the stage. I went through the doorway just to the right and down a long cement hallway with a low ceiling and pale yellow light. Noise echoed through the enclosure from all directions—the cacophony behind me, plus more voices from somewhere on the loading dock. I stopped when I reached a cinder block doorway and peered around the corner and saw two men in lime-green EVENT STAFF shirts wringing their hands over a mess of torn cardboard, dirt, and rocks.

I stepped forward out of the doorway. "What happened?"

The taller of the two guys startled and said, "It was an accident. I don't know what happened."

"Who are you?" the other guy said.

"I'm the event auditor," I announced. "Did you see two women in polo shirts back here a minute ago?"

The tall guy nodded. "We were just trying to help them unload. Their van was the wrong height for the ramp, though."

I nudged the debris with a toe, noticing scraps of green in the rubble. "Where were they unloading from?"

He pointed to an empty bay. "A van was just there."

"What kind of van?"

"Grey? Kind of funny looking."

"Did you see who was driving it?"

Both men shook their heads.

I showed them Joel Creedle's picture. "Have you seen this guy today?"

"Bill? Yeah, he's the security guy."

"Damn it." I ran a hand over my face. Of course. "What's he wearing?"

The shorter of the two men tugged at his shirt. "They made us all wear this."

"Give me your radio."

The tall guy handed it over.

I said, "How do I get Mave?"

"Just say her name. There's only one channel."

"Mave, come in."

I realized there was no way she'd hear the radio over the noise. I'd had trouble even hearing the voices coming through my phone.

"If you see Bill back here, keep him from leaving, okay? And say something on the radio. Okay?"

I clipped the radio to the waistband of my jeans and went over to the empty dock. Cold air streamed in from outside, chilling the sweat at my hairline. I saw dozens of vehicles parked back here on the expanse of cracked pavement, but no grey vans.

One earbud was still dangling at my throat. I put it back in place and said to the gang, "Creedle is the security guy. Bill. He's wearing a lime-green shirt that says 'event staff.' Or, was. There's also a van, grey. The plants came out of that."

Shelby said, "I keep seeing a lady in a green shirt. Curly red hair? Is she one of them?"

"No, she's actual event staff. Grab her and tell her to go on the radio."

I dropped to a crouch and lowered myself off the raised ledge of the loading dock and went around the south side of the Celeste Center exterior, past the short end of the open-air Congress Pavilion and the trampled-looking grassy area between the buildings. I heard voices, lots of them, and saw the massive line of people waiting to get into the expo forming from the main entrance going south; it reached the southernmost side of the building and then snaked away, under the towering posts for the SkyGlider and back toward the Bricker Building.

I lifted the walkie-talkie. "Mave, can you hear me?"

The reply was an unintelligible crackle.

"Hello?"

Crackle crackle.

I realized that I might have been beyond the range of the device now that I was outside the building.

"Shelby, tell her—" I stopped, not sure what I could tell her that wouldn't make the situation worse. "Tell her not to trust Bill or anyone he brought in."

I searched the crowd looking for a grey state trooper uniform, but even the line was no longer identifiable as a line, just a huge mob of people. I stood on my tiptoes, which didn't help. So I stuck the toe of one boot into a chain-link fence that housed an HVAC motor and climbed to the top.

From this vantage point I could see Gail Spinnaker with a television crew off to my left in front of the Taft Coliseum, no doubt having been evicted from the location at the Bricker Building by the growing crowd.

I hopped off the fence and ran the three hundred feet between us. Gail was her perky, put-together self, smiling hugely while telling the camera the incredible success story of her rebranded empire, which she now called Inspohio. Gail did love her portmanteaus. Then she saw me coming and faltered.

"Your head of security is actually a terrorist," I announced. "You need to do something."

The reporter, a woman with glossy dark hair and a wide pink mouth, looked at me like I had two heads.

Gail said, "Can we start over?"

"Um, this is live . . . ?" the reporter said.

The camera spun at me—no, not at me, at the Celeste Center, where instead of trying to get in, people were suddenly streaming out.

CHAPTER 36

Someone just pulled the fire alarm," Shelby said, "and screamed fire and it wasn't me."

I bolted toward the main entrance of the Celeste Center. "Did anyone see who it was?"

Four nos and one yes came through the phone.

Miriam said, "Someone in a green shirt. I couldn't see who."

The scene at the entrance was chaos—people pushing out while some people were still pushing in, not realizing that the one-out-one-in protocol had been suspended.

Maybe Mave. Maybe one of Creedle's crew, having a change of heart?

"The polo shirts are going towards the back, not the front," Kez said. "Should I follow?"

I said, "Everybody, just get out of the building. If any of you see Matt, grab him too."

"Roxane."

I looked up and saw my oldest brother's face ten feet away—at six-three, he towered over the rest of the crowd.

"Never mind," I said to the group. "I found him."

But then I saw something else, and my heart dropped through the pavement under the soles of my boots.

A grey van, parked just behind a pair of oak trees and the patch of grass on the north side of the doors.

———

"The van," I said. "Fuck. The van." I cleared my throat and yelled, as loud as I could, "The meeting point is to the left. Behind the Taft Coliseum."

The people in my immediate vicinity glanced at me, but no one seemed to care. Matt lifted his hand to his mouth, index finger and thumb in a circle, and made an ear-piercing whistle. "Everybody. Come on. Keep moving to the left."

"Whoever's still inside, go to the secondary entrance at the southwest corner of the building," I said to the group while Matt continued to holler at the crowd. "Tell everybody you see. Go out and keep moving south."

Andrew said, "What's happening?"

I peered in the windows of the van but couldn't see anything through the tint. I considered smashing a window, even went so far as to unsnap the strip of webbing that kept my gun firmly in its holster, but I didn't know what could possibly trigger the explosive. Besides, what would I do if I got my hands on it—defuse the bomb like MacGyver?

The only thing I could do was try to get people the fuck away from it.

Which wasn't going that well.

The end of the line, which was nearing the north side of the Bricker Building, had begun to rush forward, unaware that the goal was now to get away from the building, not closer to it. There were too many voices, some scared, some excited, phones ringing and pinging, feet on concrete—even Matt's bellowing wasn't loud enough to get the message across to people spread out across such a wide area.

I needed a visual, a gigantic flag that said GET THE FUCK AWAY FROM THIS VAN.

But all I had was four crumpled maps and nothing to write with.

I turned to the parking lot. Some people were heading that way, giving up on the event, and more yet were still coming in from the outer reaches. My vehicle was a few hundred yards away but I started toward it anyhow, thinking maybe there'd be time to herd the crowd that way.

Then I saw Matt's behemoth truck parked much closer, parallel to a rectangle of grass at the northeast corner of the Celeste Center. It sported a small trailer with a concrete machine strapped inside.

I grabbed his arm. "Give me your keys."

"What—why—no."

"Right now."

"No—"

I swiped at his pocket and grabbed them before he had time to react.

"Roxane, what the hell are you doing?"

"Sorry. Really. I'll make it up to you."

I ran through the crowd over to the truck and stepped up on the rail to get into its towering cab. I jammed the key into the ignition with trembling hands. Matt was right behind me, though, and he caught the door before I could close it.

"Scoot," he said. He put a hand on my upper arm and shoved. "I don't want you messing up my mirrors."

It wasn't exactly a fair fight, given his size. So I scooted over to the passenger side as he swung himself into the truck and revved the engine. "Now what?"

"Drive at these people. Carefully, but not too slow. Everybody needs to get way the hell down there." I pointed through the side windows to the Taft Coliseum and the rest of the fairgrounds outbuildings beyond.

"Put on your seat belt."

"Matt."

"Just do it, come on."

I buckled up and Matt pulled a sharp turn to get us facing the Celeste Center.

He revved the engine and crept forward; people scattered. In the side mirror I saw, finally, two Columbus police cruisers on Seventeeth, still trying to get into the lot.

"Now what?"

"Keep going," I said.

I leaned forward as far as the seat belt would allow, searching the crowd for anything that might give me a clue as to what was going to happen. I didn't find anything. But the plan was working—the crowd was moving back.

Just not nearly fast enough.

"Can you kind of zigzag? Like, serpentine? And faster."

My brother nodded, picking up speed as he drifted to the right and then across to the left, weaving in and out of the blue-and-red SkyGlider pylons and revving the engine all the while. Finally, the crowd began to react with some urgency. A chorus of screams went up from a group of women, their arms laden with purchases from the expo.

We were just passing the grey van.

The back doors flew open and Joel Creedle jumped out and bolted north.

He glanced over his shoulder—not at us, but at the van—as he cut to the left, heading diagonally toward the Brown Arena.

"Now," I said, "it's now. Go."

Matt stomped on the gas and drove straight at the receding crowd.

"Oh, fuck," he muttered.

A grey electric meter, the same color as the sky, stuck up out of the ground in the gap between the two pylons we were currently arcing through. There was no way to miss it.

Matt stuck out an arm in front of me but I slapped it away, screaming, "Hands down," just before the impact.

The sound of the airbags was deafening, and the cab was suddenly filled with the rubbery white cushions, a fine powdery dust, and the acrid tang of sodium azide.

"You okay?" Matt's lips said.

Before I could answer, the world exploded.

Time goes funny in moments like that. It was impossible for me to have heard the shower of gravel before the bomb went off. I couldn't hear anything. But in my memory of it, tiny rocks plinked down on the windows, first a few, then an avalanche of them, and then Matt was pushing me down into the footwell of the truck, somehow fitting his large frame in under the steering wheel. Then something metallic dropped onto the roof of the truck, skittered down, and bounced onto the concrete, and the trees were on fire, and everything was shiny wet and smoldering and the crowd of people was drifting by again, slower, stepping around bits of debris and stripes of yellow police tape, stunned silent but okay.

Suddenly, time reversed again and resumed normal speed. As the dust seemed to settle both inside and out, Matt had a hand on my shoulder, shaking me.

"—say something, please—"

I opened the door of the truck and, forgetting how high up we were, promptly fell onto the pavement below. The air smelled like burning plastic and gasoline. Then Matt was helping me to my feet, leading me over toward the brick structure to our right, pressing a folded bandana to my nose, which was somehow bleeding, which was bizarre because my head felt no longer connected to my body at all. I threw up into a concrete planter and sagged against a small metal fence.

"Just sit down right here," Matt said, easing me into a sitting position on the decorative curb.

The knee of my jeans was ripped open, the exposed skin scraped and raw.

"Is my nose broken?" I heard myself say from beneath the bandana that I held against my face with both hands.

"I'm gonna go with yes. So there goes your modeling career."

I knew that I was supposed to laugh, but I wasn't sure how.

He knelt down beside me. The airbag dust had settled on his beard and his shoulders and he had a cut under his eye, a perfect bead of blood hanging from it like a prison tattoo. He was holding his right arm funny, bent at the elbow and against his chest.

"You owe me a new truck."

I kept my hands in place against the bandana but lowered eight fingers so that only the middle ones were extended.

"There she is," Matt said.

CHAPTER 37

Aiden's eyes went the size of dinner plates when he saw my face. "Is that from the door?"

I sat down in a chair next to his bed, wincing as the thick scab on my knee snagged on the inside of my jeans, tugging against the healthy tissue around it. A broken nose was no joke, and neither were the concussion and the pair of shiners that went with it. But the skinned knee was fucking terrible. "The door?" Then I remembered what he was talking about—the door he'd slammed in my face at Rebecca's house. "No, in your dreams are you that strong."

He smirked. "Was it because of him?"

"Airbag," I said. "They save lives, but not faces. But yes, because of him, in a roundabout way." I had a lot of questions for Aiden, namely why he hadn't gone to the police when he first suspected that Joel Creedle—the him in question here—was planning an act of terrorism, or why he hadn't just called me days ago.

But there was no sense in hindsighting something like this, no explanation anyone could give that would turn it into logic and sense.

So instead, I said, "What about you, did he do this?"

The kid looked down at his hands. His chest tubes had been removed and his body had fought off the infection. But although I wore my bruises on the outside, he was banged up far worse than I was, and even after he was allowed to leave the hospital, he was going to sport psychological scars for a long, long time.

"No," he said.

I raised an eyebrow and regretted it—even my eyebrows hurt. "It wasn't your—" I reconsidered the use of the word *stepdad*. "Joel didn't do this?"

"It was the guy in the hat."

"What guy?"

"The guy who showed Joel how to use the flash drive."

"Start at the beginning."

"Well, I was spying. I knew he was doing something bad. I just didn't know what. I thought he was cheating on my mom but it was way worse, obviously."

"So you started following him. You went to the St. Clair Club in Detroit."

"How do you know that?"

"Because I was following you—at least that last time."

He smirked. "Huh."

I motioned for him to go on.

"Well, I saw him talking to this guy there. I heard them talking about the flash drive. About using it to get the people who use Constance's app to show up at a specific location. The guy in the hat told him don't lose this because it's the only copy, and Joel said he would put it in the safe at home. So I went to Walmart and bought one that looked just like it. Actually, I bought all the red ones because I couldn't remember exactly what it looked like. Then I switched them."

An imperfect, incomplete plan that ignored the existence of cloud storage or other means of copying data into more than one location. But in its way, it had worked: Creedle had to resort to stealing the Nora Health user data another way when he realized his flash drive was useless. "A blank one for the real one. That's pretty clever, Aiden. When was this?"

"I'm not sure. Before Rebecca went to Columbus."

"Where?"

"At the house."

"Describe the guy."

"I don't know, a guy."

"White, black, short, tall?"

"White, taller than me but not a lot."

"Build?"

"Huh?"

"Fat, thin, muscular, what?"

"He had on a coat. I couldn't tell."

"What kind of coat?"

"Brown."

"Hair?"

"I couldn't see it, because of the hat."

"How many times did Joel meet with him?"

"I don't know. Four?"

"Always at the St. Clair Club?"

"Yes."

"And then you saw him again when?"

"The day I got arrested."

"Where?"

"I went to your office. I got the address off that card. But you weren't there. So when I was leaving, he was out front. He saw me. He knew who I was, I guess. I don't know how. He never saw me in Detroit. It happened really fast. I was just trying to get away from him, but he was punching me and kicking me and trying to reach into my pockets. It was like he knew I had it. I finally kicked him in the nutsack really hard and managed to get away. I was so jacked on adrenaline or whatever. Then I saw this cop car sitting in traffic and I just thought, if I can get into that car, I can stick it between the seats or something and nobody will ever find it." He held up a wrist, which was scraped raw. "I forgot about how they handcuff you when they arrest you. I tried but I couldn't get it out of my pocket."

"That's pretty clever," I said. "But why not chuck it in the garbage somewhere? Throw it in the river?"

"They were following me. Who knows how many there are."

How did the man in the hat know Aiden was even in town? I said, "How did you get down here? I know your car got impounded in Detroit."

"I hitched with this truck driver."

I almost said *that's so dangerous* but caught myself. A nice suburban churchly stepdad seemed perfectly safe but turned out not to be. Conventional wisdom about danger didn't always apply. "Why here?"

"Constance had a fundraiser here. They kept talking about how they wanted to do it here, to get the most people. I saw it on TV in a hotel lobby where I was crashing. I figured, I should come down here and talk to you and you'd know what to do."

"Why didn't you call me? I would've come to get you."

"Rebecca said you can't trust the phones."

I thought of the old saying: Just because you're paranoid doesn't mean someone isn't out to get you. I said, "Did Rebecca know you had it?"

"I didn't tell her everything. But I told her I had proof. I think Joel must have found out somehow. Maybe he thought she had it, and while he was trying to get it back, he killed her. I told that cop all of this already."

"I know. I'm just nosy," I said, and he smiled. "You really can't describe the guy in the hat?"

"It happened really fast."

"How old was he?"

"Old. Older than me."

"Older than me?"

"I don't know how old you are."

"Thirty-six."

"Really?"

"I am aware that I don't look my best right now."

"I don't know. I didn't really see his face much. But he had rough hands. Oh, and glasses. I broke them."

Mariella Zervos had already seen the black-eye situation, and she handed me a gift—a pair of mirrored aviators made from metal so thin the earpieces practically bent when I folded them open. I said, "Are these from the Dollar Tree?"

"Dollar General. Just put them on. You look like a Halloween costume."

"Nice."

"Think of the children, Roxane." She gestured around the half-empty food court in the bowels of the hospital.

"Fuck off."

"Glad to hear you're feeling better, although I'm surprised that you're out and about."

I wasn't feeling particularly better when I made the decision to leave the house that morning, but I was feeling bored and irritable. My doctor had told me to refrain from driving for a week but hadn't said anything about Uber. "I just wanted to check on Nadine and the kid. Are you going to help her?"

She nodded. "I can't talk about the details, but yeah. She's willing to make a statement about Creedle, and to testify if it comes to that. I doubt it will, but good to know all the same."

"Why do you doubt it?"

"I just said I can't talk about it."

I lifted the sunglasses up.

"Okay, fine," she said, either persuaded or shamed by my appearance. "He's not talking much yet, but you can see him starting to crack. A guy like that is not going to hold up in jail pending a trial."

"Not talking much, you say."

"He's a *righteous man,* that's pretty much all I got out of him. He didn't do anything wrong, blah blah blah. He didn't break into any hotel rooms, he didn't plant any bombs. Oh, and he took particular offense to the idea that he murdered your girl, Rebecca Newsome. Apparently she used to be married to a buddy of his who still carries a torch. Did you know that?"

"What kind of question is that? Of course I did. This buddy of his was murdered in Toledo earlier this week. Does he know anything about *that*?"

"He says he doesn't."

"Here's a thought," I said, feeling petty and mean, "have you considered trying harder?"

"Excuse me?"

"This guy has all the answers. If he doesn't, we'll never know who killed Rebecca. Or who did this to Aiden. And what about Benjamin Gaskell? Doesn't his family deserve answers too?"

"What family?"

That got me. "Everybody has *some* family."

"Not this guy."

"No one?"

"An ex-wife who said, and I quote," Zervos said, fanning the pages of a notebook, "'I'm not glad he's dead, but I'm not too broken up, neither.'" She flipped the notebook closed like that settled it, and maybe it did.

CHAPTER 38

B ut I couldn't stop thinking about a few things. One, Benjamin Gaskell's body, unclaimed in the Franklin County morgue, at least until it got donated to science—an actual thing—or the city paid some local funeral home a few hundred bucks to deal with it. I preferred not to think much about what happens when we die, but in no way should it involve being stuck in a drawer on the corner of the Ohio State campus until the facility needed the space back.

And I also couldn't stop thinking about the break-in at Constance Archer-Nash's hotel room. It had struck me as odd at the time but I'd had other things on my mind. Now, it really stood out—how had this happened, given her security detail?

It was with this in mind that I dragged myself to the Hilton across from the convention center and had the front desk call up to her room.

She sounded wary when I announced myself but she said I could come up to her room on the fourth floor. She was washing a blouse in the sink when I got there, soap bubbles clinging to her forearms.

"Trip wound up being longer than you expected, huh?" I said.

Constance nodded. "I'm leaving tomorrow, but first, yet another interview."

"Hashtag blessed."

"What do you want?"

"I'm just curious about something."

She turned back to the sink, swirling the top around in the soapy water.

I watched her reflection in the mirror. "This break-in you mentioned. Was it this room, here?"

She nodded again and didn't look up.

"Where were you?"

"I was at a dinner."

"Mighty late dinner, assuming it was after you and I met."

"Yeah, it was late. Is that a crime now?"

"And you didn't notice the computer was missing until the morning?"

"Do *you* always check your computer after a late business dinner?"

"What happened that night? Really?"

She looked up, caught herself, and resumed focus on the shirt.

"I have no idea what you're talking about."

But she wouldn't meet my eye.

"You didn't sleep here. Did you?"

She looked up again, and our eyes met in the mirror.

"Constance, I don't care. I just want to find out what happened."

She closed her eyes. "I didn't— I was embarrassed, after our conversation. Yours and mine. I had a few more drinks. Too many. I don't know how many." Constance held the shirt underwater like she was trying to drown it. "I didn't go back to the room. I spent the night with a woman I met, after you left. My security guy—he stood outside in the hallway all night. It was— I'm such an idiot."

"When did you realize the computer was missing?"

"I went back to the room in the morning and my key didn't work. I had to go to the lobby for a new key. It was just this nightmare walk of shame, the whole morning. And when I finally got inside, I thought, okay, I can relax for two seconds.

And then I noticed my bag was gone, and you were calling me—I was thinking about my reputation, my campaign, my company. I don't know, okay? I don't know what happened. But I didn't want anyone to know. I still don't. I can't." She wrung out the shirt and dropped it on the counter with a thwack. "So whatever you're asking about now—no. I can't."

"This is an element of a massive crime, Constance—"

"You think I don't know that? I ruined everything."

"You don't know—"

"Can you please leave?"

She bit her lip, her eyes squeezed closed.

I patted her shoulder. "Sure. Best of luck."

It took two days for Tom to get the security tape from the Hilton, a process enmeshed in corporate bureaucracy and, apparently, cashing in on some long-due favor. "These are the highlights," he told me when he brought the video over to my place, along with a few key frames printed out.

"Nice and big for the gal with the blurry vision," I said, squinting at the jumbo time stamp in the corner of the page. I kept forgetting that squinting hurt.

The security camera had gotten a good look at Joel Creedle coming through the revolving door, almost head-on. I flipped through the first few sheets of paper and watched in stop-motion as he crossed the lobby just after one in the morning and into the elevator.

"Well, that's probably the closest thing there is to proof." I tossed the papers onto my coffee table. "Can we go to bed?"

"It's nine thirty."

"That isn't what I meant."

Tom took a breath. "I think we need to talk about some things."

"I know, and I just can't right now."

We looked at each other for a long time.

"I really am sorry. What you said the other day is totally right. Frank's gone. You're the one whose feelings I need to think about."

"I literally just said that I can't do this right now."

Another silence rolled out between us, this one hard-edged and tense.

Finally, he said, "Then maybe I should go. Until you can."

I got this tightness in my chest. "What does that mean?"

"It means, I want to do this with you. All of it. The good and the bad. I will never not be here for you, no matter what, and like we talked about earlier this year, this might not work." He gestured at the space between us. "But if it doesn't, it needs to be because we tried and failed. Not because you didn't try."

The tightness was creeping up my throat, into my sinuses. Yet another thing that hurt. "You're saying that I don't try?"

"I'm saying that you're half in, half out. I love you and I can't pretend that it doesn't bother me how you didn't return my calls for thirty-six hours after all this happened and when you finally did, it was to ask for this. Another bullshit favor. I can't go down this path with you again, where you act like you could take it or leave it because it's just sex and it doesn't matter."

"I never said it doesn't matter. All I said was that I can't have this conversation right now, and here you are, trying to make me have it. Maybe you should go."

"That's what you want."

It wasn't. "Yeah."

Tom stood up and got his coat and put it on slowly and I knew I should stop him, but I didn't. Instead, I kicked over the coffee table, the printed-out frames cascading across the floor.

The doctor had said something to the effect that there were no guidelines regarding how much alcohol was safe following a concussion, which technically could be interpreted conversely—there were no guidelines about how much was unsafe, either. I did a shot in my kitchen, experimentally, and didn't drop dead. A positive sign. But somehow it made everything seem more impossible, not less, a cheap fucking trick—for my only coping mechanism to fail me at this very moment.

Instead, I took a sleeping pill and lay in bed on top of the blankets. The glow-in-the-dark stars on the ceiling were fuzzy and pale yellow-green blobs. The blurred vision was going to go away in time. Would there be anything worth seeing when it did?

slept for fifteen hours and woke up feeling both better and worse. Better because I could see my phone clearly, and worse because I didn't have a text from Tom that said You are impossible and I'm fine with it so please, continue treating everyone however you see fit.

I made tea and went onto the back porch, where the air was crisp and cold. Fall was almost over now, that distinct but undefinable shift between deliciously cool and winter. After a few minutes, I heard Shelby open her back door and come down the steps with an actual basket of muffins folded into a cotton kitchen towel.

"You don't have to eat them if you don't want to, but I wanted to make sure you had something you could eat," she said. "Oh my god, Roxane, you look awful."

I took the basket from her outstretched hand. "I know. Thank you. For the muffins, and the compliment. Sit with me."

She came the rest of the way down the steps, avoiding the broken one two from the bottom.

"I saw that you texted me. I'm an asshole for not responding."

"It's okay. I was just worried. Like what if you were dead in there?"

"I wasn't here. I should've responded to tell you that."

"You don't have to tell me anything. It's okay."

I caught her eye. "It's really not. I don't want to be like this step," I said, pointing at the offending slat, "someone that everyone has to make special allowances for."

"You're not."

"You made me muffins because you thought I might not have any food."

"But I like making muffins."

I had to smile. "That's not the point."

"You're super banged up. I think you're allowed to take a break from texting, if that's what you need."

"There's always going to be some reason that I don't want to talk about my feelings."

Shelby looked confused. "I never know what to do. That's why I brought the muffins."

She'd been through a lot, but she was still just a nineteen-year-old kid. What Tom had said about Shelby and her father was right. I hadn't agonized over that, or debated telling her. Never in a million years would I burden her with that crap, even if I thought she knew already. Because bringing it up would mean that I knew, too. I took a muffin out of the basket and broke off a piece.

"They're carrot, like you used to get from the Angry Baker."

"Shel, you're amazing."

"I think you are."

"How are you doing, after all that excitement?"

Here she blushed a little. "It was scary, but also, right after? We kissed. Miriam and me."

It was the best news I'd ever heard. I threw an arm around her shoulders and squeezed. "Finally," I said.

After a shower, three aspirins, and a load of laundry, I returned to the scene of the crime—the living room—and returned the coffee table to its proper position and picked up the papers. Then I sat on the sofa and flipped through the rest of the pages, feeling a little guilty that Tom had taken the boredom hit and watched the security footage for me. Okay, a lot guilty, especially since all

I had offered in return was the displeasure of my company and a fight about nothing.

I was going to need to figure out how to get over myself.

I turned a page and saw Joel Creedle coming in through the front doors of the hotel, face in profile as he turned to look over his shoulder.

The next page showed a view of the sidewalk: Creedle with a hand up, pointing into the building. There was another person with him, a guy with glasses and a baseball cap, a medium-colored coat. Aiden's assailant? I couldn't see his face, but there was one more printout in the stack.

I flipped to it and drew in a breath and the papers all fell to the floor.

"You didn't tell me you wanted a ride way out to East Jesus," Kez said, frowning through the windshield at the tree-lined Powell Road.

"I think technically this is *West* Jesus." I stared at my phone—with a minimum of squinting—and willed Maggie to call me back.

James Holmer had struck me as a nobody, but it all suddenly made sense. The chemistry degree I'd noticed on his wall would've given him the know-how to make the Tannerite explosive. Marathon Petroleum, his employer, prominently featured in those clippings on the wall in the St. Clair Club.

"We need to discuss a mileage reimbursement situation."

"Why are you always trying to get more money from me? I'm not exactly rolling in it."

"After what just went down, I bet you're gonna be."

She might have been right about that. I had already scheduled three new client meetings for next week and had half a dozen phone messages that I still needed to return. My brother Matt reported that his giant, hero truck had done the same for his own business—all the shots on the news with his name and phone number had generated a lot of leads—but for the moment his broken arm precluded him from doing anything about it.

These were good problems to have.

Kez added, "I just have to do right by me, you know?"

"You're doing a great job, working for me. With me. I really appreciate it. I know I'm trash at saying so, but I do. You're smart as hell and I hope you know that."

She glanced at me, a smile twitching at the corner of her mouth. "Shit, I wasn't trying to make this into a whole thing, I was just hoping for my fifty-eight cents a mile."

"Fifty-eight cents?"

"The IRS standard rate?"

I made a mental note to start requesting mileage reimbursement from my clients. "Make a left here."

Kez swung her tiny car onto Maggie's street.

"So what's the plan?"

I pointed to the white house. Rebecca Newsome's car was still parked in the driveway, while James Holmer's truck was not.

Good.

I said, "I don't have one. We're just going to talk to her and see what's what." I handed her Deputy Carter Montoya's business card. "If anything gets wonky, call him. Okay?"

"Okay."

I was hoping she'd answer the door—a gamble, since she wouldn't answer my phone calls, but a doorbell and a pathologically stubborn detective could really wreak havoc on an infant's sleep schedule if we had to.

It turned out I didn't need to worry. Maggie opened the door right away, baby Bea squalling in her arms. My former client was pale and disheveled in flannel pajama pants and a yellowing undershirt. She didn't seem angry at me, though, just a little stunned.

"Maggie, this is my associate, Kezia Denniere. Can we talk to you for a second?"

"It's a mess in here," she said, but stepped aside to let us into her house.

Kez beamed at the screaming baby. "How old?"

"Five weeks. No, six."

"Can I take a turn?"

Maggie thrust the child into Kez's arms. In one of the most shocking twists of the week, the baby settled almost immediately. Kez shrugged with one shoulder. "I'm the oldest of five."

The two of them drifted into the living room, Kez cooing baby talk and letting Bea's sticky little hands grasp at her braids. Maggie said, "I suppose I should apologize to you."

"That's not why I'm here. Can you tell me where your husband is?"

"James? He's in Findlay, at work. If you wanted to talk to him you should have called first."

"I did call," I said, "several times."

Maggie shook her head and pulled her phone out of her pocket; the lock screen showed no missed calls. "What do you need to talk to him about?"

"I don't. Maggie, I know you said that you didn't know Joel Creedle."

"No."

"But your husband does."

"No."

"Is James monitoring your phone calls?"

"No."

"You don't use UnityView?"

"Well, we—it's just so we always know we can trust each other. It strengthens our bond."

"Except when your husband is using it to screen your phone calls for you." I showed her my five call attempts in the last hour.

Maggie tapped at her phone. "Sometimes in the house . . . I don't have a good signal. James would never do that to me. Keep people from getting in touch with me."

"Tell me this, Maggie. Did you get a bunch of calls and voice mails from me last week?"

"Just—no, just one."

"You told me you didn't want your husband to know you had hired me."

"Yes, but just because—he didn't want me worrying."

"Maggie."

"That man on the news is sick. Something went wrong in his brain, in his heart. That is not what Keystone is. His sickness has nothing to do with me or my husband—"

I showed her the printout from the Hilton's security camera, and her mouth formed a perfect O as she stared at her husband's face. Then her eyes drifted to the time stamp. "This can't be. James has been in Findlay since Sunday for work."

"Findlay," I said. "That's where he said he was on the day of your mother's accident."

"Yes, he goes up there two days a week. The big refinery there."

"It never occurred to me at the time, but he made it to St. Ann's awfully quick, for being all the way up in Findlay."

"What—he was worried, about me. He was driving fast."

"Tell me this—did he get new glasses recently?"

"Glasses?"

Her face answered the question—yes. But her mouth said, "He would never hurt anyone."

"How sure of that are you?"

"Sure." She was shaking her head. "I'm sure. He's my husband."

"How'd your mother get along with him?"

Maggie's eyes had widened. "Poison ivy," she whispered.

"What?"

"The poison ivy. What you said the first time I came to the office, about poison ivy."

"Yes."

"You had it, after you tried to help my mom."

"Yes."

"When you said that I had—it was just this fleeting thought. Like when you think you see a mouse, just in the corner of your eye. You just hope you were wrong."

"Maggie, what about the poison ivy?"

"James had it, when the baby was born." She bent forward at the waist and let out a sob. "He said from working in the yard. It's in all the pictures from the hospital, on his hands, and his arms—"

That was when the front door opened.

"What's going on?" James Holmer said, glancing from his wife's face to mine. He wore the tan coat, which must have blended into the trees that day in the park. He was flushed, a slick of sweat on his upper lip. "Maggie, is she bothering you?"

"No."

"Where's the baby?"

"The neighbor has her," Maggie said quickly.

"Why?"

"I needed a break."

"A break from our child?"

"What are you doing home? You said you weren't coming home until tomorrow."

"I wasn't—but you sounded upset last night—"

Maggie held up the security camera image.

"Is that what this is about?" James licked his lips. "Pastor Joel?"

"You said you never met him. You said the Fellowship was more than just him."

"I just didn't want you to worry."

"So how long have you been helping him with this?"

"I wasn't."

"Don't lie to me."

"I'm not."

"If you lie to me, you will never see Beatrix again."

Anger flared up in James Holmer's face. "You don't get to de-cide that."

"How did you get to the hospital so fast that day?"

"I wanted to get to you. You sounded so—so weak and scared on the phone."

It was impossible to say what Maggie's mental state had been like that day, but she was no longer either weak or scared. Her face was pink and she grasped her phone so tightly her knuckles popped out in bright white ovals. "When did you start controlling my phone with that app?"

Now James looked at me. "Why are you filling my wife's head with this nonsense?"

"I don't need anybody to fill my head with anything," Maggie snapped. She whipped her arm back so fast I didn't have time to react before the phone left her hand and bounced off James's cheekbone. "What did you do to my mother?"

"You're being hysterical, Mags, I know the last month has been hard for you. Remember what we talked about in lifegroup?"

"You argued with her that morning. I heard you. I thought—I thought it was about the Fellowship. That she was trying to start that same old fight again. But that's not what it was."

A red welt was forming on James's cheek from the phone. "We both just wanted what was best for you, sweetheart."

"What happened," I said, "did Joel Creedle tell you that she'd found out about the plan?"

James shook his head, touching a hand to his cheekbone like

the pain was just registering. "I never wanted anything to do with his plan." He spat out the last word.

"What, then?"

"He wanted my help. I kept saying no. But then Rebecca had to stick her nose into his business—your mother went behind Joel's back and helped his wife run away from him. I just wanted her to tell me where Joel's wife was hiding."

"That's bullshit. You were in on it from the beginning. The flash drive with the phone numbers. The little chemistry experiment you detonated at my office. How you almost beat Aiden Brant to death. You're in this up to your eyeballs. And what about Keir Metcalf?"

Maggie flinched as I said the name. James didn't respond to what I said, instead murmuring, "It wasn't right, what Rebecca did. Interfering like that. Maggie, you know how she could be."

"You were going to help that horrible man kill those people!"

"He has a vision—"

"What did you do to my mother, James. Tell me right now."

"I just wanted to convince her to tell me where Nadine was. That's all. That's where it started."

"So you followed her to the park that day," I said.

He nodded. Now he was the one who seemed weak and scared. "I needed to talk to her."

"You didn't just talk."

"It was an accident—"

I cut him off. "She fell backwards. That wasn't an accident."

James didn't bother to deny it.

"And everything that happened after wasn't an accident. What about Keir?"

Maggie was crying hard, gasping for air. She grabbed my arm and held on tight.

James said, "Pastor Joel asked me to talk to him."

It was important to his particular brand of denial that he could claim he hadn't meant for things to escalate, that he'd simply wanted to have a conversation. If it had been one conversation, I might've believed him. But two conversations, two bodies? "You didn't just *talk* to him. Like you didn't just talk to Rebecca either."

"You killed him? You killed *him* too?" Maggie was squeezing my arm so hard it hurt.

"You hated him, Maggie, don't pretend that you didn't—"

"You let me walk around here thinking I was crazy."

"I was doing what it took to protect my family. My child. Just look at you." James sneered. "You aren't fit to care for her. No one will ever believe you. Either of you." He straightened his jacket and smoothed down his hair. "I can't believe you just left her with a neighbor. After everything I just did for this family."

He turned and opened the front door to a handful of Delaware County uniformed deputies and Sheriff's Deputy Carter Montoya, who nodded at me, and I nodded back.

CHAPTER 40

Conventional wisdom says that people don't change, especially not overnight. But conventional wisdom also says that every day is a new chance to do better, and this was the conventional wisdom I wanted to follow. To that end I dressed nicely in the clothes I'd bought in Detroit and attempted to camouflage the worst of my bruises with makeup in the hope that if I looked like less of a train wreck, maybe I'd act like less of one too.

Let's not forget the conventional wisdom about faking it until you make it.

I got my Uber driver to take me to Bethel Road first, so I could pick up New India and good beer from the carryout across the street. Then we headed to Tom's place.

"Wish me luck," I said as I got out of the car, carefully balancing the full paper sack of food and the six-pack in its cardboard carrier. "I need it."

"Good luck. Don't forget to rate me five stars," the driver said without looking up from his phone.

I set the beer on the doorstep and knocked.

Tom came to the door and looked out at me through the pane of glass next to it. "I was thinking about going to the gym."

"I know," I said, "seven thirty is the time you think about going to the gym."

Despite his best efforts not to smile, he did, a little, and opened the door. "You said you needed time. I figured that would be more than one day."

I put the food on the counter and the beer in the fridge. "They don't make a card that says sorry for how I acted when I was concussed, so I brought dinner."

"I see."

"Talk first, then eat. Can I sit down?"

He gestured at the sofa, and we sat.

"I'm sorry. I know I'm not an easy person to be with. It's not by choice, not really. I've spent my entire life trying to knuckle under and just get through things. It makes it hard for me to realize when things are good. I'm always waiting for the other shoe to drop. In my experience, there's usually a shoe. So I'm always on the lookout for one. For what might be the shoe. As a result I've picked a lot of dumbass fights with you."

Tom nodded but stayed quiet.

"And we have this pattern where I get mad, then you come through for me, and then we both just pretend it never happened. Or, rather, I pretend it never happened, and you go along with that because you don't like confrontation, at least not with me. How am I doing so far?"

"An accurate assessment. Is there more?"

"Yes. I get freaked out when you're up front about feelings. Because, well, because I'm messed up inside and actually hearing that you care about me makes me less likely to believe it."

"Roxane, I don't know how you could not believe—"

"Let me finish."

"You have the floor."

"All of these things are my own bullshit that I need to work through and have nothing to do with you. Which is really unfair, I know, because you're the one on the receiving end. But you're amazing, Tom, and I guess I don't feel like I deserve you—I know I don't deserve you—and the only way I know how to protect my dumbass heart is to act like the stakes are low. But they aren't. Not at all. I want to do better by you. If you'll allow me." I stood up, my face hot. "Whew, okay, that's it. That's the spiel. I'm getting a beer. Want one?"

"Yes, please. Or there's whiskey."

"I know. But I heard recently that liquor doesn't solve anybody's problems. And yeah, yeah, neither does beer. But I'm trying, here."

I grabbed two beers from the fridge and cracked the lids off with the bottle opener in his silverware drawer and drank some of mine.

Tom joined me in the kitchen and we stood there on opposite sides of the peninsula, in reverse of our positions from the other night after the explosion in my office. It had been so clear to me in that moment that we worked together, perhaps because I was too stunned by what had happened to bother with the walls that my mother called me out for keeping up all the time.

I said, "I want you to be happy. And what if I can't make you happy?"

"What if you can?" He set a hand on top of mine. "I've been feeling like shit all week. I know why you were upset. I think that everything you just said? Completely true. But then I went and did something to hurt you anyway, even though that's the last thing I want to do. And I'm sorry for that."

"If there are any other secrets my father told you? Don't tell me."

"You don't mean that."

"Not really, but I sense that it would be good for my character, to not know."

"There aren't any."

"You weren't supposed to tell me that."

He leaned across the counter and kissed me, one hand on my shoulder. I could feel the warmth of his palm through my shirt and down my arms and into my belly. I said, "Does this mean we're okay?"

"Yeah."

"Better than okay?"

"We will be."

"I'll take it."

Tom said, "Me too."

The next morning I met my brothers at the Starliner Diner in Hilliard. "I don't like being seen with you two right now," Andrew said, nodding at Matt's cast and my black eyes. "People are going to think I'm responsible."

"Either that, or they'll think you're next." I put my sunglasses back on. "Does this make it better or worse?"

"Now it looks like you're a rock star and we're your groupies." Matt stirred his iced tea with a straw using his good hand. "Or he's the groupie, I'm the bodyguard. Injured in the line of duty." Then he frowned. "Fuck, bad choice of words."

I said, "So I found out something this week. Dad got some woman pregnant a long time ago. We have a half sister out there. This asshole has known about it since February, though."

Matt nodded.

"What does that mean?"

"It means, yes, I already know about this."

Andrew sat back in his seat. "You do? Since when?"

"Christ, I must have been seventeen or eighteen."

Now it was my turn to slump backward. "Mom told you?"

"What? No, God, no," Matt said, almost laughing. "Dad did."

This fact came down hard on the table, muffling us into silence for at least a minute.

"Um," I said finally, "why?"

Matt shook his head. "He was drunk, and I was there. I was

also blasted, but this kind of thing has the power to stick with you."

"Jesus. And you were mad at me, Rox, for not telling you for a couple months."

I leaned my elbows onto the table and rested my chin in my hands. "Why didn't you tell us before?"

"When? At the time? You two were kids."

"So were you."

"Yeah, well, that was on Dad—a fucked-up thing to do, to burden somebody with that information. I wasn't about to turn around and do the same thing to you guys."

Matt was six years older than I was, not so big a gap, but when we were growing up, it seemed insurmountable, like he was in another world. And as adults we were unable to bridge it, or maybe we'd never tried, not really. But Matt getting into the truck with me the other day had felt like a rope across the divide, one that we could both hang on to.

He added, "He said it so nonchalantly, too. Like an aside. Then he said, if anybody ever asks, it's yours."

I spread sour cream on my breakfast quesadilla and shoved a big piece in my mouth and chewed. "That has to be the most fucked-up thing he ever did," I mumbled around it.

"It's not a contest." Matt drowned his Cuban French toast in extra syrup. "I know he pulled some dick moves with you too. With all of us."

We ate in silence for a while. Then Andrew raised his chipped coffee mug. "To that cranky old drunk bastard who, despite his best efforts, managed to get three badass kids."

"Cheers."

"Cheers."

And we drank.

ACKNOWLEDGMENTS

The most important acknowledgment goes to the readers who are so enthusiastic about Roxane Weary as a character. Writing this series is the best thing ever. Thanks, especially, to my book club ladies, to amazing librarians like Erica O'Rourke in Cook County, Illinois, and to bookstore owners like Denise Phillips of Gathering Volumes in Toledo, Ohio (name checked in this very novel, because that's how much I love her store). Shout-outs, also, to Glen Welch and the Book Loft for putting this series in the hands of even more Columbus readers.

Huge thanks to my agent extraordinaire, Jill Marsal, for always advocating on my behalf.

Thanks to my team at Minotaur, especially my editor, Daniela Rapp, and my publicist, Kayla Janas.

I also want to thank my Faber team of Angus Cargill and Lauren Nicholl. Angus always catches the throwaway lines at the ends of my chapters, where I go on just that much too long. He's always right. I'm thrilled that I didn't accidentally give any of my characters the name of a prominent UK car service this time.

I am a very lucky writer for many reasons, including the fact that my work has been recognized with some awards. Thanks to the Golden Crown Literary Society and the Private Eye Writers of America and the tireless volunteer staff who power those organizations.

Thanks to Mark Miller, who knows why. Similarly, thanks

to Ric and Debbie Cacchione, Russ and Debbie Frost, Bill and Susan Kerwin, Megan and Lori Brandstetter, Erin, Jim and Anne Schroeder, Sharon Santino, Lisa Schunemann, Donna and Shannon McCall, and Jennie Eyerman, for showing up for me in a way that I'm still so, so grateful for.

Thanks to my MWA Midwest fam and my Pitch Wars fam for always having my back.

Thanks to my fellow "Unlikeable Female Characters," Layne Fargo and Wendy Heard: we still need to get the matching jackets.

Thanks to my parents for their unyielding support, especially for asking questions they already know the answers to at book events to get the conversation started.

Finally, thanks to Joanna Schroeder, who shows up and pays attention every day. Fwoosh.